Behind The F

A Novel by

BETH A. FREELY

Behind The Eyes Of Dorian Gray

A Novel By

BETH A. FREELY

Copyright 2005 by Beth A. Freely Carpenter
Second Edition Copyright 2020 by Beth A. Freely
The Muses Funhouse
www.themusesfunhouse.com
932 Thistle Ridge Lane
Arlington, TX 76017

All rights reserved, including the right to reproduce this book or portions thereof in any form whatsoever. For information about this book, please contact Beth A. Freely at brauch@themusesfunhouse.com.

This book is entirely a work of fiction. The names, characters, places, and incidents depicted herein are either products of the author's imagination or are used fictitiously. Any resemblance to actual events or locales or persons, living or dead, is entirely coin-cidental.

Dedication

To my family for always encouraging and inspiring my imagination, to my friends for all of their criticism, good, bad and indifferent, and to everyone who helped me beat this book into shape.

With special love to my daughter, Caitlyn Rose. Your continued support, patience, and love while I write is the best motivation any author could have. I love you both.

Prologue

LONDON, 1893

The portraits that hung along the staircase leading from the foyer at street level up to the first floor of the townhouse were carefully removed from their places on the wall. The canvases were painstakingly cleaned, the frames cleared of the layer of dust that tarnished them, before being packed away in heavy, wooden crates for transportation and storage. The artwork was in remarkable condition, the colors still vibrant, the lines still crisp, each with an engraved silver plate identifying the individual the paintings captured for time immemorial. When the portraits were all packed, the handlers moved on to the sitting room and then every other room within the three-story building.

The old townhouse had seen better days. Some of the plaster was now freeing itself from the ceiling high above the oval library, the brown stains of water damage marring the surface. The circular staircase in the corner was rusting, and many of the gaslight fixtures that were evenly dispersed throughout the three-level structure no longer worked. The hardwood floor was worn, the chimney needed fixing, and the lingering smell of mildew clung to the air. It needed work and a good airing out, a loving hand to restore the interior to its grandeur, for the outer structure was still quite sound. That was assuming a loving hand could be found.

The very last portrait was found in an upstairs room, covered with a cloth of deepest purple. The handlers quickly moved it to the foyer for packing, never uncovering it until the very last minute. There was no silver plate to indicate the identity of the individual in the painting. The packing crate was left bare and unmarked, and the men that handled it did so quickly, almost as if they were afraid it would burn them. There was an aura about the richly painted portrait, an aura of evil that the superstitious handlers did not care for.

It was a full-length painting, and, when the cloth was removed, an exquisite oil of a beautiful man in his mid-twenties was revealed. But there was something bizarre about the portrait. It was considerably older than the rest, yet the clothing the man wore in it was of the present day. A light ruffle of white peaked above the flowered gray waistcoat, his overcoat and trousers made of a slightly darker pinstripe. Even in the portrait, his boots shined, the white of the spats a bold slash against the black of the foot. The chain to his gold pocket watch was visible above his pocketed right hand, a finely crafted walking stick with a silver tip clutched in his left, on which his family ring of deepest sapphire and gold glittered on his middle finger.

But it was the man's eyes that caught one's attention. Deep brown, set above chiseled cheekbones, they stared at a person and seemed to follow them through the room, as old portraits were wont to do. They made a person miss the full, red lips that were carefully placed above a strong, goateed chin and the carefully shaped mustache. Or even the dark hair that seemed to fall playfully across the right side of his forehead before making its way along his cheek to caress his shoulders. The eyes made all forget everything else in the portrait, as if the unidentified man was peering into a person's very soul.

It was whispered that the young aristocrat in the painting was the owner of this large townhouse. But no one could verify the rumor. The valet had long since fled the city, returning to his home in the Cotswold's, and none of the house staff could be found. The house had stood empty for two years, after the owner's mysterious death, no one coming to claim it, no one wanting it.

Now, the house was cleaned, the furniture covered, the books that lined the walls neatly arranged and dusted. The musty smell still clung to the air, but it was not as strong as it had been. No one knew who sent the missive instructing that the work be done. No one asked or cared. Closing up the house was simply a few extra shillings in the handlers' pockets, and they loaded the portraits onto a cart and hauled them away. Some were to be given to a gallery, for they were worth a small fortune; some were sent to a London warehouse, only to be lost for all time. And one held a destiny not even the artist, who painted it could ever have imagined.

The house was ready for a new owner, if one was forthcoming.

Little did any of the handlers and cleaners know that the three-storied townhouse on the east docks of London, along the river Thames, would remain empty, devoid of life, for one hundred and eleven years.

Chapter One

L ONDON, DECEMBER 21ST

Rachael Lafferty stomped the snow from her booted feet as she stepped into the street level entrance hall of her Victorian townhouse. She took the stairs two at time in her excitement to reach the upstairs foyer, running her fingers along the newly installed banister as she went. She was waiting for a package, an item she had purchased at auction two weeks earlier. The crystal window of the upstairs door twinkled at her as she opened it and she took a deep breath of the cinnamon scented air, which wafted from the potpourri in the jar by the door. At the sight of the long crate, setting against the sideboard to her right, the portrait inside waiting to be uncrated and proudly displayed, she squealed with delight. "Oh, good, you're here!"

She hung her leather jacket on the coat rack in the corner and rushed to the crate.

Following her up to the townhouse's second level foyer, Duchess Tessa Falcon, Rachael's best friend and also her literary agent, paused at the top of the stairs, a little out of breath. "I can only wonder what would make you so enthused that you ran up these stairs." The duchess shook her red curls to free them of snow, and water gently splattered against the glass of the entrance door, causing small rainbows to appear in the beveled panes. "There's no one here." She looked around as she removed her heavy coat, hanging it on the stand beside the door. She rubbed her arms briskly through her thick black sweater, her eyes scanning the dark corners high above her. Every time she entered Rachael's home, Tessa experienced a sense of foreboding, for which she could not find a reasonable explanation. "I don't understand how you can live here. This place gives me the creeps, Rachael."

Rachael ignored her complaint, having heard it over and over so many times that she could recite it in her sleep. She loved the huge townhouse as soon as she'd seen it, and bought it right away, not even caring how much work was needed to fix it up or why it had stood empty for so long. The realtor made sure he pointed out every flaw in the building, every item that needed repaired or replaced. He had actually made the comment that the place needed a match. Rachael didn't agree. She wanted the Victorian, complete with leaking pipes and peeling plaster.

And she had restored the place in timeless fashion. The walls of the upstairs foyer and the staircase leading to the third floor were encased in dark tongue-and-groove paneling, the deep brown enriched by the small lamps she had installed to replace the decaying gaslight fixtures. Family photos lined the staircase, the smiling faces of the Lafferty clan gazing down on the room with love. The foyer opened up into a large oval sitting room and library. The spiral staircase that stood just inside the enormous sitting room shined with a fresh coat of black paint. The hardwood floors were highly polished, the wide oak strips warm and golden. Her own unique touches of scented candles and potpourri were everywhere, her extensive collection of dragon figurines covering the empty spaces upon the bookshelves that lined the walls.

To Rachael Lafferty, the Victorian was not just a house. It was a home.

"My painting is who is here," she answered as she grinned devilishly at her friend over the wooden box. "Or should I say, he is here." She slipped her fingers between the edges of the wood and pulled. "Let me get something to pry this open with." She quickly jogged from the foyer and disappeared.

Tessa's curiosity was peaked, and she took up position at the opposite end of the crate. "He?" She stared at the crate, her hands propped on her hips as she waited. "Hurry up, Rachael! Julian will be here in a half-hour to pick me up," she called in a huffy tone. She cocked her head, wondering what hideous Art Deco monstrosity was inside. As soon as Rachael returned, Tessa helped her pull the wood free, the slats falling to the floor with a clatter. The painting inside was covered by a cloth of purple which was barely visible through the packing material.

Rachael pulled the remainder of the packing material free, the straw-like substance littering the floor around her feet. Carefully they eased the portrait from its wooden confines, taking care not to catch the canvas on anything as it cleared the packing crate. They propped up the life-size portrait, which stood over six feet, and leaned it against the wall. Rachael pulled the purple cloth and acid-free protector from the gilt frame. "Turn on the light, Tessa," she instructed as she took a step back. She smiled as the overhead chandelier softly illuminated the room, casting its light upon the portrait. "Isn't he beautiful?" she whispered in awe as she propped her elbow on her arm.

Tessa looked at the portrait then back to Rachael before shrugging in boredom. "I can see why you like it. He looks like he stepped out of one of your novels."

Rachael pulled off her tan blazer, draping it on the newel post. The sparkles in her blue blouse danced as she moved back towards her painting. She tilted her head as she tapped her finger against her lips. Tessa was right, he did look like a character from one of the historical romances she wrote. She couldn't resist the childlike grin that lit her face. "Really? Which one?"

Tessa snorted in disdain as she walked away from the portrait. Her boots clicked on the wooden floor until she stepped on the Persian rug in the sitting room. The room was shaped like a huge oval, a large fireplace gracing the far wall, a lithograph copy of Vincent Van Gogh's *Starry Starry Night* above the mantle. Books lined the walls to the right and left from floor to ceiling, broken only by the entrances that were dispersed every five feet leading into the hallway both upstairs and down. The furniture was as old the house itself, original pieces that were priceless antiques dating back to the late 1800's and the glory that was Victoria's reign. They were arranged within the length and breadth of the Persian rug and provided a comfortable atmosphere for entertaining. "Any one of those tawdry gothic novels that you're so good at," Tessa replied as she stopped at the sideboard beneath the circular staircase. She poured each of them a glass of rich, sweet port wine from the crystal decanter and returned to Rachael's side, handing her one of the glasses. "So, who is he?"

Rachael took a sip of the spirit, rolling it over her tongue. It was sweet with the slightest nutty flavor, the perfect bouquet. "I don't know," she remarked wistfully.

Tessa looked at her in surprise, trying to keep the disbelief from her voice. "You bought a painting of a strange man and you don't know who it is?"

Rachael nodded, swirling the wine in the glass. "That's what I said." She moved into the sitting room, settling down in the brocade, wingback chair that stood just feet from the cold fireplace. She had spent a small fortune restoring the antiques in the house to their original splendor, the only liberty she had afforded herself being the new upholstery that covered the wing-backed chairs, love seat and sofa that graced the room. The craftsmanship that was the wooden framework of the furniture was unparalleled and needed little to no work.

They were not the only items within the townhouse she had fixed. New plaster coated the walls of the halls, fresh paint in the lightest of tan bringing them warmth. The plaster on the ceilings had also been repaired, a new decorative medallion installed around the fixture of the large chandelier that hung over the library. She had refurbished the old kitchen with the best countertops, cabinets and appliances money could buy, hiring handcrafters to create everything that was not electrical. Even the bath upstairs had been modernized, although she kept the large claw-foot tub that she had found within when she bought the house. Long, hot bubble baths were her main vice and she enjoyed them tremendously in the deep tub. Every fireplace worked with a clear chimney and vented flue, every window was storm protected, every tile on the roof new. The entire house appealed to her romantic side and the modernization gave it a breath of new life.

Rachael gazed at Tessa as she sat primly on the sofa. "Oh, face it, Tess. He could be anyone," she commented regarding the portrait she could see standing in the foyer from her seat. "So, I bought a nameless portrait. Sue me."

Tessa simply shook her head. "Now I know you are crazy." Her eyes met Rachael's and the two women chuckled softly at the unspoken jest. She finished her wine as the mantel clock chimed seven. "Well, at least you're happy. I suppose that is all that matters." She stood up, returning her glass to the sideboard. "Julian will be here any moment. I'll help you hang your mysterious man before I leave," she offered as Rachael sat her glass down. Both women passed through the wide doorway back into the upstairs foyer.

Together, Rachael and Tessa lifted the portrait of the handsome, young aristocrat. They carried it up the short flight of stairs to the landing. "Right here. I hung up the nails two days ago." She pointed to the empty space on the wall.

"Smart girl," Tessa commented. She glanced at the hangar on the back of the portrait and they lifted it into place.

The portrait fit perfectly in the spot Rachael had chosen for it, almost as if it was designed to hang there. The two small lamps hanging on either side of the painting, their pale blue shades softening the harshness of the bulbs beneath, cast a warm glow on the man's face, bringing it to life. His eyes seemed to brighten in the shadowy confines of the landing. There was a luster to his boots and the chain of his pocket watch. And, if one didn't know better, the portrait's subject seemed to suddenly stand up straighter.

Rachael stared at the portrait with tears in her eyes. He was inspiring, with his full red lips and twinkling brown eyes, and her fingers wiggled with the desire to type, a new story working its way through her body. It sent a pleasurable shiver down her spine. "Do you see it Tessa?" she asked softly. She still couldn't get over the raw beauty of the man in the portrait. She trotted down the stairs and looked up at the painting from the foyer floor. "It's as if he could just walk from the canvas."

Tessa looked down at Rachael. "You need a long vacation." She heard the soft rap of knuckles on the glass door and calmly walked across the foyer, fetching her coat. "I better not find you standing in the same spot come morning." She wrapped her scarf around her head before giving Rachael a sisterly kiss on the cheek. "I mean it," she warned as she closed the door.

Rachael took one last look at the portrait and turned away, bending down to gather up the packing material that was spewed across the floor. She tossed it all back into the crate, pausing every now and then to study the portrait of her mystery man. She could almost feel his eyes on her back as she moved about, clearing the foyer of the packing crate and inside material. That fact didn't seem to bother her in the least. She reached out and turned off the foyer light just as the door opened, letting in a gust of cold air from the street side entry on the floor below.

"See? She has moved. Rachael is not a statue, Tessa." Julian Falcon, the head curator at the British Museum of Art, remarked as he gazed at his wife as she made her way back up the stairs from the entrance hall. He swept into the foyer, his tan wool coat billowing around him as he took the stairs to the landing two at a time. He considered the painting of the unknown man with a critical eye. He motioned behind him with his left hand. "Turn on the light, love. These lamps aren't bright enough."

Tessa shrugged and with a sigh, she did as her husband requested. Standing beside Rachael they watched as Julian slipped on his small, wire-rimmed glasses and began to inspect the portrait. "He insisted on seeing it, Rachael. He turned the car around and drove back here," she whispered to her friend, not wanting to disturb Julian, who running a trained and critical eye over the canvas.

Rachael glanced at Tessa. "Oh, please," she teased as she leaned against the newel post. "You barely had enough time to get to the car."

Julian began at the bottom of the portrait and took his time, gazing over every inch of the full-sized painting. He ran his hand carefully along the gilt frame, shaking his head in disbelief at what he was seeing. "This painting is," he paused searching for the right word, "phenomenal. Definitely mid1700s." He stepped back, cocking his head before bending down to gaze at the scarlet slash of the artist's signature in the lower right-hand corner. "Rachael, where did you get this?" he asked softly. He never took his eyes from the portrait.

"At an auction about two weeks ago. I was about to leave when they brought it out." She shrugged. "No one bid on it and they were about to close the auction when I raised my little card." She smiled with glee as she waved her hand. "I got him for a song." She climbed the stairs to stand next to Julian.

"How much, if you don't mind me asking," Julian inquired as he lightly touched the canvas, feeling the rough edges of the oil paint that was used to create the masterpiece before him.

"Two thousand pounds." Rachael glanced down at him as he coughed in disbelief, withdrawing a white handkerchief from his pocket and dabbing at his lips. She could see the sparkle in his eyes and her smile faded only slightly as she sensed that the museum curator was about to confirm her suspicion. "He's worth more, isn't he?"

Julian stood up and removed his glasses, carefully folding the arms down and placing them in their case. "Rachael, this portrait is priceless." He tucked the glasses case back into the inner pocket of his coat along with the handkerchief. "Do you have any idea who this man is?" His green eyes met hers in earnest.

Tessa snorted as she leaned against the sideboard, her hands folded before her. "She has no idea, Julian. She bought a painting of a nameless man."

Julian's eyebrows rose as he gazed at his wife, turning slightly to lay a hand on the banister, motioning to the portrait with the other. "Tessa, he is not nameless." He turned back to the painting in awe, admiring the fine brush strokes that detailed the man's rich clothing and accouterments. "This painting has been missing for over a hundred years." He chuckled softly. "This is none other than Dorian Gray."

"Dorian Gray?" Tessa scoffed as she stood up and walked towards them. "Jules, that is a story. A literary classic, but a work of fiction."

Rachael moved closer to the portrait entranced, her eyes locked on the eyes in the painting. "Dorian Gray. *The Picture of Dorian Gray* was written by Oscar Wilde in 1891. It's the only full-length novel he ever produced. A beautiful, yet sad, work of fiction about a lonely and decadent man in Victorian England."

Julian shook his head as he walked down the stairs. "But it wasn't fiction," he remarked in excitement. He drew his coat back and tucked his hands into the pockets of his charcoal trousers. "Oscar Wilde was none other than the character Lord Henry Wotton, Dorian's friend and confidante. He was among the people who identified Dorian's withered corpse in one of your second-floor rooms." He ran his fingers through his hair. "Wilde had also seen the portrait before Dorian died. He had seen the old man in the painting and made sure to warn Dorian away." He shrugged. "And we know what happened," he added as an afterthought as he looked at Rachael knowingly.

Rachael stood still, stood gazing at the portrait before continuing Dorian Gray's sordid little tale where Julian had left off. "When Dorian slashed the painting in his relentless search to regain his lost youth, he signed his own death warrant. The portrait, restored itself to the image of Dorian as a virulent young man." She glanced at Julian, an odd look on her face. "At least the image of the virulent young man he still was at the time. Which explains his clothing compared to the age of the painting itself," she whispered in fascination as she lightly ran her fingers along the brushstrokes that made up the gray pinstripe of Dorian's finely tailored suit.

Julian smiled up at her. "Precisely." He pointed to Rachael. "This is why the painting is invaluable. I would have it insured, if I were you."

Tessa's mouth dropped open. "Please don't tell me the two of you believe this nonsense." She sniffed derisively. "You are both insane. You've been breathing London's foul air for too long." She turned on one heel and headed back out into the night. "I'll be waiting in the car," she called back to her husband, having had enough of legends and gothic tales based on a piece of literature.

Julian laughed as he watched his wife walk back out into the cold. "It is a fanciful story, but it is also the truth. I wrote my doctoral thesis on Dorian Gray and the portrait Basil Hallward had painted. Some of Hallward's paintings are displayed in the gallery, which is how I knew he at least was real." He looked over his shoulder, giving the portrait of Dorian Gray one last look before making his way to the glass door of the foyer. He stopped, one hand on the doorknob as his gaze lingered on the painting for another brief second before looking at Rachael. "I wonder where it has been since 1893. I suppose we'll never know. He's in good hands with you, Rachael." He nodded to her. "Good night." Julian closed the door gently behind him and the house grew silent once again.

Rachael smiled at the painting, marveling at her good fortune. "Good night, Dorian Gray," she stated warmly, chuckling at the fact that she had said goodnight to a painting. She made her way back to the foyer, locked the inside door for the night and turned off the light. She glanced once last time at the painting before stepping into the sitting room and lighting the fire. By the time she returned from the kitchen with a hot cup of Earl Gray tea, the room had warmed as the fire crackled cozily. She decided to take the night off from writing and settled on the couch with a book. It wasn't long before she was asleep, her tea cold on the table beside her, and thoughts of Dorian Gray whirling through her mind.

THE SMALL CLOCK UPON the fireplace mantel in the sitting room chimed midnight. The witching hour. The fire had burned down to low embers, emitting a soft orange glow across the hardwood floor. Only the small lamp Rachael had been reading by illuminated the large sitting room, its light not even touching the shadows that seemed to close in upon the sleeping figure on the couch. The light didn't touch the bottom of the third-floor balcony. Occasionally the house settled with a soft creak, almost as if it were sighing. Beyond that, the house was still, as if waiting for something.

Snow fell outside, blanketing London with its white radiance beneath the electric streetlamps that were evenly dispersed along the roadways. It glittered outside the glass panes of the shops and eateries, sparkling in the night. Even the city, usually bustling at midnight, was silent and still, holding its breath as the deepest dark fell upon it. Not even the inhabitants of the old city braved the cold, dark night of winter, having scurried indoors at the first sign of inclemency. It was a perfect night for staying inside to keep warm, watching the television, listening to music, enjoying one's family.

The portrait shuddered in earnest, expanding like the lungs of a newborn child as it took its first breath of air outside the womb. The paint that had been carefully placed on the canvas moved with the fabric beneath it, each stroke of the brush lengthening before returning to its proper size, stretching, retracting, stretching, retracting. A soft glow emanated from the painting, starting above the heart of the man captured for all time in oil and moving outward, illuminating the raised pigments, making them appear as if they were once again wet. The colors suddenly became brighter, warmer, fresher.

Dorian Gray became aware at the last stroke of midnight and he could feel himself finally starting to warm up after an eternity of coldness and darkness, similar to this night that gave him rebirth. His deep brown eyes began to clear, focusing on a strange, new world as he stared down into the foyer of a large home, the surroundings familiar yet strange. It took him quite a few moments to realize that the room he gazed into was the second-floor foyer of his own townhouse on the East docks of London. Yet he could not place the uneasy feeling that settled into the pit of his stomach as his gaze traversed the room, recognizing only a few pieces of the furniture that were strategically positioned along the walls.

He had no idea how long he had been trapped in his own portrait, positive that his decadent and less than savory lifestyle had damned him to the deepest pits of hell. He took a deep shuddering breath, the first since his tragic demise in 1891. It caused the canvas to move slightly, as if a soft breeze had touched upon it. It was at that time he took his first tentative step forward.

Dorian felt the pull of the canvas, the painting not wanting to give him up. Yet he was determined to become free and he forced his body to move. He reached out slowly, his hand appearing from the portrait like a white specter, his booted foot following. The colors of the painting stretched behind him, reluctant before snapping silently back into place on the canvas as the man continued his forward motion. His face became elongated as it pushed through the shroud that held him in the painting, his hair falling to his shoulders as it was finally released. The magic that surrounded the portrait shattered, the glow that came from deep within intensifying until the landing in the foyer stairwell was coated in brilliant white that disappeared as fast as it had appeared.

For a moment, the world swam around Dorian, blurring the colors that sprang to life as he stepped onto the solid landing beneath his portrait. His vision cleared and could feel the silver top of his walking stick, cold and hard beneath the palm of his left hand. He raised it into the air, studying it for a moment in remembrance before tapping its tip in the palm of his right hand. A small smile crossed his lips as he breathed a sigh of relief. He was finally free of the portrait that had haunted him for so long. He gazed back from whence he came to see his image still upon the canvas, the colors now more faded, before turning on the ball of his foot to descend the stairs.

Photos lined the wall to Dorian's left, and he pondered over each one for a few moments before moving on, the faces unknown to him, causing him to contemplate whom they could possibly be. The clothing they wore was strange to him, the women in trousers of a blue material he had never seen before. Many of the women wore their hair cut above the shoulders, something that was almost of unheard of in his day. Even the style of the men's clothing and hair was puzzling.

He paused at the last portrait on the wall, his fingers sliding slowly down the glass that covered it. It was of a single woman with piercing violet eyes and bow-shaped lips that were tilted in the softest of smiles. Her low-cut blouse revealed an ample amount of creamy skin and his eyes widened in curiosity. "And who are you?" he whispered in question, pleasantly surprised by what he saw. His cultured, accented voice was rough from disuse, yet he dismissed it knowing that a strong cup of tea would cure the raspiness in the back of his throat.

Dorian continued through the foyer, running his fingers along the small table that stood near the door. The silver plate that once held visitors calling cards still sat in the middle of the tabletop, polished and bright, but now it held a set of odd-looking keys. He picked up the keys, dangling them before him as he studied their shape. They were not the standard skeleton keys he knew. Instead, they were smaller, the shiny metal cold and jagged. He grunted softly as he replaced them in the silver plate. Turning, he gazed once again through the room, noticing the crystal chandelier above him and the fresh paint that coated the walls. Even the hardwood floors beneath his feet no longer held the scratches and scuffmarks it once did. He ran his fingers along the leather jacket that hung on the stand in the corner, the material soft, a stark comparison to the hard keys he had just handled. After a moment, he continued to the entrance door, reaching out to wrap his fingers around the bronze doorknob that beckoned him. Instead of the solid metal he expected to grip, his fingers passed right through the knob. His brows furrowed as he tried again with the same results.

"That's strange," he mumbled, staring at his fingers as he rubbed them together. Why could he handle objects in the house, yet he could not grip the handle of the front door? Was it a trick, some strange repercussion that allowed him to leave his painted prison but not his home? He blinked in confusion and once again reached out to stroke the warm leather of Rachael's jacket. He looked back to the door and tried grasping the knob for a third time. The results were still the same. He simply could not grasp it. With a disgusted sigh, he set his walking stick next to the coat rack and moved on into the sitting room.

Dorian's boots were silent up the hardwood floor as he moved through the foyer to the sitting room. One would have expected to hear the click-click of his boots as he moved, but there was nothing. He gazed around the room that had once been his favorite. All of the furniture that graced the room once belonged to him, although the upholstery that now covered it was in considerably better condition than he remembered. It was also different. Whereas his furniture had been upholstered in muted tones of burgundy and light tan, the fabric that covered the antiques were patterned with small flowers and complimented with light mauves and pinks. He looked at the mantel clock as it chimed half past twelve. Withdrawing his pocket watch from his vest pocket, he opened it with a soft click in the silent room. The mantel clock was fast, again. He snorted slightly, for the clock above the fire had never kept the proper time. Satisfied, he snapped the watch shut and returned it to his vest. Slowly he made his way around the room, touching a book here, a trinket there as he inspected every subtle nuance of change that occurred in his home.

The soft feminine moan behind him gave him pause and he turned. Dorian cautiously approached the sofa, taking care not to entangle his feet in the odd cord that ran from the room's only source of illumination to an even odder square in the wall. He gazed over the back of the couch and found himself suddenly staring into the sleeping face that graced the stairway wall. Her thick eyelashes lay softly upon her cheeks as if they were the finest black lace. Her rose colored lips were slightly parted as she slept, her cheek cradled upon a delicate hand. He watched as she shivered slightly, turning more fully on her side and away from him, drawing her knees to her chest as she curled into a ball. The book that was in her other hand slipped free, falling to the floor with a dull thud as her fingers relaxed.

Dorian walked slowly around the sofa and retrieved the volume, gazing at the title embossed on the leather binding. "*Nicholas Nickleby*," he read out loud. "A bit dry, but still very good." He peered down at Rachael before striding to the wall and replacing the book on the shelf where it belonged. He gazed over the titles, noticing many classics by Dickens, Shakespeare, and the Brontë sisters. There were also many other authors, names he did not recognize. The shelves that lined the walls of the sitting room were filled from top to bottom, a fact that comforted him. It seemed that the stranger, who inhabited his home was well-read, a pleasing thought that left intelligent conversation an option. That was assuming she could see and hear him, a fact that yet remained to be discovered.

A soft blanket was draped across the back of the chaise in the corner, and he retrieved it, snapping it open. Gently, he covered the beautiful and mysterious woman, who had invaded his home, then he reached out to lightly stroke his forefinger along the line of her jaw. Her skin was soft and warm beneath his touch, sending a jolt through his body that he was not expecting.

He smiled to himself, the simple gesture softening his features. He retreated to the circular staircase that led to the upper floor, pausing at an opening between the tall bookshelves to gaze down. He could see more clearly the subtle, yet feminine, changes that graced the dark room below, the softness of the newly remade furniture, the small trinkets that littered the shelves and tables of a womanly bent. He could not help returning his gaze to her face and he let it trace the features of the sleeping woman. "The face of an angel," he murmured haughtily, "with the body of temptress," he finished in a husky growl.

Satisfied that she would not awaken, he continued on along the balcony to peer in the rooms he once inhabited in life. He found himself inexplicably drawn to the room that once held the bane of his existence, the smallest of the three bedrooms on the second floor. It was the furthest room from the master bedroom and usually the coldest. He stood within the doorway, his eyes scanning the room. The easel that had propped up his life-size portrait for more than a century was gone. In its place before the double windows that overlooked the street was a large oak desk. An unusual two-inch thick rectangle stood on a pedestal in the middle of the desk, its surface flat and black. There was a board beneath with the letters of the alphabet scattered across in what appeared to him to be in no semblance of order. It reminded him of the typewriter he had seen a friend use to compose letters and articles that appeared in the daily press, except it was considerably more compact. A smaller box sat beside it, a red ball perched in the middle of it.

"What is this?" he queried softly as his fingers tentatively touched the ball. The rectangle flared to life, causing him to squint in the darkness as he stared at the image of a dragon, which had appeared before him. A small arrow moved across the image as he rolled the ball in its cradle, his brow furrowing. "Interesting."

Dorian lifted his hand and stepped away from the desk, glancing back momentarily before returning to his inspection of the room. His armoire, which once housed his elegant clothing, stood against the wall to the right of the desk. Carefully he opened the doors finding that now it was filled with soft angora sweaters and neatly pressed trousers, including a few of the strange blue ones he had seen in the photo. He closed the doors and moved to the window, brushing aside the curtain as he gazed upon the river Thames. The snow glistened as it fell, covering the street below. Metal and glass beasts lined the roadway opposite the river, horseless carriages of the modern age that he had read about before his death, but had never seen.

A single dark eyebrow rose as he considered how much things had changed since his death. He had the desire to feel the cold air on his skin and reached for the window latch, planning to open it wide for a brief moment to breathe the air of London. But as with the foyer door below him, his hand could not grip the latch, his fingers simply slipping through it as if he was not even there. With a disgusted sigh, he turned away from the window and once again studied the room.

Dorian's eyes fell to the bookcase beside the door and he carefully made his way around the desk to peruse the books that were neatly lined upon the top shelf. He glanced across the titles printed on the spines, stopping when one caught his attention. He picked it up and smiled. "*The Rake Notorious.* There is a term I haven't heard in a long time," he commented to himself as he thumbed through the pages of the volume in his hand. He paused, carrying the book back to the desk and glancing at the picture on the back flap of the dust jacket by the light of the computer monitor. "So," he breathed in mild surprise, "your name is Rachael Lafferty." He read the short biography. "An American nonetheless."

He closed the book and tucked it beneath his arm as he walked from the room, gazing over the balcony to spy on Rachael still sleeping below. Her chest rose and fell in deep sleep. "Sweet dreams, Miss Lafferty," he whispered before touching the fingers of his left hand to his lips and throwing her a kiss.

His footsteps were once again silent as he moved along the upper floor towards the master bedroom, pushing open the double doors and pausing. The room was just the way he remembered it. A large four-poster bed stood on the far wall, a set of round back Victorian chairs in the alcove before the window. A heavy dresser with a full mirror stood across the room from the bed and he paused at it, leaning forward to glance at himself. "Haven't changed a bit, Gray. Not one bit," he murmured as he smoothed his fingers along his mustache. His hair was still thick and a rich mahogany brown, falling to his shoulders with an impish curl, not even a hint of silver running through it. His cheekbones were still high and chiseled, his skin smooth with no lines, no wrinkles, no crow's feet around the eyes. His lips had retained the fullness of youth and his clothing still held the crisp feel of newness.

He turned away from the mirror, pleased with the reflection he had gazed upon and tossed the book onto the bed. It softly thudded on the lavender bedspread. "Not exactly my color, but it will do," he remarked off-handedly about the spread. The lamp on the night table was lit and he shrugged off his jacket and vest, tossing them casually on one of the chairs before removing his boots. He sat on the bed, his brow furrowing. The mattress was harder than he expected, but it seemed comfortable enough as he propped the pillows against the headboard. The movement caused the scent of vanilla to drift to his nose and he inhaled deeply, closing his dark eyes and savoring the smell. Leaning back against the pillows, he gracefully crossed his ankles and opened the book, quickly becoming involved in Rachael's story of the notorious rake.

The still winter night settled around the old townhouse, a comfortable silence as the snow continued to lightly fall. The impression of the house holding its breath dissipated, as if it knew its master was home. Had anyone walked into the bedroom that night, they would've seen the most unusual of sights. A hard-covered book floated above the lavender coverlet, the pages eerily turning by themselves in the quiet London night, and only the sound of invisible fingers upon paper disturbed the stillness.

Chapter Two

DECEMBER 22ND

Rachael hummed to herself as she carried the third plastic storage box of Christmas decorations from the attic of her townhouse. It was the only area of the Victorian she had not modernized, with the exception of new insulation, and it was large enough to eventually turn into a writing studio. She knew exactly how it would look when she was done with it, the walls that formed the peak of the roof covered with white board that would eventually hold her Post-It note outlines. That was assuming she could bring herself to clean the attic out. There were steamer trunks of items scattered all around it and she had yet to have the time to look through them. She paused on the landing, gazing at the full-length portrait of the tragic Dorian Gray. "Are those steamer trunks in my attic yours, Mr. Gray?" she asked playfully. She chuckled at her own silliness before continuing to the floor of the foyer.

The compact disc player in the sitting room spilled the sounds of Christmas carols through the townhouse and Rachael found herself humming along with them as she lined up the boxes of decorations. A ten-foot Douglas fir stood in the corner opposite Dorian's painting, white lights already twinkling from its boughs, keeping time with the music that was playing. She picked up the remote and turned the music up as she rubbed her stiff neck, rolling it to loosen her muscles. She didn't see the apparition that had been watching her, following her from level to level as she decorated for the holiday.

Dorian stepped up behind Rachael, reaching out to rub her neck, his fingers merely inches from her flesh when the second-floor entrance door swung open. He closed his eyes, stifling a growl of aggravation at the intrusion. He had been enjoying his quiet contemplation of her, listening to her voice as she sung with the carols that emanated from the stereo in the library. He wanted to know more about her, wanted her to slow down long enough to comfort her, to ease her stiff muscles. She had been on the move since dawn, having woken from her sleep on the sofa and returning to the bedroom, totally unaware of his presence in the house. She had made an impression on Dorian, one that he could not yet describe, but one, nonetheless.

Dorian turned his attention to Tessa Falcon, taking an immediate dislike to the woman. She exuded arrogance, and he had known plenty of women like her. They had no qualms about complimenting one to their face before cutting them off at the waist behind their backs. He had to find out what her connection was to Rachael.

His eyes narrowed as he stood before her, blocking her path as she closed the door behind her, pausing to stare at the tree. When Tessa did not scream at his presence, he simply stepped back, blending into the shadows of the corner as if he was part of them. Her lack of reaction confirmed a nagging suspicion that had plagued him the entire night and it opened another door to a myriad of questions and possibilities. He gracefully folded his perfectly manicured hands at his waist, his eyes following Rachael's every move. He was a patient man and he knew he could wait until the opportune moment before determining whether she was an asset or a liability to the young woman, who now resided in his home. For Dorian had taken an instant liking to Rachael the moment he had set eyes on her sleeping on the couch the night before.

"Good Lord, Rachael," Tessa exclaimed rudely, "do you think it's large enough?" She removed her leather gloves, laying them on the sideboard before hanging her coat upon the rack in the corner.

Dorian sighed in disgusted, and he pushed the coat out of his line of vision. He smiled as he saw Rachael silently mocking the woman as she added another strand of white lights to the back of the tree.

Tessa didn't see. She checked her cell phone before setting it by her gloves. "You always did have a penchant for excess," she sneered with a haughty shake of her head. "Tea?" she asked as she rubbed her hands together.

Rachael leaned over one of the boxes, pushing items aside as she searched for the ornaments she wanted. "I have a penchant for large Christmas trees, Tessa," she remarked as she wiped her hands on her blue jeans. She straightened, her eyes dancing as she looked at the pine. "Besides, a large Victorian townhouse deserves an equally large tree."

She turned away from the tree, shivering for a moment as Dorian slipped behind her, his hand brushing across the back of her neck. "You let the cold air in," she chided Tessa as she walked towards the sitting room. When a glint of silver in the corner caught her eye, she stopped and picked up the ornate, silver-tipped walking stick. "Where did this come from?" she asked as she studied it, rolling the finely crafted cane in her hands, taking in the minute detail of the scrollwork along its length. The handle wiggled slightly in her hand and she tugged, revealing a very sharp sword within the length of the cane. "Oh my," she giggled as she pulled it free. *"En garde!"*

Tessa backed away, her hands up in defense. "Put that away before you get hurt! Really, Rachael, the things you purchase." She snorted. "You're becoming way too involved in the research of your stories."

Rachael slid the sword back into the cane. "Did you leave this here?" she asked curiously, wondering if Tessa was playing a joke on her. The literary agent knew of her love for unique things, and the cane with its hidden sword would've been a perfect gift.

"Hardly." Tessa waved her hand in dismissal. "I would suspect that one of the delivery men left it." She turned away, walking deeper into the sitting room.

Dorian stood on the landing beneath his portrait. "Not highly likely," he muttered in annoyance. He never expected anyone to see the cane, and his curiosity was peaked. How could they see his walking stick and not him? It simply defied reason and logic, and added to the mystery that surrounded both him and his release from the portrait. Were the two tied together? They almost had to be. He stroked his mustache as he watched the two women, his mind racing in contemplation of his sudden freedom.

Rachael turned her head towards the stairs. "Did you say something?" she called as she set the cane back in its place. When Tessa didn't answer, she shrugged and followed her friend through the house, to the kitchen in the back. She leaned against the island counter as Tessa filled the kettle and set it on the stove. "How was dinner last night?" she inquired, attempting to make small talk as Tessa prepared the ceramic teapot. "Was that new restaurant as good as everyone said?"

Tessa shrugged. "It was all right. The service was slow, but the quality of the food made up for it." She looked at her friend as she leaned across from her. "Where is my manuscript? You were supposed to have it to me two days ago. I cannot keep putting off the publisher, Rachael."

Dorian stood outside the kitchen, listening to Tessa berate the younger woman. He shook his head as he walked away, pausing as he continued listening to the conversation.

"Do you hear footsteps?" Tessa asked suddenly as she looked from the kitchen door into the hall. She walked to the entrance, glancing up and down the curved corridor. "Hello?"

Rachael snorted. "Great. Now you're hearing things, Tess." She poured tea into the cups she had set on the table. "And you talk about me."

Dorian smiled to himself as he continued back to the foyer, sure that the sound of his footsteps could still be heard in the kitchen. He had enjoyed the discomfort he heard in Tessa's voice when she called out. He gazed at the enormous tree skeptically and wondered just how close to Christmas it was, and he peered into the boxes of decorations Rachael had set out. He bent down, resting one arm on his gray trousered knee as he lifted a small glass ornament from the box.

The small, strange, gray box the woman called "Tessa" had lain on the table chirped and he stood, picking up the cell phone and staring at it. He let his eyes slide sideways at the laughter that erupted from the kitchen, before sliding it into his pocket and returning to his inspection of the items before him. He picked up a whimsical ornament of a teddy bear and shook his head. "No, no, dear Rachael, these will never do."

He stood and made his way up the staircase, heading for the attic. Dorian was surprised to find the old steamer trunk that held his decorations still in the farthest corner of the attic, right where he had left it after he had celebrated his last Christmas on Earth. He ducked beneath the rafter, opening the trunk carefully after blowing away the debris that covered the lid. He reached in to push aside the decaying packing material, and it crumbled to dust in his hands, giving him pause, remembering the feeling of his demise as his body decomposed the same way. His lips thinned as he brushed his hands on his pants, pushing the memory away, his eyes resting upon the purpose of his journey to the attic.

Reverently, Dorian lifted from the trunk the porcelain angel that had graced his own tree at one time. Her velvet dress was faded, and he half expected it to disintegrate when he touched it. Yet it didn't, the tight seal of the trunk protecting it from the ravages of time. He rubbed a gold curl between his fingers before setting her aside and gathering up the now antique crystal ornaments that were stored within. He stood and felt the phone in his pocket vibrate. Shifting his gifts to Rachael into one arm, he retrieved the small device and tossed it in the trunk, shutting the lid before leaving the attic.

When he returned to the landing, he tilted his head to listen for Rachael and Tessa. He could hear their voices drifting from the kitchen and raised in argument, discussing what he could only assume was a scene in the newest of novels that the author was penning. He did not like the arrogant tone Tessa took with Rachael, yet he knew that he was powerless to do anything about it.

Or was he? He looked at the coat hanging on the rack behind him and set the ornaments and angel aside, and, picking up his cane, he unsheathed the sword. With two quick slashes, he let his displeasure be known, shredding Tessa's coat. Content for the moment, he returned to the tree and began to put the ornaments on it.

"Fine, fine. Let the scene stand as is. Who am I to argue?" Tessa's voice floated from the entrance of the sitting room into the foyer. "And, about this party, I still think you should allow me to have it at the estate. There is no way you are going to be ready." Her boots clicked on the hardwood floor as she crossed the sitting room. "Besides, this place is..." She stopped just within the doorway, her mouth hanging open, her words dying on her lips.

Rachael sighed as she pushed past Tessa, not seeing what had silenced her friend. Rachael pulled her long hair into a ponytail. "Yes, I know, Tessa. Creepy," she finished sarcastically, glancing back at her and wiggling her fingers. She laughed as she stopped walking, turning to look at Tessa. "What's the matter? You're always teasing me about this place being spooky. Can't I have a little fun back?"

Tessa had paled visibly. "Spooky? Right now, the word *haunted* comes to mind," she managed to stammer. "Okay, Rachael. Pack up your belongings and let's go. You are not staying here," she ordered as she set the teacup she had been carrying on the sideboard. She picked up her gloves, her brow furrowing as she bent over to peer under the piece of furniture. "Where's my phone?" she asked in a panic.

Rachael started to follow Tessa, stopping mid-turn as she saw what had caused Tessa's sudden panic. "By your gloves," she answered breathlessly as she covered her mouth with her hand, tears springing to her eyes. She stared lovingly at the angel in her red dress atop the tree, slowly reaching out to slide her fingers over a crystal ornament of a partridge. "Tessa, she's beautiful." She cradled the bird in her hands, looking at the other woman. "And these ornaments. Where did you find them?"

Tessa straightened, staring at the ornaments that Rachael was admiring and touching ever so gently. "Nowhere," she remarked, the slight hitch of fear marring her cultured voice.

Rachael laughed. "Oh, stop it, Tessa. C'mon. Tell me. How did you do this?" She walked over to the door, swinging it open and gazing down into the entrance hall. "Come out Julian. The game is up, I've seen the tree," she called out into the empty space.

She stepped through the door, leaning over the railing to peer into the lower entrance hall, her lips pursing when she didn't see Julian hiding from her.

Dorian leaned on the balcony railing above the library. He had a clear view down into the foyer from his vantage point and was utterly amused. After spending the night reading the novel Rachael had penned, he knew she would love the ornaments that survived in the trunk upstairs. He leaned his hip on the rail, clasping his knee, enjoying the fear that emanated from Tessa.

Tessa shook her head vehemently as she pulled Rachael back into the foyer, pushing the foyer door shut as her hand clutched her friend's arm. Red strands of hair stuck to her cheeks, her eyes wide with terror. "We did not do this, Rachael," she insisted as she pointed to the decorations on the tree. "I'm telling you, this house is haunted."

She was facing Dorian, never seeing him as he observed them from the upstairs balcony. "Let's go. Now." She grabbed her coat and screamed as she held it up, looking at the slashes down the back. "You wretched poltergeist!" she yelled.

Rachael's eyes widened as she took Tessa's coat, gaping at the torn fabric. "Tess, I'm sorry. I...I must have done this when I was fooling around with the cane." She removed her leather jacket from the rack. "Here. I'll buy you a new one, I promise," she apologized, chewing her lower lip in worry.

Tessa stared at her in horror. "This place is haunted, and I'm not staying." She grabbed her coat from her.

Rachael shook her head sadly as she gazed at her friend. "Get a grip, Tessa. I've apologized for your coat. What more do you want?" She watched as Tessa pulled her ruined coat on, visibly shaken by finding her clothing ruined in such a fashion.

Sighing in resignation as she turned away, wiping the tears from her eyes, Rachael knelt next to the box of her grandmother's beloved ornaments, searching for ones that would complement the crystal gifts that glittered on her tree. She took the first one and slipped a slender green hook in the loop on top, hanging it up before gathering another ornament. "If you don't want to admit to buying these, then don't." She sniffed in hurt as she stood, setting the second ornament on a branch. "And I'll replace your coat."

Tessa grabbed Rachael's arm roughly, spinning her around to face her. Her eyes were fervent as they silently begged with her friend. "To hell with my coat, Rachael. Julian and I did not do this. And your house, dear, is most definitely haunted.

"It is not safe," she finished in a hurried whisper, her eyes darting around the room. "Please."

Rachael jerked her arm free, her jaw clenching as she protested adamantly, "No. I'm not leaving my home." She chuckled ruefully, shaking her head. "The party is in three days. I've already sent out the invitations and booked Grace." She turned away sadly. She knew Tessa was wavering between fury and fear and she did not want to get into a heated argument with her over a bunch of decorations. It was bad enough she was agitated over her friend's reaction and she hid the shaking in her hands that agitation caused by continuing to place the decorations on the tree. "Feel free to come if you wish, but not if you're going to be uncomfortable." She paused a moment, hanging her head when Tessa slammed the door, rattling the glass.

Rachael's Christmas spirit had been dampened by her friend's outburst, and she truly was sorry for destroying the coat. There couldn't possibly be any other explanation for the mysterious cuts that marred its woolen surface.

She reached out, retrieving the stereo remote from the sideboard and walked to the doorway of the library. She set the remote on top of the stereo after turning it off, the sudden silence of the house pressing in on her. She didn't mean to upset her friend, but the townhouse was her dream home. She had put too much sweat and tears into modernizing and restoring it as best she could to its original grandeur. She was not about to give it up. Not even for a ghost.

She turned and looked around, hoping maybe to see her invisible housemate. But she saw nothing, no spectral image, no wavering shadows, no mist. "Thank you for the angel and ornaments," she said softly. "They are a beautiful gift." She sighed and finished decorating the tree with red and white velvet bows, before packing up the boxes and returning them to the attic.

Dorian walked slowly down from the balcony to the landing, where his portrait hung, watching Rachael as she reached out to extinguish the chandelier above them with a flip of a dark switch on the wall. He reached up and unbuttoned another button of his white shirt, tucking his hand in the pocket of his trousers as he stepped back, giving Rachael room to pass him on the landing. "You are quite welcome, Rachael," he replied. He watched her pause on the stairs and glance around before continuing on her way with a slight shrug of her shoulders. He remained gazing at the tree as he heard the water turn on in the bath, filling the claw foot tub. "Beautiful," he commented. Turning on one foot, he made his way back to the master bedroom to gaze out the window.

People were bustling in the fading light of day, carrying packages, moving along with harried expressions upon their faces. Dorian leaned against the window frame, not understanding what the hurry was. He had always enjoyed the parties that were held during this time of year, remembering how anxious he had been to receive certain invitations to the fêtes that occurred. He suddenly found himself yearning for those lost days of his youth, when his life was simpler, easier, before he allowed Basil Hallward to paint that damned portrait. It wasn't the first time he had felt that way.

Dorian heard the soft splashing of water and turned to look towards the door. The lost days of his youth were not the only yearning that plagued him, for he found himself longing to be with Rachael Lafferty. It suddenly occurred to him that she was the first woman he'd been interested in since Sibyl Vane—the young actress whose death he had been ultimately responsible for.

However, his attraction to Rachael presented him with a problem. He was now a ghost.

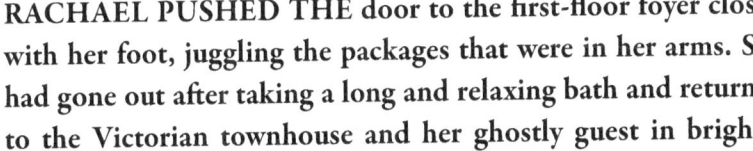

RACHAEL PUSHED THE door to the first-floor foyer closed with her foot, juggling the packages that were in her arms. She had gone out after taking a long and relaxing bath and returned to the Victorian townhouse and her ghostly guest in brighter spirits than when she had left. The more she thought about the apparition that apparently resided in the house, the quainter the idea became to her. Her ghost was obviously thoughtful, as she gazed at the antique ornaments that were mingled with her grandmother's. She grinned.

"I'm home," she called out loud, not the least bothered by the fact that she was probably talking to herself. She glanced at Dorian's portrait, still amazed at her wondrous find.

Carefully, Rachael set the parcels in her arms down beneath the tree. There were packages galore within the paper shopping bags, each of them neatly wrapped in festive paper and bows. A bouquet of fresh cut flowers peaked out of one of the bags, and she picked them up carefully, unwrapping them from the paper the florist had put them in and arranging them neatly in the crystal vase upon the sideboard. They were a perfect combination of red and white roses, difficult to obtain in the winter months, unless one knew where to find them. She leaned over and breathed in their scent, before hanging her jacket upon the rack.

"Welcome home, Rachael," Dorian commented from the landing. He had heard her enter the townhouse and made his way from her office to see what she had brought home. He heard her humming to herself as she moved through the sitting room towards the kitchen. He gazed into the bags, smiling as he reached into the first one and withdrew a small box, placing it beneath the tree. By the time Rachael returned to the foyer, each package had been carefully arranged beneath the huge Christmas tree, the bags folded and neatly stacked on the stairs. And Dorian had slipped into the shadows to await her reaction.

Rachael stopped before the tree with her hands propped on her hips. "Well, I see you are a bit impatient," she chuckled as she gazed at the gifts beneath the tree. The white lights nestled within the boughs were twinkling at her, another surprise from her invisible guest. "And we seem to have figured out the mystery of electricity, although you probably just saw me plug the light strand in, didn't you?" She gathered up the bags that were on the stairs, pausing in thought as she enjoyed the smell of roses and pine that permeated the foyer. "Thank you," she offered quietly, before returning to the kitchen to put the bags in the pantry and pick up her cup of tea.

Dorian watched as she climbed the circular stairway toward the second floor, waiting as he saw the light in her office turn on. He moved to the sideboard to select the most perfect of red roses, before finding his way into the kitchen. She would return to refill her teacup, and he placed the small leather notebook on the island counter, the red rose placed atop its cover, a stark contrast to the darkness of the leather. "You say you know my story, Miss Lafferty," he remarked to himself as his fingers smoothed the leather of the book. "Well, then, here is side that no one has ever seen."

The notebook was his personal journal, the pages yellow and brittle, faded with time. He had discovered it in the attic while she was absent from the house and decided that it would be the most appropriate of clues to his identity. Once again, he slipped into the shadows, gazing out the small window near the table at the Thames. He had no idea how long he stood there before she returned, but her shocked gasp and the sound of ceramic hitting the floor behind him made Dorian turn to face her.

Rachael stared at the notebook and rose, before turning around to see if she could discover who had left it. She searched every room of the townhouse, returning to the kitchen in curiosity. She slowly picked up the shards of ceramic that had recently been a teacup and deposited them into the rubbish, then returned to the island to stare at the notebook.

Cautiously, she reached out to run her fingers along the embossed leather cover, her fingers tracing the same path Dorian's had only a short time earlier. The leather was worn in the center of the book, as if the owner's fingers had traced the design that was once there over and over. She picked up the rose and raised it to her nose, breathing in the flower's heady fragrance as she opened the cover of the book to gaze at the first page. "*Property of Mr. Dorian Gray*," she read the refined handwriting within, setting the rose aside. She retrieved another teacup, almost afraid to turn the page of the notebook and glance at the secrets within. Yet, the writer's imagination within her took hold and she made her way into the sitting room to curl up in one of the wing-backed chairs to read.

Dorian stood behind her chair watching as she slowly turned the first page. He saw a small shiver slide down her body when she looked up. Backing away, he kept to the shadows as she gathered the soft blanket she had found herself beneath earlier that day when she awoke. She wrapped it around her like a cape as she sat back down and began to read aloud from where the book had opened in her lap:

> *March 12, 1890. Oscar came to visit me again and although his company does not upset me, I find myself craving solitude all the more. It could be that the portrait continues to age no matter what I do to stop the haggard lines that appear upon my brow. Is it not enough that I must bear the weight of my deeds upon my conscious? Is it not enough that I must remember the joy of my youth, yet never experience it again, even though physically I have not aged a day since Basil finished the damnable painting? I have seen too many of my contemporaries pass beyond this realm, yet I am not given such reprieve.*

Rachael took a sip of her tea and she turned the page, intrigued by the story that unfolded on the pages in her lap. An additional story of Dorian Gray that no one else, except for her, seemed to be privy to.

Dorian knew the words within by heart and he paced along the outer edges of the sitting room, keeping to the shadows. He made sure his footsteps remained silent on the hardwood floor, for Rachael had yet to acknowledge that she heard him as he moved about with her in the townhouse. He whispered the words in unison with her as she continued reading:

> *I have wasted my life in the pursuit of hedonistic pleasures, giving up the comfort that would have been afforded me had I not fallen to the wayside of sin and debauchery. I fear that no matter how hard I try to make amends for what I have done, it will never be enough. It will nev-*

er satisfy the bloodlust of the cruelest of Fates, who have cursed me. In my own naïveté of youth, I have damned myself to immortality. The fear of my own mortality has given way to a new fear.

He paused in his pacing, gazing back at Rachael. She was staring straight at him, a disturbing look on her beautiful face. He finished the passage softly in the soft light of the lamp at her side: *"The fear of never being able to enjoy the fortitude and wisdom that is born of old age."*

Rachael slowly closed the notebook and stood up, placing it beneath her arm as she let the blanket fall from her shoulders to the chair. She walked past Dorian, paused at the tree long enough to unplug the lights, and stopped on the landing to gaze at his portrait, tracing her finger along the line of his painted jaw. "Maybe you weren't as selfish as people thought you were," she muttered to herself. "Young and naïve, an example to others possibly?" she pondered. She sighed and headed up to the office.

Dorian watched her from the doorway as she settled before the device she referred to as a computer. Her hands operated the machine with expert capacity, and she seemed to slip into a world of pure imagination. He looked to the right, retrieving another book from the shelf and slipping from the room, leaving her to her thoughts and creativity. It was almost twenty-four hours since he had stepped from the portrait. He began to wonder what the next twenty-four would bring.

Later, Rachael staggered to her feet as she pushed away from her desk, the notebook that had mysteriously appeared in her kitchen temporarily forgotten. She glanced at the clock. It was almost three in the morning. She had been sitting in front of the computer trying to work for almost four hours, and she had accomplished absolutely nothing. She was exhausted, both physically and emotionally. Between decorating the house, dealing with Tessa's irrational outburst, and fighting a case of writer's block that had been plaguing her for weeks, she was ready to settle beneath the heavy down comforter that decorated her bed.

"Sleep. I just need some sleep," she mumbled as she stepped from the bathroom, her body functioning on autopilot well enough to get herself changed into her nightgown. She yawned as pushed down the light switch, trudging into the hallway. Her right foot met something solid and she blinked, bending down to feel for the unknown object. She walked into her office and turned on the light. In her hands was her copy of *The Rake Notorious*.

"What are you doing in the hallway?" she asked the book, hoping beyond hope that it would not answer, especially considering that her house was certifiably haunted.

Rachael carried it to the bookcase and slid it back onto the shelf. There was another hole in the row of books and her brow furrowed as she ran her fingers through the empty space. She tilted her head, reciting the titles that sat on the shelf, trying to jog her cloudy mind as to the title that was missing. "Now where did you go?" she asked as she gazed beneath the shelf, blinking sleepily. She peered beneath the armoire and then her desk, running her fingers through her thick hair as she stood in the center of the room, bewildered. She scratched her neck and shrugged. "Great, I have a ghost that reads," she stated quietly. "Or, Tessa snagged it for some reason."

She closed the door to her office and turned to trudge up the corridor towards her bedroom. She stopped, slowly turning on one foot and gazing down into the foyer. The lights of the Christmas tree twinkled at her in the darkness of the house, casting dancing shadows across the foyer floor and along the staircase wall. She was positive she had unplugged the strand. "Fine. I'll leave it on. Obviously, you enjoy it and who am I to argue? Besides, you'll just turn it back on," she muttered.

Rachael rubbed her eyes with the heels of her hands as she headed back towards the bedroom. Once again, she bumped into something that was blocking the hall. Except, this time, it wasn't just her foot that connected with an object, it was her whole body. She reacted before the fear of an intruder in her home could take hold; she lashed to the right with her hand, before following with her left. A pair of strong, masculine hands wrapped around her wrists as she let out a startled scream and kicked her attacker, her foot connecting with a solid shin. Her attacker grunted and released her. Her hands now free, she pushed the man into the wall and fled into the bedroom, throwing herself across the four-poster bed. She pulled the drawer of her night table open, her fingers fumbling through the drawer before wrapping around the can of mace she kept hidden within for such an occasion.

"Wait! Please!" Dorian called, following her into the bedroom, just as confused and bewildered as Rachael. He saw her slide back off the bed, the can in her hand as she swung her arm around, aiming it towards him. Instinctively, he slapped at her hand, knocking the can from her and sending it bouncing across the room.

They stared at each other for a brief moment before she lunged towards Dorian, again. Taking a step toward her, he threw up his arms, grabbing for her wrists, but missing. The small area rug beneath his foot slid forward, knocking them both off balance. He couldn't stop his forward momentum towards the bed, and he fell on top of her, pressing her down into the mattress with his body.

He grabbed her hands as she smacked at him, pounding her fists into his shoulders, and pinned them above her head. "Stop!

I will not hurt you, Rachael," he said, his voice husky and slightly breathless from the exertion of defending himself.

Rachael froze, her heart slamming wildly in her chest as her gaze met and locked with the warm, brown eyes of Dorian Gray. "You're...you're..." His solid body was warm above hers, and she could feel the softness of his gray trousers upon her legs. She watched in amazement as his jugular pulsed in his neck. Even his breath was warm against her cheek and she shook her head. "It can't be. You're a ghost," she finally managed to stammer. "You're *my* ghost."

"Obviously, I'm a bit more...corporeal than either of us expected," Dorian replied.

He was as shocked as she was by the revelation, yet he could not discount his good fortune. He could smell the vanilla that surrounded her in a soft, fragrant cloud, and he released her wrists, pushing himself off of the bed, away from her, hoping to hide the sudden and strong reaction his body had to the lushness of hers. Gazing down at her on the bed did not help, for she was wearing nothing more than a thin white satin nightgown that only accented her very womanly figure and soft curves.

Rachael sat up, her cheeks stained red as she gathered her robe into her hands, the look of appreciation on Dorian's face having been noticed. She stood and pulled it on, tying the sash as she slowly walked around Dorian. She tentatively reached out and touched the ruffle of his white shirt. The silk slid through her fingers, soft, warm, her eyes catching a glimpse of his chest beneath the material.

"How is this possible?" she asked, looking at the vest and overcoat that was draped over the chair before the window. "Where did you come from?" she whispered as she touched his face, expecting her fingers to pass through him. Instead, they met the smoothness of his cheek.

Dorian smiled slightly as he caught her hand in his, raising it to his lips and kissing her palm, before turning her hand over. His eyes sparkled in the dim light of the moon that shone through the window, his lips lingering longer than was proper on the back of her hand. "I came from the portrait," he answered, his breath warm on her skin, causing the slightest of trembles to course through her.

"You, Rachael Lafferty, brought me home."

Chapter Three

DECEMBER 23RD

The mantle clock chimed four in the morning. Dorian clicked his pocket watch shut as Rachael swept back into the sitting room, an elegant silver tea service in her hands. He stood by the fireplace, enjoying the heat from the blaze within as he absently swirled the tip of the poker around in the ash. He gazed into the flames, watching as they sent sparks flying up the flue, a log cracking and falling in the grate. He glanced over at her, watching as the shadows danced along the length of her satin robe, accentuating her figure beneath the thin material. He turned back to the fire, kneeling to position another fragrant log in the grate.

He was not one to question why he was suddenly corporeal, thankful for the gift and already making plans to take full advantage of it. After all, he had a beautiful woman residing under his roof. Now the question remained, who else could see him? Was there a reason Rachael could see and feel him, a reason why he was corporeal? Dorian doubted he would ever get an answer to that particular question. At least, none seemed forthcoming. He could feel his body coming alive and he smiled to himself as he peered over his shoulder once again to watch Rachael.

Rachael set the tea service on the accent table that stood between the two wing-backed chairs. She poured a cup for herself, the porcelain of the teapot warm from the brew within. She began to pour a second cup for Dorian when she paused. "I know this may be a strange question," she started, her eyes tracing the line of his back, falling on the curl of hair upon his shoulder. "But can you drink tea?" she asked curiously. She sat on the edge of the chair, her fingers tracing over the notebook that she had carried from her office when she and Dorian came down to the sitting room after their unusual meeting in the bedroom.

Dorian put the poker back in the rack beside the hearth and stood up, brushing his long fingers together to clear them from the ash that lightly coated them. He stopped by the chair opposite her, his hand casually draped along the back. "I don't know," he answered honestly and sat down. He crossed one long leg over the other, before accepting the china cup and saucer from her. "Thank you." He took a sip, swallowing hard, coughing as he leaned forward, attempting to stop the tea from sloshing down his front. "It's hot," he exclaimed.

Rachael stood quickly, gathering up the tea towel and exchanging it for the cup and saucer. "It should be. If it's not, then this teapot isn't worth the money I paid for it." Her eyes met his as she sopped up the tea that had fallen to the floor and she blushed slightly, as he took the towel from her to wipe his hands. "I'm sorry. That was a bit rude of me. Are you okay?" she inquired, taking the towel back from him before sitting down in her chair.

"Yes. I just burned my tongue and throat," Dorian answered, clearing his throat to help ease the burning. "I do believe that accurately answers your question, Miss Lafferty." He brushed a small piece of lint from his trousers. Waiting for his tea to cool, he leaned forward, perched on the edge of the chair, his elbows propped on his knees. His long hair fell about his face like a dark satin curtain, hiding his expression.

"It's Rachael," she remarked after a few moments of silence. "You're not in the nineteenth century anymore, Dorian." She smiled to herself, gazing down into her cup of tea, the scent of Earl Gray drifting up to her nose. "*We're not in Kansas anymore, Toto,*" she whispered.

"Pardon?" Dorian looked at her, the slightest turning of his head allowing her to see his eyes.

"Nothing. A line from a movie," she answered bashfully.

"Movie?" A look of confusion marred his brow as he sat up straighter, then leaned back in his seat. "It is quite apparent that many things have changed since my demise." He once again tried his tea.

"Oh, you have no idea," Rachael responded before falling silent, the stillness that grew between them becoming awkward. She sipped her tea, deep in thought. How could Dorian have solid form? Most ghosts were not corporeal, at least in the sense that he was. And how could he have come from her beloved portrait? Her brow furrowed as her mind wrapped around the implications. Was it because of some strange supernatural intervention that his portrait aged while he did not? At least, that was according to the story that Oscar Wilde had put to paper. Had his essence, his soul, been captured and locked in the portrait a little over a century ago?

Could that be why she had been so captivated by the work of oil and brush that had become the portrait of Dorian Gray? Or was there truly more to Dorian's abrupt appearance than met the eye? She set her teacup aside, rubbing between her eyes for a moment in an attempt to stave off the headache that was threatening to erupt in her temple. She gazed over at him, studying him in his antique clothing that fit him so perfectly. "Dorian, did you say that I brought you home?"

Dorian nodded as he stood up. "Yes." He raised his hand, his ring glinting in the soft light of the lamp on the end table. He turned to her. "This was once my home. Not as elegant as *Selby* to be sure, but still mine."

She knew the *Selby* he referred to had been the estate left to him by his grandfather, and it would have been long lost to the ravages of time and expansion of the city of London.

"This was where I resided for over a hundred years." He slowly walked the outskirts of the oval, one hand running fondly over the bookcases that lined the walls from floor to ceiling. "It was here that the man, who became my eventual biographer, learned my unusual life story." He paused behind her chair, leaning forward to whisper in her ear haughtily, "And in all that time, I never aged." He saw the shiver go down her back, causing her to briefly tremble, whether from fear or excitement he was unsure. He returned to the mantle, opening the glass door that covered the clock sitting there and adjusted the time.

Rachael turned in her seat to gaze over the back of the chair at him. "You never aged once the portrait was completed," she clarified. She gripped the arm of the chair so hard that her knuckles were white. There was something about him that gave her pause, a feeling of anticipation combined with a touch of fear that kept her focused upon the man standing at her hearth. She reached behind her and picked up the notebook. "You left this for me, then."

Dorian peered down at her, his eyes narrowing slightly. "I thought it would give you better insight into who I was. Obviously, I missed the small fact that you seem to already know my story." He approached her slowly, his body poised ominously behind her chair as he leaned into her. "Just how much do you know of my life?" Though he had read the original manuscript, he was curious as to what lies, what fabrications Oscar might have added afterward to sell his novel.

Rachael swallowed hard, turning away from him and sipping at her tea. "Your friend, Oscar Wilde, told the tale of a highly impressionable, young man. A man, who became intrigued with a life of decadence and debauchery." She glanced over her shoulder, noticing how he clenched the back of her chair as tightly as she had done a few moments earlier. "It is a story about a lonely aristocrat whose portrait aged when he did not." She stood up, quickly walking over to one of the bookcases and reaching up to gather a volume in her hands. She turned to Dorian, holding it up so that he could see the title on the front cover. "You, in your search for absolution, gazed upon what your portrait had become and proceeded to slash it to bits."

She closed the distance between them, handing him the book and catching his stare above it. "When you did, your body rapidly decomposed and the portrait restored itself. Only instead of it repainting itself to the way Basil Hallward had originally captured you, it portrayed you as the young man you were the day you died, dressed in the clothing of Victorian England." She licked her lips in excitement, thrilled with the prospect that he was here, with her. "Whatever magic that painting contained in the first place must have captured your soul within it." She shrugged. "Assuming you believe in that in the first place."

Dorian's lips tilted slightly in a grimace. "You've seen my portrait," he snarled. "And before you I stand. To haunt this house." He tossed the book to the couch, leaning on the chair. "So, we must both believe in that...magic."

Rachael retrieved the book and replaced it on the shelf. "I've always believed in ghosts but you're the first I've ever met." She smiled nervously at him. "Granted, you're also a bit more solid than even I could've imagined, but apparitions have been known to move objects, hide things..." She let her comment hang in the air between them.

Dorian stroked his fingers along his mustache, tapping his finger against his lips in thought. "Tell me then, Rachael, do you believe that this is my penance for the sins I committed in life?"

"Perhaps," she replied softly. His eyes were cold as they gazed at her, slowly softening as he studied her features.

Dorian noticed the soft blush that stained her cheeks and reached out to tuck an errant strand of hair behind her ear, rubbing the lock between his fingers for a moment before releasing it. "What year is it?" he inquired, allowing his annoyance to fade.

Rachael froze at his touch, pausing for a brief moment before answering him, "We are in the 21st century." And she told him the current date.

Dorian stepped away from her, once again restlessly pacing the spacious sitting room. "I just passed in the year of our Lord 1891," he stated with certainty. He tucked a hand in the pocket of his trousers as he inspected the collection of dragon figurines that were perched on a shelf. "I have been trapped in that painting for well over one hundred years." He traced the delicate wing of one of the mythical creatures. "Over a century." He turned away, continuing his review of her belongings. "I find it curious that you are the only one who seems able to see me."

Rachael followed him around the room with her eyes. "How do you know?"

Dorian lifted his shoulders languidly. "Your acquaintance Tessa looked right at me. As a matter of fact, she hung her coat on the rack in front of me, as I stood in the corner, obscuring my vision." He snorted in disdain. "Through me would be a more apt description."

Rachael's eyes widened. "You ruined her coat!" she exclaimed in realization. "Somehow you slashed her coat with that cane...sword in the corner!"

"Did I?" he asked as he tilted his head slightly, his eyes challenging her. When she did not reply, he smiled coldly. "I'm sure the look she bestowed so graciously upon me is one that I shall see quite often. It is clear that she does not like me."

Rachael could hear the hurt in his voice even if it was not expressed on his face. She walked over to him, her bare feet patting on the rug. "She doesn't like your portrait, Dorian. She doesn't even know you."

"Neither do you," he pointed out sharply.

"That's neither here nor there," Rachael answered in dismissal. "Tessa wasn't impressed by the painting. But I wouldn't take it as a personal insult. She's seen too many paintings since Julian became curator at the museum. I'm sure I wouldn't be impressed either if I was in her position." She laid her hand on his arm, trying very hard to understand the man before her. "Tess doesn't warm to people easily. And she was very against me purchasing this place."

Dorian raised a single eyebrow. "My home is not good enough for a bestselling author? A woman, who has more imagination than most people and knows how to convey it expertly on paper?" he inquired haughtily at the mere but very poignant insult. He shrugged her hand off his arm and moved past her to gaze over the books behind her couch.

It was at that precise moment Rachael remembered the whole story behind Dorian Gray. He was portrayed as conceited, haughty, a true aristocrat in every sense of the word. A man, who believed his position and stature in the society of Victoria's England would protect him from any sin he took part in. He was a man, who had committed murder with no remorse and ran from the evil he had so heinously participated in throughout his years. Evils that eventually distorted the portrait that had become his conscious so much that he was compelled to destroy it in a vain effort to regain his lost innocence.

Yet Rachael could see behind the arrogant veneer that surrounded Dorian like a suit of armor. There was a lonely man in there, someone whose beauty and grace had distanced him from his peers, causing him to be adored by those around him, but never truly loved. Someone who, at one point in his life, cared about his friends and family but had forgotten what it was to be able to express it. He gazed coolly at her as she studied him. Giving in to the desire to comfort him, she calmly closed the distance between them to cup his face in her hand. She saw the brief flash of curiosity in his eyes. "Of course, your home is good enough, Dorian," she assured as she stepped away from him. "I'm comfortable here." She twirled around with a warm laugh, the satin of her robe whirling around her ankles in a white cloud. "I can write here. I can live here. If I get tired, I go to the window and watch the barges moving along the Thames or take a walk along the docks and feed the seagulls."

"Your personal Eden," he sneered cruelly. "Away from the world."

Rachael kneeled on the couch, her waist even with the back as she nodded. "You have no idea what this townhouse is to me. Why do you think I took the time and energy to restore it? To repair the damage I found in it for being empty for so long?" She shook her head slightly, her long brown hair falling about her shoulders. "It's home, something I've been trying to find since I left my parents' house." She reached out to grab the ruffle of his silk shirt, tugging on it gently, forcing him to take two steps towards her. "And I have the good fortune to now share it with a very corporeal Victorian ghost."

"You should be afraid of me, if you know my story," he replied, the slight sadistic edge to his voice as he thread his fingers in her hair. "I happen to be a very complicated man." He crushed her soft locks in his fist. "You might find me to be stifling, even possessive. You may not want to remain here."

Rachael licked her lips. "Well, that's for me to decide, isn't it?" she stated with conviction.

Dorian laughed cruelly. "Read my journal before you make that decision, Rachael."

"I am my own woman, Dorian. No one tells me what to do, what to feel, what to say. Not my agent, my family, no one," she snapped, her own voice filled with haughtiness.

He gazed down at her, his fingers tightening in her hair slightly. "Tessa seems to feel differently."

"Tessa is not my keeper," she answered succinctly. She slowly walked her fingers up his chest, knowing by the pressure his fingers exerted that she was playing with fire. She was not going to give in to his scare tactics. It would take Dorian Gray more than his idle threats to frighten her away. She laid her fingers upon his lips as he opened his mouth to speak, silencing him. "You don't order me around and you leave me alone when I am trying to write, then you, Mr. Dorian Gray, will have the best roommate London has to offer. Deal?"

Dorian's eyes narrowed slightly as he removed her fingers from his lips. "On one condition. You afford me the courtesy of moving freely throughout this dwelling when I please, to do as I please."

"Done," Rachael answered, wondering exactly what he had in mind with his words. And even if she did know, there was nothing she could do to prevent it. He was a ghost after all.

Dorian's lips tilted in a cool smile, but the heat that filled his eyes caused her face to redden in a becoming blush even more. He released her hand to cup her cheek in his palm, her skin warm, soft, and feminine. He pulled her towards him with the hand that was still entangled in her hair, lowering his mouth to within a breath of her own. He paused, feeling the gasp of her breath, the pounding of her heart before allowing their lips to touch. "Then you have a deal, Miss Rachael Lafferty," he answered her before kissing her passionately.

He stepped away from her, a satisfied smirk on his face as he bowed to her and swept from the room on silent feet.

Later that day, Rachael furiously pounded on the keyboard of her computer, her fingers a blur of speed as she attempted to keep up with the idea that was flowing like a raging river within her mind. It didn't matter to her that she had a total of three hours sleep, having retired to bed at six in the morning after contemplating Dorian's stolen kiss a little over an hour earlier. She could still taste him on her lips, a combination of tea and pure maleness and she didn't restrain the girlish giggle that escaped from her as she typed.

The fact that her very handsome Victorian ghost had stolen a kiss did not bother her. After all, as she had told Dorian, she was her own woman. His kiss had actually helped break the writer's block that had plaguing her for weeks. In the hours she had sat in front of the computer, she had managed to complete the manuscript Tessa had been bothering her for a day earlier. She saved it, burnt it to a compact disc, and hit the print button, then pulled off her headphones before standing up for a much-needed stretch.

"I take it your newest novel is now finished."

Rachael actually jumped with a startled squeak at Dorian's soft inquiry, turning towards him in embarrassment. "Don't do that," she laughed as she tried to hide the surprise from her voice while feeling the heat in her cheeks. He leaned against the doorframe, his arms crossed over his white silk shirt, his gray vest unbuttoned. He wore a bemused look, his lips twitching as if he enjoyed her discomfort.

"And yes, I finished it." She neatly stacked the pages of her book on her desk as her laser printer spit them out one by one. "Thanks to you," she added.

Dorian's eyebrows rose as one as he pointed to himself with a delicate hand. He pushed away from the doorway, slowly moving into the room with the singular grace of a cat. "And what, pray tell, did I do to help you finish your masterpiece?" he questioned. He stopped within inches of Rachael, purposefully invading her personal space to keep her off balance. His eyes narrowed slightly as he waited, caressing her cheek with his finger. "I'm sure my mere presence in...my home was not the cause of your inspiration." He watched her expression carefully, gauging her reaction to the word *my*. He still considered the elegant townhouse his, but the idea of sharing it with Rachael was an appealing prospect. Even if he was just a ghost.

"Well, no," Rachael answered nervously. She found herself unable to move away from him, the desk chair pinning her in place. His claim on the house did not surprise her, and she was more than happy to allow him the pleasure of still referring to it as his own. She would have to make sure though that he eventually gave in and at least referred to it as *theirs*. Especially considering the amount of money she had invested into the property. She reached behind her, gripping the back of her chair as Dorian leaned into her.

"Ah," Dorian breathed softly. He slid his hand to the back of her neck, applying just enough pressure with his fingers to still her. He could feel her pulse beneath his palm, and he let his lips tilt upwards as he lowered them to hers. "Then, could it have been because of this?" His mouth descended to hers in a possessive kiss, one that brooked no argument to the fact that he was staking his claim. It was a kiss filled with passion, and hunger.

"Rachael?" Tessa's voice made its way up to the author and the ghost. "Rachael, are you up there? Answer me, for I refuse to take one more step into this haunted house of yours!"

Dorian ended his kiss with a deep-throated snarl. "Then don't, Mrs. Falcon," he commented nastily, casting a glance to the door. He never released Rachael, his free hand falling to her waist.

Rachael gasped in shock, staring at Dorian. She knew that he did not like Tessa, but he had yet to explain to her exactly why. At least she knew the dislike was mutual. Until she could figure out what bothered her ghostly companion about her friend, she resigned herself to playing mediator. If Tessa had any idea just how haunted the house was, Rachael would have a *bone fide* fight on her hands.

She gently pushed Dorian away, ignoring the icy glare he bestowed upon her. "Yeah, I'm up here," she called from the doorway, her voice cracking slightly. She cleared her throat and looked back at the ghost. "Please, be nice," she pleaded in a desperate whisper as she swept past him, the disc and the hard copy of her book in her hands. She paused beside him for a moment, her eyes fervently begging him to behave. She squeezed his hand briefly before walking from the room, once again silently petitioning him to be a gentleman.

As soon as Rachael released his hand, Dorian clenched his fists in irritation, reigning in his formidable temper before turning to follow her from the room. "Oh, I'll be as nice as I possibly can manage," he whispered to himself. He saw Tessa's head appear as she ascended the circular stairway in the sitting room to the second level and he moved into the deep shadows that lined the wall. She passed him, pausing and looking right at him before hurrying her pace and entering the bathroom. He smiled coldly as he changed direction and followed, stopping just within the doorway to watch Tessa twist her long red hair into a tight bun.

"If you finished it, then why don't you join Julian and me for dinner tomorrow night?" she called out to Rachael, who had slipped into the master bedroom for a moment. "You cannot possibly enjoy being in this townhouse by yourself day in and day out." She paused, once again looking through Dorian as she gazed towards the doorway, never seeing the ghost as he leaned casually against the doorframe, his eyes narrowed in irritation. "And don't give me any nonsense about not being alone." She reached for the clip she had laid on the countertop. "A ghost does not compose a suitable companion for anyone," she finished.

"Give it a break, Tessa. I'm fine here. You know I enjoy my solitude," Rachael called back, going around the balcony to the other set of stairs.

Dorian took a step forward just as Tessa's fingers almost touched the ornate clip. With the slightest tilting of his wrist, he snapped his forefinger along the inside of his thumb and flicked the clip from the counter. He smiled as the item skittered across the tile floor to land behind the commode. "Who are you to judge what composes a suitable companion?" he asked conversationally as he leaned against the wall opposite the counter. "And if Rachael enjoys her solitude, why do insist on disturbing it?"

Tessa stared at the clip now lying on the cold tile. "Fucking ghost," she hissed as she walked over to the commode, leaning one hand on it as she bent down to retrieve the clip. Her fingers stretched towards the clip just as it moved. It went flying away from the commode and skidded beneath the claw foot tub, hitting the baseboard before coming to a stop under the far side of the tub.

"Dammit," she growled as she marched over to the tub. She adjusted her tight skirt before kneeling on all fours to reach beneath the bath, dust bunnies and cobwebs brushing against her hand. Her fingers closed around the clip and she stood up, smoothing her skirt with shaking hands before clearing the dust and cobwebs from her hair clip. "Why don't you just go to hell?" she remarked as she returned to the counter and the mirror above it.

She reached up to her hair, her chin tight to her chest as she secured the clip in her red locks. Satisfied that it would not go anywhere, she lifted her gaze and froze, her eyes locking with the reflection of a man behind her. The man from Rachael's beloved painting. His expression held all of the arrogance that was spoken of in his story and she could not control the trembling in her hands.

Dorian could tell by the look of shock that shifted to abject terror on Tessa's face that she could see him. That small fact delighted him, and he decided to test a theory. He stepped closer, holding out his hands so that he effectively pinned her between his body and the sink, only a few inches of space separating them. Not only was he corporeal to Rachael, he was also very solid against Tessa Falcon. "I have lived in hell, darling Tessa," he whispered in a sarcastic tone. "I much prefer the comforts and luxuries of my own home and the beautiful woman, who now owns it."

Tessa swallowed nervously before whirling around to face Dorian. But no one was standing there. She waved her hand, feeling only bone numbing coldness in the space the ghost was occupying. Slowly, she turned back to the mirror, the trembling in her hands consuming her body as a bloodcurdling scream climbed up her throat and escaped her lips. She could still see Dorian in the mirror.

Dorian stepped up to her, slapping his hand over her mouth and silencing her scream before it alerted Rachael. This was a game he could enjoy. He had read about ghosts that could manifest themselves enough to terrify the inhabitants of a home, poltergeists that moved things and caused physical harm. He was simply delighted with his newfound power and abilities, especially if it meant that Rachael could truly be under his keeping.

"Now, now, Tessa. There is no need for that," he whispered. He slowly drifted his other hand up her arm to rest on her shoulder, his next words sharp and cruel as he leaned forward to breathe in her ear. The strength of his convictions regarding Rachael caused his jealousy to flare to life, inwardly startling him. He didn't let it show, the expression on his face full of malice. "She's mine. I already own her most valued possession, not that she even realizes it yet. I hold her heart in the palm of my hands. Soon, I will lay claim to her body and you will be nothing more than a fond memory in her mind." He stared at her in the mirror, his brown eyes cold, the line of his full lips curling into a mocking smile. "She needs no one but me now. Oh, you may sell her books to the highest bidder with no regard to her feelings on the matter. And you may gain her international prestige and recognition, but only I can give her what she truly desires." He let his hand slide from her mouth. "Do you know what that is, Tessa? Do you know what our beloved Rachael most desires?"

Tessa shook her head, her eyes wide with fear. "You're a ghost. You cannot give her anything."

"Can't I?" Dorian asked. He tilted his head as he studied her in the mirror, his fingers running along the line of her neck. Her flesh was warm, her pulse racing beneath the coldness of his palm. He closed his fingers slowly, testing to make sure they would not simply slip through her slim neck as they did the doorknob and locks of the windows before squeezing with just enough force to make Tessa reach up to grasp his invisible hand as she choked. "I am a jealous man. I have found the one thing that made my entire debaucherous life worth living. And I will not tolerate anyone coming between Rachael and me."

He pushed her roughly into the sink, her forehead hitting the glass of the mirror. It cracked, a jagged edge slicing into the pale skin of Tessa's forehead. "Remember that when you enter my home," he finished, releasing her. He adjusted his shirt as he exited the room, ignoring the sobs that came from Tessa as she tried to stave off the blood that seeped from the cut in her forehead. "Remember that, Tessa," he repeated as he casually descended the stairs in search of Rachael.

Chapter Four

CHRISTMAS EVE

Dorian Gray was well aware of the fact that Rachael was extremely furious with him. What he viewed as a friendly warning to Duchess Tessa Falcon, his dear Rachael did not. He enjoyed watching Tessa run screaming from his home— no, he corrected, forcing himself to accept that fact that Rachael lived there and it was now *their* home—babbling incoherently as she swept up her coat and rushed into the wintry afternoon. Rachael's manuscript lay forgotten on the sideboard near the door. There were long, angry, red marks marring her pale neck.

He had watched the entire incident from the balcony, never moving from his position even when Rachael swarmed down upon him in righteous anger for what he had done. He was not even fazed by the sharp smack of her palm against his cheek when he explained his motives to her. What truly bothered him was when she slammed the door to the master bedroom, locking herself within and exploding into a tirade of the vilest curses he had ever heard leave the lips of a woman, which were followed by the sound of glass breaking.

But it was the wrenching sobs that escaped her room through the thick oak doors that pierced something deep within him. He stood outside her door until they faded, a tightness clenching his chest and the heart he had longed thought turned to stone.

He had forgotten what is was like to feel affection towards another, and it made him realize that there was something more to him than just the faded existence that came with being a ghost. It made him realize that he could still hurt and be hurt.

Rachael's Christmas party was the next night and he believed he had found a means to regain her good graces before then. Her happiness had suddenly become the most important thing to him, and he would not have that ruined because of his petty jealousies. No matter how cruel he had been in life, he had always tried to consider the feelings of the fairer sex in his dealings with the world. Even if he did not always succeed, he at least tried. Now, he was once again on the wrong end of his territorial nature. He had allowed his temper and the sharp whip of his tongue drive a wedge between Rachael and himself simply because he did not like the way Duchess Falcon tried to run the author's life.

In a way, he had done the exact same thing with Sybil Vane over a century ago. He had seen the shining star in the actress, he had seen a brilliant and promising thespian in the making and had fallen madly in love. But that love had caused Sybil to throw away her career, to stop pretending she was the heroine, to see the actors around her for what they were. Had he stopped and not acted before considering the consequences of his actions, his cruel words that he regretted for the rest of his life, Sybil Vane may not have killed herself. He didn't expect Rachael to take her own life, but the thought of her shunning him was a sobering one. "Should have considered that before you scared dear Tessa away, Gray," he mumbled angrily to himself as he made his way back to the sitting room.

Dorian sank into the deep wing-backed chair before the fire, his fingers steepled as he gazed out over the room in deep thought. He remembered a time when he had been a kinder soul. Many of his peers and acquaintances had described him as having a simple and beautiful nature, although thoughtless at times. In retrospection, he wondered if the thoughtlessness was more from his naiveté of the world, or if it had been from the hidden jealous streak that taunted him from before his meeting with Basil Hallward, the artist who had painted the portrait that now hung above the landing. Or had the long conversations he carried on with Oscar regarding the mysteries of life and love jaded him so much that he stopped considering the world around him and only worried about himself?

Dorian sighed as he stood up, the mantle clock chiming six in the evening. He made his way silently back to the kitchen to check the thick steaks that were now cooking in the modern stove. It was a simple plan he had devised. He would simply woo Rachael to distraction until she listened and forgave him. He turned the steaks with a fork, having already burned four of them to a blackened mass before figuring out how the modern appliance operated. He was very out of his league with the electric devices that now dominated his kitchen. It was the only room in the townhouse that Rachael had completely renovated and, at first, he did not recognize it. He closed the oven door and listened, trying to discern if Rachael had left the confines of her office before gazing down at the vegetables that cooked on the stovetop. He was pleasantly surprised to see they were cooking evenly, and he turned his attention to the bowl of strawberries that waited for him on the center counter. If he had been required to do this during his life, he would've starved. He concentrated on cleaning the fruit, setting them in individual bowls before adding heavy cream to them. He carried them to the table he had set in the sitting room, lighting the candles and shaking out the match in his hand. He tossed it in the fire with a grim smile, satisfied with the meal he had created and the ambiance he had attained with the intimate setting.

"Now for some music," he commented huskily to himself. The thought of having Rachael completely in his power made his body tense in anticipation. Dorian bent over the stereo, staring at it in consternation. Next to the computer the author created her manuscripts on, it was the strangest device he had ever seen in the modern world. He found the power button and jumped when the room suddenly filled with the sound of very loud music that came from the radio. Annoyed by his own reaction, he stabbed at the button marked CD and sighed when silence once again filled the room. He did not understand how she could listen to that horrendous racket. Perusing the selection of music that was housed in a shelf above the stereo, he carefully selected a disc that would provide the right atmosphere. He slipped the disc into the holder, closed it and waited, turning the dial that controlled the volume until soft strains of Bach permeated the room.

Dorian straightened, blinking at the compact disc player. "What ever happened to a bloody simple string quartet?" he muttered in irritation as he climbed the stairs. He saw that the door to the master bedroom was thrown wide open and he gazed into the room, noticing the rumpled bedcovers and Rachael's clothing strewn across the floor. He made his way to the spare bedroom and listened intently, the tap-tap of her typing audible through the door. The faintest sounds of music could be heard, and he was positive she was wearing the unusual sound-making machine upon her head. She called the contraption a Discman and the device that covered her ears, headphones. Whenever she was writing, she had them on, claiming the music helped her concentrate. He snorted at the thought.

Reaching into the pocket of his trousers, Dorian removed the note he had penned earlier, tacking it to the door with his penknife. It was only a matter of time before Rachael would emerge to find herself a cup of tea. He returned to the kitchen to finish the dinner he was painstakingly preparing. He hummed along with the symphony playing in the sitting room. His mood had much improved. There was no way she could resist his peace offering.

A few minutes later, Dorian finished setting the last plate of steaming food on the table when he heard the familiar squeak of the hinges to the spare bedroom door as it opened. He shrugged on his vest and overcoat, retrieving his cane from the foyer corner before settling comfortably in the wing backed chair to wait. He looked the epitome of a proper Victorian gentleman, which was exactly the image he wished to portray. He smiled mischievously while he inspected his perfectly manicured nails, his free hand clasping the silver top of his cane. His eyebrows rose as he whispered to himself, "Let the seduction begin."

"DEAR GOD IN HEAVEN, what happened?"

Tessa turned away from the mirror over her dresser, her hands covering the marks at her throat. She couldn't hide the bandage that covered the gash in her forehead, or the red rims of her eyes from crying. She stared at Julian, clasping her shaking hands together. "Julian! I…I didn't think you'd be home for another hour," she managed to stammer as she licked her lips in nervousness. He had gone to Portsmouth on business the day before and she had assumed she had plenty of time to hide the marks around her neck before he returned to take her to dinner.

Julian sat his suitcase down near the bedroom door, studying his wife. "The conference let out early," he remarked offhandedly, concern filling his voice. His brow furrowed as he tilted his head, his eyes scanning her neck, then darting to the bandage on her forehead. He had never seen Tessa so disturbed in all the years of their marriage and he knew whatever had happened to her had to have been something serious to make her behave the way she was. He tossed his overcoat onto the chair to his right and approached her, his eyes narrowing. "You look like you've seen a ghost." He reached out and brushed his fingers across the bandage. "What happened, Tess? Did you have an accident? Have you gotten get medical attention for that?" He gently took her chin and turned her head. "Who did this to you?" he asked sharply.

Tessa irritably slapped his hand away, not wanting his coddling. She hated that the most about Julian. It was his one flaw that irked her. "No, I did not seek medical attention," she snarled as she pushed past him, gathering up her satin robe and sliding it on. The welts left by Dorian's fingers were still a vibrant red on the pale and freckled skin of her neck. She walked over to her dressing table and sat down, picking up the soft bristled brush and began to run it through her hair with furious strokes. "And, for your information, I did see a ghost."

Julian had poured himself a brandy from the decanter near the window and had just taken a sip of the spirit when Tessa made her declaration. He spat the liquid from his mouth in shock, his eyes meeting hers in the mirror. "Please tell me you're joking, dear," he exclaimed with an air of disbelief as he brushed the liquid from his shirt. The narrow-eyed and thin-lipped glare she gave him spoke volumes. "You're not joking are you, Tessa?" he whispered.

Tessa spun on the stool, pointing forcibly to her neck, the fear evident in her eyes. "Does this look like I am joking? Does it?" she shrieked. "Never again will I step foot in that damned townhouse of Rachael's! Never!" Her hands shook so badly that the brush slid from her fingers to fall to the carpeted floor with a muted thud.

Julian sunk slowly to the edge of their bed, holding up his hands to placate his wife. "Tessa, you're not making sense, darling. Tell me what happened. From the beginning," he soothed. He wanted to pull her into his arms to comfort her but knew better than to even try. At times like these, she was cold and unapproachable. He sipped at his brandy, waiting for her to talk.

Tessa took a shuddering breath, calming herself, the memories of the event replaying in her mind like a slow-motion movie. "I stopped by Rachael's yesterday to gather the manuscript she completed. I invited her to dine with us tonight and while I was in the bath fixing my hair, I was attacked," she stated succinctly.

"Attacked? By whom, Tessa? Did someone break into the townhouse? Rachael lives alone and I'm sure she would not attack you," Julian commented dryly, concerned for his wife's sanity, which was clearly hanging in the balance. "You're saying that a ghost that is haunting Rachael's townhouse accosted you." He leaned one arm back on the bed, propping himself up casually. He had hoped that Rachael would accompany them, as he wanted to engage her in conversation regarding her prized portrait of Dorian Gray. The board of directors wanted to see it, to display it in the gallery and it was an exciting opportunity for all involved. He continued when she didn't answer. "And didn't she apologize for ruining your coat?"

Tessa's mouth dropped open. "You don't believe me, do you?" she accused, her voice going up an octave.

"Well it is a fanciful story, love," Julian sighed as he sat back up. He set his glass on the night table before gracing her with a patient look, as if he was speaking to a recalcitrant child. "Tessa, you've made no effort to hide your disdain of the house, so making up a story about a…"

Tessa stood and crossed the room, slapping Julian. "How dare you!" she snarled. "I was attacked!"

"Yes, I can see that. Did you report it to the constable?" Julian asked sharply, rubbing his cheek. She saw her face redden in embarrassment before she turned away from him. It was enough to rile his anger. "Dammit, this is the exact reason why I do not like you going to that part of London. There are muggers all over those docks."

"You imbecile," she hissed. She bared her neck for him, making sure he could plainly see the red welts upon her neck. "These were made by the fingers of Dorian Gray, not some poor street urchin, who had the desire to rid me of my purse!" she snapped in frustrated shock. She could not believe that her own husband would not believe her. "I would be sent to the nearest hospital for psychiatric evaluation if I had reported this to the police!"

Julian stared at her. "Tessa, *Dorian* is a painting. Nothing more," he sighed.

"He is a ghost, Julian, a violent one at that." She took a deep breath, tilting her chin and gazing arrogantly down her nose at her husband. Something snapped within Tessa, turning her fear of Dorian Gray into outraged defiance. "He threatened my life. It seems that he is under the impression that Rachael is his to do with as he pleases and obviously will go to no extent to make sure I remain out of her life."

Julian shook his head, reaching down to untie his shoe. "Out of her life?" He snorted softly. "And I suppose he caused whatever is beneath that bandage on your forehead as well?" He glanced up at her still not sure if he believed her. "Tell me, Tessa, how do you propose that this..." He waved his hand as he sat back up. "...ghost could've caused you physical injury?"

Tessa's mouth moved for a moment, but no sound came out of it. She turned away from Julian unsure of the answer herself. She bent down to gather up her hairbrush, returning it to her dressing table. "I do not know. But I do know what I saw, and what I felt," she responded, her last word resonating in a snarl, "and so help me, Julian, I will do everything in my power to get Rachael away from that...that...menace."

Julian stared at her back, his brow furrowing in contemplation as she vowed her vengeance. He had heard of ghosts that could move objects, poltergeists that could scare families from their home. He rubbed his cheek again where she had slapped him, watching her in the mirror. Whether Tessa was telling him the truth remained to be seen. Considering her reaction to the day's events, he wasn't sure what to believe. He stood up and laid his hands upon her shoulders. "All right," he began slowly, using a soothing and placating tone in an effort to ease her apprehension. "How do you plan on convincing her?"

Tessa shook her head, her hand rubbing her sore neck. "I do not know. But I will find a way." She promised as she shook her head. "I will find a way."

Chapter Five

Rachael rubbed her eyes tiredly as the door swung open to her office. She had tried to get a hold of Tessa, but the Duchess refused to answer any of her calls. It irritated Rachael to no extent, adding to her anger at Dorian. She had wanted to apologize to Tessa on the ghost's behalf, to try and explain to the other woman what had happened, how she had discovered her invisible roommate. She had also hoped that maybe Tessa could help her discover just how and why he was so solid. She growled softly as she pinched the bridge of her nose, ready to lash into Dorian yet again for his inexcusable behavior.

She moved to take a step from the room that had been her silent sanctuary from the horror of what Dorian had done, when she stopped at the sight of Dorian's penknife stuck firmly in the wood of one of the door's panels. She could smell food cooking, the delicious aroma drifting upward to greet her rumbling stomach. She questioned herself, wondering if she had started dinner and forgot about it. She could see the flickering of the lights on the Christmas tree, for the sitting room was dark except for the fire that was burning in the hearth and chasing away the cold of night. There was also something else flickering below her and she raised an eyebrow in curiosity. She leaned over the balcony rail to see a table set for two, her silver candlesticks holding her cranberry tapers, and they were burning brightly.

Puzzled, she looked back at the penknife in the door, pulling it free and letting the note fall to her hand. She unfolded the piece of paper to find an invitation, written in a straight and even hand, the wording cultured and refined. She read:

> *To Miss Rachael Lafferty. Your presence is requested at a dinner tonight with Mr. Dorian Gray. Formal dress is required and has been provided for you. Dinner will be served at eight o'clock sharp. Your humble servant, Mr. Dorian Gray.*

She stared at the note in disbelief. "*Mmm.* Sucking up, Dorian?" she whispered in a strained voice. Her lips pursed as she tapped the invitation against the palm of her hand. She knew Dorian's story a little too well, knowing the type of man he had become as he aged. She was still furious with him, and he was going to find that she was not one of the graceful ladies of Victoria's realm that simpered and fawned over a well-versed apology. As a matter of fact, she intended on making it very difficult for him to gain her forgiveness.

Rachael sighed as she noticed the door to the master bedroom standing ajar and made her way into the room, freezing at the sight that greeted her. A beautiful Victorian-era gown in black sateen and lace hung from one of the bedposts, its elegant train just brushing the hardwood floor. A pair of shoes sat below them, not very high in the heel and decorated with simple black ties to go around her ankles. On the dresser to her right was a pair of diamond earrings and matching choker, sparking in the soft light of the night table lamp. Petticoats and undergarments that would fill out the skirts of the gown were laid out neatly upon the bed, as well as what she would only assume was a whalebone corset. "Oh my," she remarked in shock as she ran her fingers over the sateen skirts. "You've been busy, my dear ghost." She caught the faint scent of cedar on the clothing and marveled over the fact that the dress and its accouterments had remained intact for more than a century. "Someone knew what they were doing when this was packed away."

There was no label on the gown to indicate the size, but Rachael suspected it was close to her own. "Okay. I'll play your little game, Mr. Gray."

Taking the utmost care with the antique clothing, Rachael slowly donned the undergarments and dress. It was a bit more difficult getting into the corset by herself, but somehow, she managed to get it on and adjusted correctly. She was sure it was looser than was proper, but she didn't care for it helped fill out the dress to perfection. She gazed at herself in the full-length mirror behind the door after donning the earrings and choker. By the time she swept her hair up atop her head, she looked as if she had stepped out of one of her own historic romance novels. She ran her fingers over the pendant that hung from the choker as she turned from side to side to study herself, completely amazed at her transformation.

Rachael made her way down the staircase, the train of the gown secured by a thin loop around her right wrist. Her shoes clicked on the hardwood floor, a bit tight, yet comfortable. She licked her lips nervously as she looked around the room, ignoring the growling in her stomach at the smell of food. Somehow the gift of clothing and jewelry had tempered her fury with her ghostly roommate, replacing it with a sense of anticipation. She moved deeper into the dark room, breathing in the soothing scent of the cranberry tapers. "Dorian?" she called softly, smoothing down the skirt of the gown.

Dorian turned from his place at the hearth, a glass of sherry in his hand. His breath caught in his throat at the sight of Rachael, and, for the first time he could remember, he was speechless at the beauty before him. He had found the dress in the attic the same day he had discovered his journal, and he could smell the odor of cedar as he laid the dress out to air and allow the wrinkles to smooth. His accurate assessment of her size thrilled him as he gazed at the creamy swell of her breasts above the edge of the bodice, the pendant nestled in the hollow of her neck. It beckoned to him and his eyes slowly met hers as he tossed back the rest of his sherry.

"You look...beautiful," he complimented after a few moments. He set his glass on the table as he moved past it, reaching out to take her hand. As soon as she slipped it into his, he raised it to his lips, lingering longer than what would've been deemed proper. "I must ask for your forgiveness," he whispered as he trapped her hand over his heart. "What I did was inexcusable, and I truly did not mean to frighten your friend." It was a lie, and they both knew it, but he knew the words, once uttered, would be a small step towards soothing Rachael.

The words were sincere in her ears, but the sentiment was not reflected in his chocolate brown eyes. "What you did was cruel, Dorian. You could've seriously hurt her if the mirror had broken. You're lucky it didn't, and she simply cut herself on the corner," Rachael replied angrily.

Dorian's lips thinned. "I am a cruel man, Rachael, and I make no apology for that." He let his expression soften and smiled in apology. "Unfortunately, I have a very jealous nature and it took a hold of me in that moment." He tucked her hand into the crook of his arm, leading her to the finely laid table. He held out the chair for her, waiting until she was seated. "Would you care for a glass of sherry?" He held the bottle out for her inspection before pouring the amber liquid in the finely cut crystal glass at Rachael's right hand.

Rachael nodded. "Please." She took a sip as he set it aside, letting the liquor roll over her tongue, savoring the flavor. "I forgot I had this." She noticed that he had donned his vest and overcoat, his hair curling around the collar of his white shirt impishly. She was finding it very difficult to maintain her ire with the ghost. Between his gifts, the shock of the elegant dinner he had managed to prepare, and his stunning beauty, she could feel her resolve dissolving.

Instead, she tore her eyes from him, gazing at the plates of steaming food before her. Each plate held a perfectly broiled steak with a crisp medley of vegetables for color. A small desert bowl of strawberries and cream sat above the main course. "Did you do this?" she asked in awe as he took his own seat, silently berating herself for uttering such a foolish question. Considering no one else had been in the house that she knew of, he was the most logical choice for the meal before them.

Dorian picked up his utensils, pointing to Rachael with an amused smile. "Even an aristocratic, arrogant…SOB can still be cultured and cook," he answered. He took a bite of his steak, content to let her believe that his skills were more than they were. He nodded as he sliced another piece from the steak. "Superb." He took a sip of his sherry and leaned back in his chair, watching her from above the rim of his glass.

Rachael looked down at her plate, slicing into her steak, her words from their argument the night before coming back to haunt her. She blushed furiously and set her fork aside before raising her glass in a toast. "Touché, Dorian. Touché."

Dorian inclined his head towards her, tapping his glass to hers. A comfortable silence descended over them as they ate, his eyes never leaving her face as they enjoyed the meal. When she dabbed her lips with her linen napkin, he rose, once again offering his hand to hers. "Dance with me," he demanded softly.

Rachael looked up at him for a moment. "Dance?" she asked in shock as she looked up at him before glancing at the compact disc player. "We...we need more appropriate music."

Dorian waited, his hand still extended. "I am lucky I managed to determine how to operate your music maker in the corner. Do you have something more than the discs displayed there?"

Rachael chuckled and she stood up, lifting her skirts so as not to trip over them as she made her way to the stereo. She opened the bottom of the stereo cabinet and leaned over the collection of compact discs, flipping through them before finding one that she believed would suit his needs. "A waltz, then?" she asked as she turned on the receiver, sliding the disk into the cradle of the player. She glanced at him over her shoulder and he nodded. She set the track to play and turned back to him.

Dorian waited until she slid her right hand into his left before placing his right hand upon her waist. He looked at her, lifting his hand to hers. "Hold your hand here and your skirts will not get entangled in your feet." Satisfied she would not trip them both up, he swung her into the waltz, guiding her into the foyer where there was ample room to navigate. The lights of the tree made her diamonds sparkle, the skirts of her gown flaring behind her as they moved as one. He was enraptured with her beauty and grace as they moved together and the most beatific of smiles lit his face, his eyes dancing as he gazed down upon her.

Time seemed to slip away, returning them both to the days of yore, when things were simpler and courting was an art. Rachael was very aware of Dorian's hand at the small of her back, the warmth of his palm against hers as they twirled in time with the music. She had noticed his small nod of appreciation over the fact that she knew the steps of a waltz and she felt her cheeks flush as he intently studied her. She allowed him to lead, as was proper, gazing back up at him. His eyes smoldered as they traced her face, moving as one to the soft tones of the *Blue Danube*. It was a romantic moment, filled with promise as they let the moment sweep them along. She wanted to drown in the depths of his gaze, wanted to fall into his embrace. She wanted to melt into his world.

When the music ended, and Dorian slowed them to a stop, their hands still locked. Time froze, a soft intake of breath that was held as they gazed into each other's eyes, the anticipation of what could happen next washing over them. He slid the hand that had rested upon her hip along her arm to her neck, resting at the base of her head as he drew her to him. He felt the soft tremble that went through her slender body, her soft breath against his own lips. Her eyes closed as he kissed her deeply and with an unbridled passion. It was at that point in time that he understood, realizing that Rachael Lafferty had stirred something within him. She had stoked the embers of desire that had been smoldering in his veins since the night he set eyes on her lying on the couch. He felt her body relax and soften against him, pliant, and, for the moment, willing. Without warning and her permission, he lifted her into his arms and carried her upstairs, her hands wrapping trustingly around his neck.

Rachael clung tightly to Dorian, feeling suddenly detached from reality, as if she was in a dream of her own creation. His mouth drifted across her cheek to trail down her neck in soft butterfly kisses as he pushed the door to the bedroom open. She gazed at him as he set her down, the look of pure hunger upon his face causing a strange stirring within her own body. The sensation grew from deep inside, a spark that had ignited into a slow burning fire. She knew what he intended, what he wanted, and the fact that he was a ghost, invisible and airy to everyone but her, sobered her slightly. "Dorian..." she started, falling silent as his face darkened, indicative of everything she had read about him. The passion, the menace, the cruelty that he possessed became very apparent in that single expression.

Dorian lifted his hand, his forefinger held up in warning. "Do not say a word," he cautioned. "Say nothing." His eyes drifted to his journal on the nightstand, open and face down to a page within. Gathering it up, he quickly read his own neat hand, discovering where in the story of his life Rachael had stopped. He remembered that night vividly, one that had taken place shortly before he had met the divine Sybil Vane, when he was still innocent with a lust for life. The night of passion he had detailed within the pages called to him, insisting that he show the woman, who stood before him, now, dressed in the manner of the Victorian era, just how viral he was.

His eyes lifted slowly from the pages, and he tossed the book aside, stepping up behind her as he noticed the full-length mirror behind the door. He turned her so that they were both gazing at their reflections, her back to his front.

"Her beauty could never compare to yours," he whispered into her ear, his lips lingering along her neck. "She was too gentle, too meek, to enjoy the gifts I bestowed upon her." He reached up to brush the backs of his fingers along Rachael's cheeks, caressing the length of her neck before turning his palms down to drift the length of her arms.

Rachael was entranced and he smiled slightly as she took a step back to stand closer to him. "She was too innocent, to naïve." He entwined her fingers in his and raised her hands above her head, forcing her reach backwards to wrap them around his neck, leaving the line of her body exposed. "You are not innocent, are you, Rachael?" he whispered, his eyes locked with hers in the mirror. "You are not naïve."

Rachael shook her head in answer. He was weaving a spell around her, one that contained the promise of heated passion and sharp pain. He pulled her back against him, watching transfixed as Dorian slowly ran his hands up her body to cup her breasts through the elegant clothing molded to her flesh. Her breath caught as he teased her, closing her eyes with a soft moan as he applied enough pressure with his thumbs to make sure she could feel his caress through the fabric of the elegant gown and the undergarments beneath it. She threaded her fingers into his hair and clenched them into a fist, pulling gently.

Dorian exhaled sharply, an evil smile drifting across his face as his eyes narrowed. "Open your eyes, Rachael." He couldn't help but to use an exact quote from one of her steamy novels. "Gaze upon the man that will nail you so thoroughly that you will never want for another again," he growled huskily. Confidence oozed from his every pore and he dropped his hands back to her hips, grinding his own against her and making his intentions so clear that she could not argue. Or deny him.

Rachael's eyes flew open at his crude words, recognizing them from *The Rake Notorious*. It was almost as if she had written that book with Dorian in mind, capturing the ghost's manners in frightening clarity. The heat that exploded within her was mind numbing and she turned her head, her mouth seeking his.

She had stepped into his world and there was no going back. She had to know what it felt like to have him, in all his viciousness and conceit. She wanted to find out if his claim of being the only man she would ever want again was true. It didn't even matter to her that he was a ghost without a true form.

He turned her around roughly, his mouth dominating hers in a voracious kiss as his fingers dug into the soft flesh of her upper arms. She grasped his coat, pushing it off his shoulders in a feeble attempt to gain the upper hand in the game he had started, feeling him working at the fastenings of her gown. She felt cool air hit her back when she broke his grasp, her eyes flaring in challenge as she allowed the gown to fall to her feet, drifting around her in a cloud of black. If she did nothing else, she would prove to him that she truly was her own woman, the only person who controlled her destiny. The only person who could give him permission to take certain liberties with her.

When she turned to step free of the gown, Dorian let out a low laugh, enjoying her defiance. She was not some pallid maid that would allow him to do to her what he desired without uttering a word. He expected she was going to be as demanding between the sheets as he was. He reached out to pluck loose the ribbon that held the corset tied together, and then ripped the offending garment from her body, laying bare the prize he was determined to claim. He spun her around, his eyes drinking in the creamy orbs that had been hidden from view and he licked his lips.

He casually began to unbutton his vest, watching in fascination as she slipped from the underskirts to proudly stand before him in the tiniest patch of red lace he had ever seen. He licked his lips as his eyes drifted slowly down the sleek lines of her body, taking in her soft and toned curves. "You are a wicked tease, Rachael Lafferty," he commented as he tossed his vest to the chair before the window. "A vicious spider that has caught me in her web," he purred as he dawdled over the buttons of his shirt, before pulling it free of his trousers and letting it drop to the floor. He moved towards her, stalking her like a dark jungle cat with its prey in sight, catching her in his embrace before roughly pushing her onto the bed.

Rachael gasped as he landed on top of her, his mouth claiming the prize it hungered for. He continued lower, sliding his body along hers as his tongue mercilessly teased her flesh, until she was gripping the bedcovers, her whole-body shivering beneath his ministrations. He nipped at her sensitive skin as his hands caressed her body with a familiarity that would've been unwelcome had it been anyone but him. He pulled her hands above her head as he continued his exploration.

Her body was alive, fire heating her blood, stirring within her something she had long sought yet had been denied until now. She arched her body against his, craving the contact of skin against skin, let out a sob of desperation.

Dorian's dark eyes never left her face as he kissed and licked the softness of her skin. He lifted his head, his eyes narrowing slightly. "Patience. Give it time, my love. It will be worth it." He continued to ease his way down her body, his hands trailing behind his lips as he removed the last article of clothing she wore, letting her panties slip from his fingers as he stood. "Never have I had a woman so wanting. So..." he paused as he unbuckled his belt, sliding it free from his pinstripe trousers, "...wanton. Are you a wanton whore, Rachael? Or have you been denied even the lust of the flesh because of the prestige you so seek, forgetting what pleasure is? How it feels? What it is like?" he snarled nastily.

Rachael watched him intently, his words piercing her heart in all their cruelty. He was right, for it had been far too long since she had enjoyed the company of a real man and not one of her imagination. But how real was Dorian Gray? Real enough, for he was the ghost of a man that had been dead for more than a century, a man that walked from the painting that hung upon her wall at the stair landing. It was an absurd thought, one that she refused to even contemplate as she pushed away the voice in her mind that begged her to run, to get as far away from the apparition she had somehow managed to conjure. She whimpered softly as she backed away from him, moving up the bed to rest on her pillows, her eyes heavy with passion. "Dorian," she whispered.

Anger flashed across Dorian's beautiful face and he strode around the bed to stand alongside of it. He leaned forward, trapping her as he placed his hands on either side her body, invading her personal space. He watched as she pressed herself deeper into the pillows in an attempt to put distance between them. It did not work as he followed her, their faces mere inches from each other. "Did I not tell you to say nothing, Rachael? Did I give you permission to utter my name?" he whispered.

When she shook her head in answer, he stood up and returned to the end of the bed. He removed his boots, allowing them to drop to the floor with a heavy thud, his trousers joining them as he leaned a knee on the bed. He grasped her ankles, pulling her to him as he loomed over her, his body tight, taut. "If it is a sin to enjoy the pleasures of the flesh that tempt us so, then I will gladly be damned for eternity." He reached between them, finding the core of her womanhood and teasing her with no remorse, inhaling her intoxicating scent. "There have been very few things in this world that I have desired to possess. You, my sweet, wanton Rachael, are one of them. And right now, the only thing I want to hear escape your lips are the moans I cause."

Rachael slowly smiled at his words, seeing them as a challenge as she reached up to grasp his hair in her hands. She tugged his mouth down to hers and plundered it, her body responding to what he was doing to her. She could feel his passion pressed against her thigh and she shifted beneath him, allowing him to settle more firmly in the cradle her body created for him.

They fit together perfectly, as if they had been made for each other, to join together now across the expanse of space and time. She could feel the imminent reaction of her passion building and she arched her back, her mouth finding the soft hollow of his neck. She could taste the warmth of his skin, the musky flavor that was distinctly Dorian's indelibly marked upon her taste buds for all time. His hand continued to torment her body and in the back of her mind, she struggled with the fact that he was a ghost. A very corporeal ghost that knew how to play her body like a finely crafted instrument. She felt the wave of passion wash over her and she cried out before sinking her teeth into his flesh as she rode out the ecstasy he had brought on.

Dorian slowed the movement of his hand, his eyes tracing her face as he enjoyed the ache in his flesh her teeth had caused. "*Mmm*, a biter. My Rachael likes to play rough," he observed hoarsely, his voice thick with passion. Drawing his fingers to his lips he licked her sweetness from them before threading them in her hair, roughly pulling her head back and exposing the line of her neck. He clasped her wrists in his other hand, his body poised above hers as he swirled his tongue along her pale flesh from the edge of the choker to her chin. She didn't fight his roughness, her eyes flaring in stark provocation, daring him. "Tell me, Rachael. I want to hear you beg. I want you to beg for what only I will ever give from this moment forward," he demanded coldly. When she didn't respond, he pulled her hair harder, her sharp gasp turning into a low moan. "Say it," he insisted through clenched teeth.

"Take...me...Dorian," she managed to beg. Her body tingled, his hands so tight around her wrists that her fingers were going numb. At that moment in time, the thought that the casual observer would only see her writhing and naked body upon the bed, and not her ghostly lover, never entered her mind. She was caught in the here-and-now, any danger she was in from the dominating man poised above her long gone. "Please," she begged, her breath coming in quick gasps.

"Gladly." Dorian plunged deep within her with a low, deep moan of satisfaction. How long had it been since he had the pleasure of a woman's body? Since he had a woman warm and willing beneath him? He made a silent vow that as long as Rachael was in his life, he would be with her every night.

She matched his every move, her body arching into his as he pummeled her in passion, his mouth exploring every inch of her sweet body that he could reach. He growled angrily as he released her hands, wanting to be deeper within her, wanting to touch her core, her soul, so that she understood he now owned her. He slid his hands beneath her hips and lifted her until his own release was milked from him by the woman he was determined to possess in every way possible. His eyes locked with hers, his heart pounding frantically in his chest as he smugly smiled in deep-seated satisfaction.

Rachael met his gaze after a few moments, her eyes still heavy-lidded with passion. Her expression hardened momentarily before she bucked beneath him and rolled, pinning Dorian beneath her. The look of shock on his face made her chuckle as she ran her forefingers down his chest, scraping her nails over his own dark nipples.

"You truly are a harlot," he moaned as his lips tilted in a smile. He gripped her hips as she sat up, watching as she released the pins from her hair, allowing it to fall about her face in soft waves.

"No, Dorian, I'm not. As I believe I informed you earlier, I am my own woman. I take what I want, when I want, very much like you." She leaned down, teasing his flesh with her mouth. "And right now..." She threaded her fingers in his hair and tugged, letting her lips fall to his neck. "...I want to hear you beg." Her eyes narrowed as she moved above him, turning the tables on him, playing the game he had started in her own way. "Because I have not forgiven you yet."

"Forgiven me for what?" he asked haughtily, his fingers tightening around her hips.

"What you did to Tessa." Rachael moved again, returning the sweet torment he had imposed upon her. "And you will be paying for that indiscretion for a very long time."

Chapter Six

CHRISTMAS DAY

Rachael Lafferty hurried through the Victorian townhouse, beaming. Nothing was going to spoil her good mood, not even lack of sleep or the delicious soreness her body suffered from Dorian's impassioned lovemaking the night before. She ran her fingers through her hair before pausing to adjust a wide swag of evergreen that Dorian had helped her place along the mantelpiece.

She turned on her stereo, the orchestrated sounds of Tchaikovsky's *Nutcracker* flowing through the room. She smiled at Dorian's questioning gaze as he descended the stairs to meet her in the upstairs foyer. "What?" she asked with sheer delight, leaning on the newel post to gaze up at him. He was absolutely beautiful, even more so in his ghostly form than in the painting that hung over the landing behind him. She could've sworn she could see an aura about him as he moved closer to her, a satisfied and very smug expression on his face that sent a wealth of very erotic images spinning through her head. She blushed slightly as she grinned.

"Nothing," Dorian commented casually, keeping a steady gaze upon Rachael as he approached her. "You never cease to amaze me with your choice of compositions to listen to." He dropped a tender kiss onto her forehead and retired to the sitting room with another of Rachael's novels in his hands. He gracefully settled in the chair before the fire after pouring himself a half a glass of sherry that now sat on the table to his right. He opened the book, licking his forefinger to ease the turning of the heavy pages held within. He gazed languidly above the book to watch the author move about the room in her haste to finish her decorating. She had been at it since arising early that morning, adding the final touches to the festive finery. She was beginning to give him a headache with her frenetic pace.

"Rachael," he admonished softly, "stop fussing. You put even the most favored hostesses of my time to shame with your elegant trimmings and refined décor."

Rachael blushed at his high praise as she gazed at him over her shoulder. She was in too good a mood to let the gentle scolding that was hidden in his praise upset her. "I cannot help it, Dorian. I want everything to be perfect for tonight." The front bell chimed, and she set the last of the ornaments on the bookshelf before her, dusting her hands against each other before heading towards the door.

He snorted before responding sarcastically as he returned his attention to the book in his hands. "If you wanted things to be perfect, then you should not have invited that viper, Tessa."

She stopped in her tracks to glare at him. "Dorian," she hissed in warning.

He leaned his chin on his hand in boredom. "I only speak the truth," he replied as he turned the page with his other hand, his dark eyes moving along the page.

The bell chimed again, causing Rachael to turn on the ball of her foot. "We don't have time for this conversation, Mr. Gray," she admonished, pushing his words from her mind. "I'm coming!" she called as she threw open the glass door to the second-floor foyer, hurrying through it to go downstairs and greet her guest.

"Without me? That's not very ladylike of you," he teased as he looked up, a sinister smile tilting his lips.

He set the book aside and stood up and followed Rachael to the townhouse's street entrance. He took a tentative step forward, pleasantly surprised that he could pass beyond the entrance. *That's very interesting,* he thought to himself as he made his way to the landing and turning. He could see a shadowy figure through the small grate, which was set eyelevel in the doorway. Why was it he could pass beyond the threshold if the door was open, yet he could not grasp the door handle or a window latch? Was it because the door led ultimately to the outside? He had no problems opening the doors to the bedrooms or the bath and it was another piece of his mysterious puzzle. Did it have more to do with Rachael's influence and presence or was it simply the limitations of his ghostly body?

He let out a soft growl of languid passion at the thought of the night before, wondering where the limitations of his ghostly body were while they were tumbling between the sheets. Not that it bothered him in the least that the limitations had been missing.

He watched Rachael a few steps below him, pausing to adjust the garland that decorated the banister. He descended the stairs quickly to catch her around the waist, pulling her tightly against him. He knew she had heard his words and nipped tauntingly at her neck. "You should at least wait for your lover. You never know who could be at that door." He nuzzled her, sliding his teeth across her soft skin. "They could be dangerous," he growled in a low, seductive voice.

"Stop it, Dorian," she laughed as she tried to extricate herself from his arms. She turned her head, kissing him, hoping the quick show of affection would content him for a few moments.

"My caterer is already late and I'm running out of time. I'm sure she doesn't want to be stuck here any longer than she has to be, since it is Christmas day." She wiggled in his grasp, pointing to the door in exasperation. "That's probably her now."

He shrugged lazily, drifting his lips across the line of her jaw as he held her. "Caterers are notoriously late, yet they manage to set a table with precision and perfection with moments to spare," he purred. "You have plenty of time and if they are ignorant enough to agree to do a Christmas party, thereby being apart from their family at this time, then it is their own loss," he finished coldly.

The bell chimed again, and Rachael pulled away. "Easy for you to say," she laughed as she threw open the door. She felt his hand fall to the small of her back as she greeted the woman, who stood waiting outside. "Good afternoon, Grace."

Grace Limpaney turned to face Rachael and grinned widely. "Aye, that it be, Miss Lafferty. I was beginning to think you weren't home when you didn't answer, lass. Old Grace was about to leave and run to the local pub to call you." She paused in her ramblings with the slightest of yelps when her eyes met Dorian's over Rachael's right shoulder. She blushed and then winked at them. "I didn't know you had company, Rachael," she teased lightly as she pushed past them into the house.

Rachael watched her as she made her way up the stairs to the first floor. "Excuse me?" She realized Dorian had slid his hand into hers, his fingers gripping hers tightly in a silent warning. She saw Grace staring pointedly down at Dorian, appraising him like a mother hen. Rachael's eyebrows rose in realization and she laughed. "Oh...yes, well...um..." She shrugged. "You caught us."

Grace looked down at them with a hearty chuckle, setting down the warming platters she had been carrying on the floor of the second-floor foyer to shrug out of her coat. A portly Scottish woman with a mothering disposition, she had quickly agreed to cater Rachael's party, even on Christmas. She lived a street over from the dockside homes in a cozy and quaint duplex with her nineteen cats and curious nature. "A young lady such as you should have fun. And I truly believe Christmas is for you younger ones." She gathered up the platters as Rachael and Dorian gained the upper landing and moved deeper into the townhouse. "Oh, it be for the wee ones too..." She let her words drop off as she glanced at the tree. "My word, Rachael, 'tis a beautiful tree." She sniffed for a moment as she studied the ornaments. "And such fine antiques. You are blessed, lass, blessed."

She continued on to the kitchen, leaving the scent of gingerbread in her wake. "Yes, a grand party it shall be tonight, Rachael Lafferty. And such a man at your side!" She laughed heartily as she set the warming trays on the counter. "Aye, you should have fun with your friends if your family can't be with you." Her eyes met Dorian's over Rachael's shoulder, the ghost having wrapped his arm around the author's waist. "Don't you agree, young man?" She grinned broadly at Dorian.

It was quite apparent to Rachael and Dorian that Grace could see him. He blessed the woman with his most charming smile as he reached out to take her hand. "Whole heartedly," he answered smoothly as he raised Grace's hand to his lips.

Grace let out a delighted squeal. "Oh, a cheeky one you've got there, Miss Lafferty!" she commented as she set out the platters and bustled from the room, giggling to herself as she returned to the entrance to gather more of the warming trays.

As soon as Grace had left the room, Rachael looked up at Dorian. "How can she see you?" she asked as she arranged the food on the huge table to her left. She knew Grace had set the heavy dishes down in order to gather up the rest from their place outside the entrance door, and she moved the dishes to the end of the table to make room for more.

Dorian lifted another tray and set it beside the first. "That is a good question." He turned to Rachael before stepping into the doorway to watch Grace as she came through the sitting room, humming to herself with the music that played from Rachael's stereo. The woman walked right through him, causing them both to shiver. He stared at Grace in shock, a strange tingling coursing briefly through him. He had never felt anything like it before. It was a distressing feeling that he would prefer not to experience again. His eyes locked with Rachael's, and he remained perfectly still.

Grace stopped and looked curiously back the way she had come. "There's a draft there Miss Lafferty. You should be finding where it's coming from." She set the additional warming trays next to the first on the table, withdrawing a box of matches from the pocket of her smock. "Where is your handsome suitor?" She set the basket that had been on her arm in the chair and withdrew the small round containers of Sterno, lighting them before carefully arranging them beneath the warming trays. The smell of delicious food wafted through the kitchen, and she shook out the first match.

Rachael looked at Dorian, who casually leaned in the doorway, one hand tucked in the pocket of his trousers. He allowed a single eyebrow to rise, motioning elegantly with his free hand for her to answer Grace. She balked for a moment as she glanced at Grace, then back to Dorian, wondering what sort of fabrication she could come up with to explain Dorian's sudden absence. "Well…he…um…" She was at a loss for words. She could see the look of stark lust in his dark eyes that remained from Grace's reference to him being her suitor. Rachael scratched her cheek nervously. "Can I help you?" she offered in an attempt to change the subject, taking the matches and lighting one, holding it out to the can of Sterno.

Grace glanced at Rachael knowingly as she set the can in place, nudging the younger woman. She could tell Rachael was embarrassed at being caught with a young man in her home. "It's all right, Miss Lafferty. Love is strange game played best between young ones such as ye'selves. You have to learn how to give your man what he wants without losing a part of yourself." She shook out the match and smiled, straightening. "Run along, dear. You have a party to prepare for. You let me do what you hired to me to do. I'm sure you'll be wanting to look your best for your guests." She chuckled softly. "And your handsome man."

Rachael nodded with a smile. "All right. I'll be right back, Grace." She hurried from the room, taking off at a run up the circular staircase, and traversed the upper balcony until she could see the entrance to the kitchen. She stopped and leaned on the railing, her brow furrowed in contemplation.

Dorian had followed her at a slower pace, stopping beside her to lean on the railing, matching her stance. "What a quaint woman your caterer is, Rachael," he commented as they watched Grace move about the kitchen as if she owned it. "How do you propose to explain me to her?"

"I don't know," Rachael answered honestly as she shook her head. The slight movement caused wisps of hair to flutter around her face when a thought occurred to her. She slowly gazed at the ghost, her eyes narrowed slightly. "I want you to touch me as we go back into the kitchen."

"Touch you?" Dorian responded as he stared at her skeptically. "And, pray tell, the reason I should do as you ask other than for the simple fact that I would want to?" he inquired, his tone slightly obnoxious. He turned to lean his hip against the railing, setting his elbow along the top and clasping his hands together.

Rachael stepped back out of view as Grace bustled from the kitchen to retrieve something else from her car. She chewed her lower lip for a brief moment, causing it to redden and pout seductively. "Call it a hunch," she whispered.

"A...hunch," Dorian repeated as he trapped her against the wall. He resisted the temptation to capture her mouth in a lingering kiss. "If you wish." He took her hand and allowed her to lead him back into the kitchen, playfully nipping at her neck as they stood at the center island, his arms wrapped around her waist.

Grace entered the room, her arms filled with fine lace doilies. She laid them beneath the spoon holders before the warming trays. "There you are." She wiped her hands on the towel she had tucked into her smock as she gazed at them. "Introduce me to your young man, Miss Lafferty."

Dorian smiled at Grace, his eyes slightly narrowing in mischief. "I am Dorian. Rachael's fiancé." He let his eyes linger tenderly on Rachael's face, even though his mind was churning. Her hunch had been correct. If he was in direct contact with Rachael, then others could see him. Touch him. It did not explain how he had been able to manifest himself physically in Tessa's presence. Nonetheless, he knew it would make for an interesting conversation at a later time, and maybe give Rachael and him some more insight as to why he was no longer trapped in his own painting.

Rachael blanched slightly at his words, clearing her throat to cover her shock at his bold proclamation. She gazed up at him, seeing the challenge in the depths of his brown eyes, openly daring her to deny his words to the woman that accompanied them in the kitchen. "We're announcing it tonight, Grace," she remarked nervously, her hands gripping the counter so tight that her knuckles were white.

Grace clasped her hands together. "Oh, I'm just tickled for the two of you!" She walked over to hug Rachael and Dorian.

"I love weddings," the older woman gasped, dabbing at her eyes with her smock edge. She stepped back away from them, turning to hide the tears of joy. "So, Dorian, what do you do? For you must be able to care for our Rachael here," she asked while fussing some more with the table settings until she had regained her composure.

He dropped a tender kiss to Rachael's cheek. "I'm an actor," he easily lied. "I was not even supposed to be in London, but the weather has caused me to remain here."

Grace took a good look at him, noticing his period clothing. "Ah, that would explain your costume." She tapped her lip with her finger for a moment. "Do you not have a change of clothing with you, my dear boy?"

"Alas, I do not. I do not live far from London. Upon visiting Rachael last evening, I was caught unprepared," he replied sliding his hand up her back to her neck, rubbing the tense muscles he found there, before continuing, "I think I shall be a bit overdressed for tonight's festivities. Would you not agree?"

"Dorian," Rachael warned. "I do not think Grace is worried about your attire for tonight."

Grace waved away her comment. "My George was about your size, I should think. Let me pop around home and see what I can find for you that would be more suitable for your party." She bustled from the room, mumbling and chuckling to herself about wedding arrangements and courteous men that were a rare find.

As soon as the door closed, Rachael sighed. "Your fiancé?" she asked him in disbelief.

Dorian casually shrugged as he slipped past her to inspect the food that had been laid out for their guests. "I thought it was most appropriate," he answered during his perusal when he slowly turned his head towards Rachael in a move that was very reminiscent of a snake eyeing its quarry. "And I am overjoyed at being able to escort you to your party tonight."

Rachael could tell by the set of his jaw and the tone of his voice that he would brook no argument from her in regard to his presence at her side. She let her lips twitch as she walked over to him, smacking his hand as he reached for an *hour d'oeuvre*. "You better hope Grace has something that will fit you. Unless you want to field questions about the style of your clothing," She leaned forward to place a light kiss on his lips. "Or attend my party in your birthday suit." She swept from the room, her step lighter at the thought of Dorian at her side and the whispers of curiosity that would ensue because of it.

He watched her leave, gazing back down to the food that was making his mouth water. A calculating smile spread across his face as his mind ran through the guest list. "This should be a very interesting evening," he whispered before indulging in one of the stuffed mushrooms. "Very interesting indeed."

KITTY KENDALL SLOWLY walked through her little two-bedroom house on the outskirts of London, contemplating the party invitation in her hands. Having just finished the entire Christmas gift exchange ritual with her parents, she was glad it was over when they left. It wasn't because she didn't like Christmas. On the contrary, it was her favorite time of year. But she much preferred celebrating Yule, the Pagan version of the holiday. There was less commercialism, more celebration, and quite a bit less stress.

She smiled as she scratched behind one of her cat's ears in passing, the silver-tabby sitting on the small sideboard in the hallway like a striped and furry king. She knew that Rachael's party would be the talk of the literary world for months to come, but she was unsure if she was up to the social niceties that her attendance would require.

She walked into the kitchen and placed a kettle of water on the stove for a cup of tea, her ankle bracelets of small bells tinkling with her steps. Her feet were bare on the cold stone floor and she hummed to herself as her big brown doe-eyes searched the cabinet above the counter for the type of brew she wanted. One of her cat's batted at the soft fabric of her broomstick skirt and she picked him up, nuzzling her round face in his soft black fur. She set the cat down. "Poe, you're shedding," she remarked as she brushed his fur from her cream-colored peasant blouse. The cat gave her an insulted look, meowed once at her, and gave her a good view of his backside as he walked away.

Kitty laughed at his antics, her eyes landing on the party invitation she had placed on the table when she walked into the kitchen. She knew Rachael would be expecting her, regardless of the fact that Kitty never responded as required. It was an unspoken given between the two women. She had met Rachael at a supernatural and paranormal convention a few years earlier, and the two women felt an immediate kinship. Kitty had read Rachael's tarot cards that day, surprising her when the cards told her that they were destined to meet, that the young witch would help Rachael with an unusual problem in the future. The unusual problem had yet to present itself, but Kitty was patient. While they both waited, they enjoyed each other's company and friendship.

She carefully measured out the loose black tea leaves into the strainer, humming to herself as she looked at the clock on the stove. It was four o'clock, and in less than two hours, the party would be starting. The kettle began to whistle, and she poured the hot water from the kettle into her mug. The steam curled as it rose from the basin of her cup, warming her face with its heat and the aroma of the tea. She raised the mug to her lips and sipped at the hot liquid, making sure it was the way she liked it before dropping the strainer into the sink. She turned on the ball of her foot to sit at the table and found four pairs of eyes staring at her. She lowered the mug for a moment. "Now what are the four of you up to?" she asked the cats that stared at her from where they sat on the table. They had been silent while gaining their perches on padded paws that whispered through the house.

One of the cats, a seal point Siamese with piercing blue eyes named Michelangelo, simply meowed at her, his gray paw firmly placed on the invitation, his dark blue eyes gazing upon Kitty like a wizened old soul. The tabby, Raphael, pushed Kitty's deck of Tarot cards towards the front of the table from its place behind him, his tail swishing back and forth in irritation as he stared at her with his brilliant green eyes, daring her in challenge. Poe, a solid black cat with amber eyes and the youngest of the four, and Bela, a pure white cat with pink eyes, an albino stray she had rescued from a busy street, sat flanking the others, waiting, looking at her expectantly. Kitty had named the cats after her favorite figures in history: two artists, an author and a movie star. It never ceased to amaze her how Poe and Bela's names fit them. Poe had an attitude and Bela was a bit of an actor himself. Michelangelo and Raphael usually just ignored them, acting as if they were better than the others. She loved all four of them dearly.

"All right, all right," Kitty mumbled with the merest hint of mirth as she sat down, gathering up the cards. "Let's see what we have and then I'll decide whether or not to go to her party." With a seeming sense of satisfaction, the cat's settled more comfortably on the table to watch, leaving her enough room to spread out the cards for a reading.

Kitty held the cards tightly, her eyes closed as she concentrated on the energies that flowed around her, through her, and into the cards. She laid them out in a very simple pattern, one that would give her more insight into the events that could happen at the party. She had seen the guest list. She had actually helped Rachael write out the invitations, so she was quite aware of the variety of individuals who would invade her friend's home. There would be agents and authors, publishers and booksellers, friends and lovers. The only people who would not be there would be Rachael's family. Rachael's only living relative resided in the States. Her parents had been dead some eight years.

So, when Kitty turned over the *Lovers* card, she paused in curious contemplation, her hand hovering over the deck sitting before her. She had been so focused on Rachael herself instead of the party that she was not even aware that the cards directly pointed to the famous author in every which way. She stood up while gazing down at the cards. The *Magician* was on one side, the *High Priestess* the other, the *Lovers* in the middle surrounded by six more cards that were seemingly insignificant within the reading.

"What is this all about, Rachael? You forget to share a secret with me?" she whispered to herself in question. She took the last swallow of her tea before gazing into the bottom of the mug. The pattern of the few leaves that had escaped the strainer left her with a foreboding feeling. The tea leaves combined with the cards that still looked sightlessly up at her from the kitchen table were enough to make Kitty suddenly decide to attend the Christmas party.

She hurried from the kitchen, heading for the stairway and her bedroom upstairs. She wasn't going to wait until time for the party to arrive. She was going to get there early to see what was going on. She had the distinct impression that Rachael Lafferty was going to have some explaining to do.

It didn't take the young woman long to get to the dockside Victorian home and she simply swept through the street level entrance door and up the stairs to the first floor without even ringing the bell. Kitty felt the presence at once. A strong spirit that almost bowled her over with his masculinity and haughtiness, her eyes immediately fell to Dorian's portrait on the landing wall causing her to gasp in shock, her hand rising to her throat. She knew immediately that the man in the painting was the same presence she felt suddenly inhabiting Rachael's home.

"Kitty?" Rachael saw her friend standing in the foyer, pale as a ghost with her dark hair flowing around her round face like wisps of fog. She followed the woman's gaze to the portrait before hurrying over and inserting herself in the other woman's line of view. "Snap out of it, Kitty. It's just a painting," she said feigning nonchalance. She could almost guarantee that Kitty knew something was amiss and probably sensed Dorian as soon as she walked into the house.

Kitty's brown eyes were on Rachael as she began to laugh, remarking, "No. No, I don't quite believe that." She swung the heavy, black wool cloak off her shoulders and hung it on the coat rack in the corner, before moving past the Christmas tree and all its lights to stare up at the painting again. "Where is he? I want to meet him."

Rachael knew better than to play the fool with Kitty. It was well known that Kitty was more than she seemed; the woman had a sixth sense that defied all logic, called a witch by some. The author knew her friend had talents that went beyond the mere realm of normalcy and many times she had valued Kitty's judgment and opinions almost more than she valued her own. As a matter of fact, she was not surprised that Kitty asked to meet Dorian immediately.

"He's in the sitting room," she answered in defeat as she motioned Kitty in the direction of the sitting room.

As Kitty pushed past Rachael into the sitting room, she adjusted the lace shawl she donned when she'd changed her blouse. She didn't think it would be appropriate to arrive at a Christmas party covered in Poe's black hair. She stopped in the middle of the room when she sensed that foreboding feeling she had earlier intermingled with the arrogance and confidence of the masculine entity that was standing before her. Her eyes took in Dorian standing at the fireplace, a curious expression on his face.

An intrigued smile crossed Kitty's lips, and she gazed back at Rachael. "And how long did you plan on keeping your ghostly roommate a secret?" she inquired merrily as she clasped her hands at her waist. "I mean, really Rachael, he is much better looking than that portrait makes him out to be. One can only capture so much on the canvas."

Rachael blushed slightly as she walked past Kitty to stand next to Dorian. "You're the last person on this Earth I could keep him a secret from."

Kitty laughed. "You are quite right in that." She slowly stepped towards them. "Especially when I laid out the cards and discovered him."

Dorian gazed at the newcomer, his eyes narrowing slightly, his jaw tensing imperceptibly. "She can see me?" he asked cautiously, turning to face Kitty more fully. His eyes met Rachael's for explanation, wondering how this other woman could see him. He wasn't touching Rachael; there was no physical contact between them. What was the reason? If he had been curious before about his mysterious appearance and the events that had transpired since that night, then he was even more intrigued now to understand the whys and wherefores of his newfound life.

"Of course, I can see you," Kitty answered. "I am more in tune with the supernatural than most." She held out her hand. "Kitty Kendall. And you can only be Dorian Gray." She saw the confused look on Rachael's face, and she continued with a sly wink. "Tessa has been complaining about the portrait since she first laid eyes upon it."

"Oh," Rachael remarked softly. She realized that she was not touching Dorian in any fashion and froze. "Wait. We're not touching, and you can still see him?" She asked when she saw the incredulous look Kitty shot her and answered her own question. "Never mind."

Dorian took Kitty's hand and raised it to his lips, brushing them ever so slightly across the soft skin of her hand. "I am delighted," he stated seductively, turning on his infamous charm. He knew it worked on Rachael, and he wondered who else it would work on.

"I'm sure you are," Kitty breathed. His hand was ice cold, yet solid, his lips no warmer. It was if his body still held the coldness of the grave within it. His breath, though warm, was causing the gooseflesh to rise along the length of her arm. She could see the suspicion within the depths of his eyes, the carefully restrained agitation that permeated his being. She couldn't resist the impulsive laugh that escaped her lips as she gently squeezed his hand once, before sliding it free. "Oh, you are trouble," she remarked. "Yes. You are most definitely trouble." Her eyes twinkled as they passed back and forth between Dorian and Rachael.

Dorian studied Kitty as she moved to the couch, sliding off her shoes to tuck her legs beneath her. "Have we met before, Miss Kendall?" he asked softly with suspicion, retrieving his glass of sherry and sitting in one of the wing-backed chairs. She was vaguely familiar to him, but he could not place why.

Kitty shrugged, an easy lifting of her shoulders that made her mass of thick brown hair flow like water upon the shoreline. "Maybe in another life, Mr. Gray. I know I would remember you if it had been in this one," she replied in a matter of fact tone that was very indicative of her beliefs.

Rachael leaned her hip on the arm of Dorian's chair. Kitty is a witch..." she began in explanation.

Kitty held up her hand. "I much prefer the term neopagan, although sorceress has a deliciously wicked tone to it, wouldn't you agree?" she teased, leaning her chin on the palm of her hand as she gazed at the ghost. He was the first one of his kind that had ever crossed her path, and she was completely fascinated with him. She could already tell that there was much more to Dorian Gray than met the eye, and she was definitely going to get to the bottom of that mystery.

Dorian sipped at his sherry, his eyes meeting Kitty's over the rim of his glass. "Most definitely," he answered dryly, his lips twitching. He liked Kitty. Liked her immensely.

Rachael relaxed slightly, her hand resting on his shoulder. "She's a powerful witch, if you can believe everything that is said about her."

He raised an eyebrow. "Is that so? Do you know any hexes, curses, that type of thing?" he inquired pleasantly. "I know of a few people that would benefit from having one placed upon them. It might allow them to gain unique insight on another's plight before snapping to hasty judgments."

Rachael squeaked in protest at his comment, shaking her head. "I give up," she whimpered.

Kitty never moved, unaffected by the seriousness of his words. "I don't like to boast, but I have a wonderful little hex that causes the most uncomfortable rash on the backside in my spell book."

"Kitty!" Rachael gasped before laughing. "Don't encourage him." She had been around the witch enough to know that she could do the things she claimed. Granted, she also prayed she would never be on the receiving end of one of Kitty's spells.

"I was being quite serious," Dorian sniffed before draining the last of his sherry.

"So was I," Kitty agreed with a casual smile.

Rachael sighed, taking his glass and moving over to the small liquor cart to refill it. "Well, at least you get along with one of my friends," she off-handedly remarked to Dorian. She placed the stopper back in the decanter before turning to face them. "She has helped me with some research for one of my novels." She handed him his glass. "Kitty, can I offer you a glass of port wine?"

Kitty sat more upright and smiled at Rachael. "Oh, why not. I usually don't indulge in spirits..."

"Rachael does," Dorian growled as he gazed at the author hungrily.

Rachael's face reddened at his comment and she knelt to pick up the glass that had slipped from her fingers, thankful that it did not break.

Kitty did not comment on Dorian's declaration. "Since it is Christmas, a glass of port would be nice. Thank you." She couldn't see the expression on Rachael's face, but it was not needed considering that the look on Dorian's was enough to know that the cards she had read earlier had been right on the mark.

Rachael handed the younger woman a glass before perching on the edge of the other wing-backed chair. "Kitty also keeps me in supply of my favorite soap and potpourri," she commented casually, trying to steer the conversation away from mortifying topics.

"Handmade," Kitty supplied as she twirled the liquid in her glass.

"Ah yes, that wonderful vanilla scent that seems to cling to my dear Rachael. Please, do not stop creating that," he requested in appreciation before rising to step over to where Rachael sat. He pulled her to her feet, sliding his arm around her waist. "I cannot seem to get enough of it," he added huskily, his lips brushing softly along the softness of her neck.

"Dorian," Rachael softly admonished, trying to hide her face in his shoulder. She looked up as the front door chimed and sighed softly. "Well, the party is about to begin. Care to join me?" she asked him.

"It would be my pleasure." Dorian set his glass on the cart and took Rachael's hand. He smiled at Kitty. "Please excuse us. We'll return in a few moments, I'm sure." Tucking Rachael's hand in the crook of his arm, he escorted her through the room to greet their guests in the second-floor foyer.

Kitty caught the glance he cast her and raised her glass to him in a silent toast. To the casual observer, Dorian was simply the man at the hostess's side. But Kitty saw the glow that surrounded the ghost when he touched her friend. She watched as he nodded and acknowledged each guest, shaking hands, being polite, his perfectly manicured left hand never leaving the small of Rachael's back. She didn't know what it meant yet, but she would find out. And she knew that the evening would turn out to be quite entertaining.

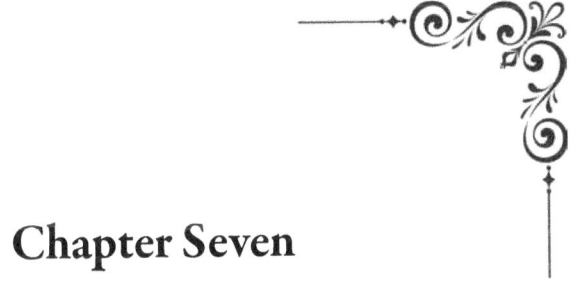

Chapter Seven

C HRISTMAS DAY, 9 PM

The Christmas party was turning out to be a huge success. Almost all of the invited guests had braved the winter weather to attend, complimenting Rachel on the wonderful job she had done restoring the townhouse. Small groups milled around the second level, some around the Christmas tree, some in the sitting room, others in the kitchen. A trio of publishers had taken up a spot at the circular staircase, discussing the extensive literary collection that lined the walls of the combined sitting room and library, arguing over the merits of leather binding as compared to the newer material that was now being used. Everyone loved the decorations, a few making the comment that the house appeared to be part of one of Rachael's novels, a true Victorian feel in the air with the fresh pine garlands and poinsettias in red and white. Rachael could not deny that all the work she had paid for to restore the old Victorian townhouse to its original splendor was well worth the money.

The partygoers were all well-dressed, even though Rachael had specified the dress code as casual. She should've known better, knowing the professionals she had invited. Many of the women wore long skirts or pantsuits, designer labels that would've been more appropriate at a theater opening than a simple Christmas party. The men ranged from suits and ties to warm sweaters and slacks, each with their own unique style that complimented their dates. All of them were cheerful, the worries of the everyday world having been left at the door.

Rachel smiled shyly at the whispers that made the rounds through the large sitting room, the sound a gentle buzz above the dulcet tones of orchestrated carols emanating from her stereo. She caught many of them discussing her newest novel, relishing the fact that they had the honor of reading the initial draft. She even managed to listen in a quiet conversation about the construction of the townhouse and the color scheme she had used to make the restoration fitting with the time it was built. But the whispers that caused her face to flush the most concerned the man at her side. Speculation abounded over whether or not Dorian was a friend or if the author had found a suitor.

Dorian's presence and charm had struck every man and woman alike. Rachael's guests enjoyed talking with him at great length about the various classic works that he was quite familiar with. The clothing Grace had provided for him clung to his tall frame like a second skin and unless one knew who he was, one would have thought that he was every inch the modern Renaissance man. He stood beside Rachael wearing a cream cable knit sweater and tight blue jeans with deep brown leather loafers to complete his ensemble. He had pulled his hair back at the nape of his neck, revealing more fully his chiseled face and perfect lips. When he laughed at a joke one of the guests had made, it was all Rachael could do to keep from pulling Dorian Gray away and up to her bedroom, the party be damned.

That particular thought vanished as she turned and stiffened slightly, her eyes meeting that of Julian Falcon's. The museum curator accepted a glass of wine from Kitty as he entered the room.

Dorian had felt Rachael's body tense and nodded to the couple he had been speaking with. Sliding his hand from the middle of Rachael's back to her hip, he pulled her more fully into his embrace, tucking her possessively beneath his shoulder. He dropped his head slightly, his lips caressing her ear. "Well, well," he whispered as Tessa entered the room behind Julian. "It seems dear Tessa decided to grace us with her auspicious presence after all."

"*Shush*," Rachael scolded Dorian, the heat spreading through her body at the intimate embrace she found herself in. Taking his hand, she pulled him towards her friends, a feat completed best by weaving through the other guests. "Be polite, Dorian. I know how one of your breeding can be when you set your mind to it."

Dorian snickered behind Rachael but kept the sharp comment that lingered on the tip of his tongue to himself. He studied the curator, having never met Julian, and wondered just how familiar the man was with his unique story. He held Rachael's hand tightly as she hugged the man with her free arm.

"Tessa, Julian. I'm glad to see you both made it to the party," Rachael exclaimed as she hugged Tessa.

Julian nodded, handing his glass of wine to his wife for a moment as he cleaned the moisture from his glasses and answered, "We were beginning to wonder if we would. I've never seen so much snow in London." He perched his glasses back on his face and smiled at Rachael, his eyes drifting across her face to lock with Dorian's. He held out his hand. "Julian Falcon, curator at the National Museum."

Tessa glared at the couple from over the rim of her wineglass, staring suspiciously at Dorian. He looked very familiar and a gnawing feeling gripped her stomach. She lowered her glass, allowing the champagne to fizz on her tongue before swallowing. "I didn't know you had a date for the party, Rachael. Who is your friend?" she asked sharply, very uncomfortable around the man that seemed to be courting her friend. She had tried to convince Julian to remain home. She was too afraid to enter the haunted

Victorian townhouse and didn't want him to be within its walls either, but her husband had pleaded his case in the most logical of manners. He had managed to assure her that nothing would happen to her as long as she stayed among the guests, and she knew she could not argue with him.

Rachael blushed slightly as she clasped Dorian's hand tighter in her own, steeling herself for the forthcoming introductions. Tessa's sharp tone sent the warning bells in her head to ringing, but there was nothing she could do to stop the inevitable. She gazed up at Dorian as she spoke. "Tessa, Julian, I'd like to introduce you to Mr. Dorian Gray."

Dorian took the hand Julian had offered, savoring the shocked look that crossed the curator's face. He noted the quick darting of Julian's eyes to the portrait that hung on the landing and then back to him. He shook the curator's hand firmly before offering his hand to Tessa. He waited as she hesitantly accepted it, then raised the back of her hand to his lips, his dislike of the woman before him carefully concealed behind a mask of propriety and nonchalance. He released it with a slight smirk before maneuvering Rachael before him, sliding his hand to the small of her back. The dress she wore was cut low in the back, her skin warm and soft beneath his palm. He kept the biting comment he was contemplating uttering from leaving his lips. "It's a pleasure to meet you both," he managed with an air of arrogance and pride. "Rachael has nothing but high praise and compliments for the two of you."

Tessa jerked her hand back, unconsciously wiping it along the folds of her skirt. Her eyes glinted coolly at Rachael's escort. "Dorian Gray." She huffed with spite and walked over to the sideboard, setting her empty glass upon it as she considered the other guests in the room. She kept her voice low, nodding to Kitty as she passed, before returning to her husband's side. "How interesting. You look remarkably like that horrid portrait gracing Rachael's stairwell." She leered at the couple before allowing a cold smile to tilt her lips as she stared at Dorian in challenge.

Dorian returned her smile, but his brown eyes remained cold and dark. The sharp edge of his voice held a barely restrained disdain. "As well I should. I have been told repeatedly that I am the image of my great-grandfather, for whom I was named."

Julian scratched his chin in thought, oblivious to the sharp tones both his wife and Rachael's escort took with each other. "I didn't think your great-grandfather ever married, Mr. Gray." He waved his hand briefly, keeping his tone light. "At least it is never mentioned in the book detailing his life." He tapped his fingers against his lower lip. "He was contemplating it though. With an actress I believe."

Dorian nodded politely, pleased that Julian was familiar with Oscar Wilde's version of his life. "Her name was Sybil Vane. A...strikingly beautiful woman with a wondrous talent for portraying the most tragic of Shakespeare's heroines." He tucked his free hand in the pocket of his jeans as he continued perpetuating the lie of his own life. "Her suicide at my great grandfather's cruel declaration that she had killed his love was enough to convince him that marriage was, indeed, a bad proposition."

"Ah, so it did happen that way," Julian commented thoughtfully with a nod. "So, then he didn't marry at all."

"No, Mr. Falcon. He did not." Dorian paused as a mischievous twinkle in his eyes appeared. "But that is not to say he did not have numerous dalliances in his long life that could have produced quite a few bastard children."

Tessa's eyebrows rose at the word *dalliances*, the hackles at the back of her neck, too. She watched as Dorian kissed Rachael's neck with more familiarity than was deemed proper, even in the modern age. It was obvious by the look of adoration and the unusual flush that stained her friend's cheeks that Dorian and Rachael's relationship was more than just casual.

For some reason, the notion irked Tessa. She strode over to one of the wing-backed chairs and settled into it as some of the guests filtered into the kitchen to sample the fare prepared by Grace. She crossed her long legs, her hands primly settled in her lap as she stared at Dorian. "So, how did you meet Rachael, Mr. Gray?" she inquired in mock sincerity. The unsettling feeling in her gut intensified as she recalled the solidity of his fingers, the warmth of his lips on the back of her hand. If this man was the ghost that had attacked her, how come people could see him and why was he so corporeal? The questions swam in her head, waiting to be answered.

Dorian accompanied Rachael to the other chair, offering her the seat as he remained standing next to her, lounging on the arm as his right hand massaged her neck with gentle fingers. "That is an interesting story." He leaned closer to Rachael, his breath ruffling the soft strands of her hair. He could tell his actions were irritating the duchess and he reveled in the power he wielded as he continued lavishing affection on the author. "I was trying to locate my great grandfather's portrait," he began, enjoying the charade that he had planned with Rachael on the event that Tessa would appear at the party. "Unfortunately, I arrived at the auction only moments after Miss Lafferty purchased the painting." He sighed in mock disappointment then smiled warmly at Rachael as she gazed up at him, her eyes pleading with him to take care of where he tread. He continued with a slight wave of his free hand. "So, I procured her address from the auction house, and came here two days ago to discuss the terms of purchasing my family's treasure back from such a charming woman." He took her hand in his, raising it to his lips to caress them against her knuckles as he entwined their fingers. His tender gaze hardened as he returned his ghostly stare to Tessa. "We've become quite good friends since. She has been gracious enough to allow me to stay here in the house until I return home."

"Has she?" Tessa looked to Rachael for confirmation, not believing the nod Rachael gave her in answer. "And you've become good friends in such a short time?" she asked derisively, her voice tightening further.

"Yes. We have." Dorian's eyes bore into Tessa as Julian mimicked his position, settling beside his wife. The ghost reached up and stroked a finger along the line of his goatee, as Rachael rested her hand on his thigh. "Lady...it is Lady?" He waited until Tessa inclined her head in the affirmative. "Lady Falcon, do you have an issue with me? Have we met previously?" he asked innocently, waving his hand casually in question. He couldn't quite contain the dripping sarcasm that echoed in his voice. "Did I upset you at a previous meeting?"

Tessa leaned forward on her seat, smoothing down her skirt. "Possibly, Mr. Gray." She reached up to tuck an errant strand of her red hair back into the French twist at the back of her head. "I am truly surprised you do not recall meeting me before." She snorted maliciously. "You left quite the impression."

"Tessa, what has gotten into you?" Julian asked, gazing down at his wife. "You are being very rude to Mr. Gray and I'm sure Rachael does not want her party ruined because of your surliness." He glanced apologetically at Rachael, patting his wife's shoulder in an attempt to calm her.

Rachel sighed, trying very hard not to bolt from the room and the conversation. She could tell that Tessa was intentionally goading Dorian, trying very hard to make him show his proverbial hand and reveal who he really was. She squeezed the hand that rested on his blue-jeans clad thigh in warning.

"Really?" For Rachael's sake, Dorian kept up the pretense of being his own great-grandson, when he really wanted to lash out at Tessa once again. "Where would we have met before, I wonder?" He furrowed his brow as he feigned mulling over their former meeting. "Was it at White Chapel?" he offered with a rising of his eyebrows.

Tessa laughed haughtily. "Nowhere so prestigious, Mr. Gray. Do not insult my intelligence in such a manner." She let the haughty expression remain on her face as she gazed at Rachael, knowing that her friend was very disturbed by the course of the discussion. She watched as Rachael's jaw clenched and the way she kept her eyes averted away from them.

Julian noticed some of the other guests pausing to eavesdrop upon the conversation. "Tessa, really. Mr. Gray is just trying to determine where the two of you might have met. You're acting like a shrew," he commented softly. He gazed at Dorian and Rachael. "I must apologize for my wife's comment."

Dorian shrugged. "I meant no insult," he replied quietly, the lie slipping from his tongue with ease. He glanced sideways to see one of the couples that had attended the night's events motioning to Rachael. "You have guests leaving, Rachael."

Rachael leaned forward and waved as the couple motioned for her to remain seated. She smiled at them before looking over to her friends. "Tessa, what has gotten into you tonight?" she asked cautiously, alarmed by the other woman's complete maliciousness toward Dorian.

"I'm sure it's nothing your...friend couldn't explain," Tessa responded as she shifted in her seat. The way she said the word *friend* was like a venomous bite from a lethal snake. She studied her hands, her rings glinting in the light from the table between them.

Dorian had managed to compose himself, although the tight clenching of his jaw indicated otherwise. "I am sure I would have remembered meeting someone as beautiful as you, Lady Falcon," he stated, fighting to keep the sarcasm from his voice.

Rachael felt his hand tense above hers, and she could sense the arrogant fury that was building within him. She tightened her grip upon his, standing up. "Dorian, I think we need some more sherry," she stated, her concern very evident in the soft tone of her voice. "And champagne. Would you be a dear and help me?" Her eyes bore into his, their depths slightly panicked as she attempted to diffuse the situation before it became out of hand.

Dorian rose with her, his eyes drifting from her face down her neck to settle upon the creaminess of her chest. "Gladly," he purred. He looked to Julian as he wrapped his arm around Rachael's waist. "Excuse us for a moment," he commented in the most elegant of voices. He escorted Rachael across the room to the hall, casting a callous glance over his shoulder at Tessa.

Tessa rose as they disappeared, shrugging off Julian's hand with a sharp jerk of her shoulder. She followed them into the dark corridor refusing to silence the suspicious thoughts that were racing through her mind or temper the anger that was aimed at Dorian. "Rachael, a word, if you don't mind," she called sharply, stopping just within the doorway.

Rachael stopped, closing her eyes as a feeling of foreboding overcame her. Slowly she spun on the ball of her foot to look at her friend. Dorian's hands on her shoulders were her pillar of strength, a comforting weight and a source of willpower for the inevitable confrontation to come. "What do you need Tessa?" she asked sweetly, not wanting to argue with her friend.

Tessa approached cautiously, standing her ground as she pointed to Dorian with an accusing finger. She never raised her voice above conversation level, not wanting to attract any attention. She ignored the laughter that drifted from the other room, pausing only to acknowledge the man that slipped past them on his way from the kitchen. She smiled politely to him as he nodded and as soon as they were alone, she attacked. "Are you sure he is who he says he is, Rachael?"

Rachael tilted her head, pretending confusion by the other woman's words. "I'm quite positive, Tess. What is this about?" She folded her arms over her chest and waited, as stubborn as the literary agent that had helped mold her career over the years. She knew Tessa would cause problems with Dorian no matter what cover story they spun as to his identity. Especially since Tessa was notoriously suspicious of anyone new in Rachael's life. Of course, what Dorian did to Tessa a few days earlier didn't help their mutual cause.

"I don't trust him," Tessa snapped, punctuating every word that left her perfectly painted lips. "Not one bit."

This sparked Dorian's curiosity and he snarled nastily, "Why do you not trust me, Lady Falcon?" His tight grip upon Rachael was the only thing that kept his formidable temper in check.

"Because I doubt anyone would trust another person who had tried to kill them," Tessa hissed in accusation. She saw Rachael's eyes flick to something over her shoulder and she gazed back to see Julian wishing the partygoers a good night on Rachael's behalf as they left.

"Tessa, that's a bit uncalled for, don't you think?" Rachael protested. She reached up to free her hair from the clip that held it in place, easing the headache that was threatening to spill forward in a blast of pain. She was astounded that Tessa would be so bold to attack Dorian during her Christmas party, especially with so many people in the house. It was enough to put her immediately on the defensive and she snapped back, "How could you just stand there and insult one of my guests like that?"

Tessa's head whipped around and she closed the distance between them in three steps. She shoved her finger in Rachael's face. "Don't you dare play coy with me Rachael Anne Lafferty!" she spat icily, her voice rising as she glared at the couple. "You know damn well he is not what he appears to be!"

The silence that descended upon the townhouse was actually deafening. The other partygoers had heard her outburst between the tracks of Christmas music that was playing, and everyone stared towards the corridor the two couples were standing in. Julian turned to look out over the room, laughing nervously. "Don't mind them. A bit of a disagreement over the hero of Rachael's latest novel." He strode into the room. "Who needs a refill?" he asked, pouring himself a drink from the bottle of wine on the sideboard.

Rachael waited until she heard the conversation resume in the other room to lash at Tessa. "How dare you!" she snarled in fury.

"It is the truth. You're simply too blind to see it," Tessa accused.

Dorian's eyebrows rose, his lips twitching in amusement. "Is that a fact, Lady Falcon?" He laughed wryly, silencing Rachael with a firm squeeze of his long fingers on her shoulders. "For someone, who seems to know nothing about me, I find your accusations very insulting. Tell me," he started coldly, "what exactly am I if not who I say I am?" His eyes narrowed in menace, his body tense in anger, the circling motion of this thumbs along the line of Rachael's neck the only indication of his restraint.

Tessa's eyes widened as he rebutted her, before narrowing into catlike slits. She focused in on his long fingers, the way his thumbs moved up and down along the neck of her friend. She could almost feel them wrapped around her own neck again and she swallowed hard, choosing her next words with care, waiting until the crowd that had gathered near the entrance dissipated, Julian helping to avert their attention away from them. "You, Mr. Gray, are a potentially violent apparition," she answered, pausing for effect, "who seems to think he can insert himself in our lives as if he belonged here."

Dorian allowed the mask of pretense he had carefully perfected fade from his face, leaving his chiseled features in cold hard lines that could not have been mistaken by even the most casual observer as a very dangerous expression. His cultured voice was a low snarl, confirming any suspicion that he was a formidable opponent, and a very dangerous one at that. "Obviously you did not take my warning seriously, Tessa."

Rachael shook her head in frustration as she interrupted their verbal sparring. "Tessa, this not the time or place for this."

Tessa scoffed, waving Rachael's protest away. "Now is the perfect time." She snapped in retribution, "He is a ghost! He cannot be trusted and is a danger to all around him." Her rage was evident in the stance she took before them.

Dorian ran a finger along his lower lip, regaining his composure and pulling his rage back under control. "I think the matter of trust is Rachael's to decide." He graced Tessa with a smug smile. "Not yours."

Tessa actually laughed with contempt, making sure she was well out of the range of his hands. Or Rachael's for the look on her face was one that presaged a sharp slap. "That is where you are gravely mistaken." She lowered her voice further, her threat filled with malice and hatred. "Do not mess with me, Mr. Gray. Rachael is not the only person who has friends that dabble in the world of the supernatural. I still carry the marks of your fingers upon my neck and I would be more than delighted to see you returned to the hell that you originated from," she hissed, pulling aside the collar of her emerald green sweater, revealing the bruises from his fingers that were still very visible, a dark smudge of purple against her pale skin.

Rachael's eyes widened at the sight, her mind immediately recalling her own marks that Dorian had left. "Tessa, please," she pleaded. She tugged at the sleeves of her gown, attempting to hide the bruises upon her arms. Granted, hers were from a night of unbridled passion, but Tessa would never see it as such.

Dorian saw what Rachael did and he reached out to gently stroke her cheek with the back of his fingers. He knew the motion was soothing to her and he felt the trembling that was coursing through her body stop. "It's all right, Rachael," he remarked affectionately as he stared at Tessa over her shoulder. He lowered his head, his breath warm along the gentle curve of her ear. "Lady Falcon is simply concerned for your welfare." He paused as he turned his head in a snakelike motion, his eyes pinpoints of fury in the dim lighting of the hall. He let a vicious smile crease his lips. "Welfare which is now in my keeping."

Tessa choked at his words, her throat constricting at what he was implying towards her. "Your keeping, Mr. Gray?" she finally managed in defiance. "I'd hardly say that her welfare is any concern of yours," she chastised.

Dorian nodded slowly. "Alas, but it is. And as long as she resides beneath the roof of my home, then, yes, my keeping," he reiterated. He kissed Rachael's cheek, rubbing his own against hers in a manner that made Tessa's blood boil.

"Stop this! Both of you!" Rachael growled, staring at Tessa before turning her steely gaze up to Dorian. "You are acting like children!"

Tessa ignored Rachael's reprimand. "Your home?" she nearly screamed. She clenched her hands into fists at her sides, doing everything she possibly could to keep from physically lashing out and him or grabbing Rachael and forcing her from the townhouse. "I do not believe your name is on the deed, Mr. Gray!" she spat as she leered at him in challenge.

Dorian straightened, waving a hand dismissively. "A mere technicality that the executors of my estate failed to rectify. But I assure you, Rachael trusts me. Implicitly." His voice was as cold as an iceberg, hard and sharp like the edge of a knife. He allowed the full extent of his aristocratic upbringing to surface, each word dripping with righteous arrogance. "I would not advise you coming between us, for it would most assuredly be your undoing."

The maliciousness and the manner in which he delivered his words shook Rachael to the bones. "Dorian!" she gasped in shock. Her hand rose to her chest as it heaved heavily from her anxiety, and she turned to look up at him in shock. "You cannot be serious! You cannot stop my friends and family from seeing me or being within my home. No matter how jealous you may get."

Dorian cupped her cheek, his voice softening into affectionate tones that were as smooth and warm as velvet. "I mean it Rachael. Your safety and happiness come above all else in my eyes. I truly think what we shared last evening proved that." His eyes gazed at her, filled with naked lust and stark desire. When they flicked to Tessa, they hardened once again. He smirked haughtily at her, like a boy, who knew the dirtiest and most private secret about the person with whom he was conversing.

Tessa paled and she felt every strand of hair on the back of her neck rise, sensing the danger that stood before her. The wicked malice that spewed from Dorian Gray was cause for great alarm. Rachael was in graver peril than she originally thought. "Last night?" She dropped her voice to a lethal whisper as she finally closed the distance between Rachael and herself. "What did you do Rachael?" she hissed in question, her disapproval very apparent in her stance and expression.

Rachael blushed, her cheeks as dark as a rose on a summer morning. "I don't think that's any of your concern, Tess," she managed to stammer in a low murmur, unable to meet her agent's eyes.

Tessa looked down, noticing the mark on Rachael's right wrist. She grabbed her arm, shoving the sleeve back. "This is none of my concern?" she snapped, her tone causing Rachael to wince. "So, am I to believe that you did this to yourself?" She grabbed Rachael's other hand, glaring at the wrist. There were perfect imprints of long, slender fingers circling the author's arms. Her eyes widened and then narrowed at Rachael before dropping her hands. "Don't tell me you shagged a violent, homicidal ghost!"

Dorian's eyes widened at Tessa's claim. "Shagged?" He looked at Rachael curiously, his lips turning up in a smug smile. "Is that what we did, my love? We *shagged*?" He let one of his hands drift down to her waist, snaking around her and pulling her tightly against him. He ground his hips against hers in a provocative manner, the tips of his fingers brushing the underside of one breast as he splayed them along her stomach. He lowered his lips to her neck, nipping gently at her tender skin. His eyes locked with Tessa's. "I much prefer the term...nailed," he growled seductively. Tessa's expression of horror made him laugh, the sound cold and menacing. "Too bad you didn't hear her screaming my name in the throes of ecstasy."

Julian turned to look at them, catching the tail end of Dorian's comment. He choked on his drink. "Who was screaming whose name?" he asked weakly. He was unsure if he wanted to butt in on the conversation, very aware that he had missed something of importance.

"Tessa," Rachael whispered, shaking her head. "I don't think this is appropriate conversation," she pleaded, her eyes glancing to some of the guests she could see from her position in the hall.

"You fucked a ghost!" Tessa yelled in shocked disgust, pointing to the bruises that marred Rachael's flesh. "Tell me, Rachael, did you have him before or after you found out he tried to murder me?" she inquired her voice thinning with the spite and anger she had presented to Dorian earlier. Marred and distorted by rage, her shrill tone dripped with venom.

"Damn you, Tess," Rachael sobbed through clenched teeth, tears teetering at the edge of her eyes, her throat constricting from a stifled sob. She was at a loss for words and unrepentant of her actions with Dorian.

"I had no idea you were so hard up," Tessa sniffed in disdain. "I'm sure we could've found you corporeal company if you needed a fix that badly."

Dorian let out a cold laugh. "I hardly think anyone you could have found for my dearest Rachael would have satiated her appetite the way I did." His brown eyes narrowed into thin slits. "And which I will continue to do, much to your chagrin. Who Rachael invites into bed is most assuredly none of your business. You've interfered in her life far too much to suit my tastes and I will put a stop to it." He held Rachael possessively, brooking no argument as to the claim he had staked upon her heart and body.

"Are you threatening my wife, Mr. Gray?" Julian asked sharply, stepping between Tessa and Rachael. He was beginning to wonder if maybe Tessa's attacker truly was in the room with them.

Dorian shook his head slowly. "No, sir. I'm merely stating a fact.

Rachael was about to reply to her friend's question when Kitty stepped into the hall. Dorian tightened his hold on her, and she mustered up a weak smile for the woman. "Kitty is everything all right?" she asked, stuffing down the explosive emotions she was experiencing.

The witch stepped deeper into the hall, peering curiously at the four of them. "Oh, yes. Jonas was looking for you. He mentioned something about wanting to talk to you in regard to the cover art of your newest novel." She could feel the tension in the air and was disappointed that she had obviously missed a very interesting conversation.

Rachael nodded. "I forgot all about that. Thank you." She gripped Dorian's hand tightly in hers.

Dorian's hard expression never changed. "You should go attend to your guests, Rachael," he remarked in a warm and tender tone. He tucked her hand in the crook of his arm, sweeping her past Tessa and Julian, taking Rachael back into the sitting room where people still lingered.

Kitty allowed one eyebrow to raise in question, noting the scowl on Tessa's face. There was definitely something more going on than a festive Christmas party. She followed Tessa's gaze, her eyes falling on Dorian and Rachael, putting two and two together. She did not know Tessa as well as she knew Rachael, having only met the agent shortly after Rachael had bought the townhouse. But Kitty knew Tessa well enough to know that, based on Tessa's demeanor, she did not like Dorian Gray.

Dorian's charismatic laughter drifted back to them over the music that was still playing, and Julian watched as his wife's jaw clenched. Someone had put another compact disc in the player, the sounds of the *Nutcracker Suite* echoing throughout the rooms, sending its Christmas cheer. He reached out to tuck a piece of red hair back behind Tessa's ear, gazing at her in concern. "Tessa, love, is everything all right? You seem a bit perturbed."

Tessa moved into his arms, settling there for a moment of comforting. "Perturbed. I'm more than a bit perturbed, Julian." She looked up at him, her green eyes flashing with anger. She managed to keep it in check, not wanting to lash out at her husband over Rachael's foolishness, but her body was tense from the confrontation. "And no, everything is not all right. Something is terribly wrong."

"Such as?" Julian prompted as he rubbed his hands along her back. He pushed his wire-rimmed glasses back to the bridge of his nose as he waited. He agreed that there was something odd happening around them, something he could not explain, but he had no information to ascertain what has occurring. "Tessa, you've been acting very unusual the last few days. I know the attack shook you up, and of course the appearance of Mr. Gray has not helped the situation. Talk to me, please?"

Tessa pulled Julian further into the corridor, hiding in the shadows where no one could see them, but where they could still see the partygoers as they spoke with Rachael and Dorian. Her eyes followed the ghost, twin daggers in the dark. "I was telling you the truth, Julian. I was attacked by a ghost, who looked very much like Rachael's new suitor." She shook her head in exasperation. "To have him suddenly show up, real, corporeal..." She fell silent.

"Well, that's surely odd, his sudden solidity," Julian teased with a tender smile. The look Tessa fixed him with sobered him, and he cleared his throat.

Tessa swallowed. "I cannot believe that Rachael would..." she hesitated, wondering if she was crazy, "...align herself with someone she barely even knows. That is not like her."

Julian pointed to the couple in question. "She is certainly taken by him, Tessa, but I hardly think that your accusations were called for." Tessa gave him a withering glance and he rubbed his chin with his finger. "Tessa, it is quite possible that he is exactly who he claims to be. I mean I realize he's not been here that long but surely Rachael would've introduced him to you while you here."

"That man was not here when I stopped by to pick up her manuscript. No one was here," she insisted profusely.

"Then he must have arrived long after you left," he reasoned, trying to placate his wife.

Tessa sighed, raising her hand to silence Julian. "The ghost was that Mr. Gray, but he was dressed in the clothing of that hideous portrait."

"Tessa, you must be mistaken," Julian began.

"I am not mistaken." She glared at him furiously. "I peered over my shoulder, but no one was there. No one. But when I returned my gaze to the mirror, he was there. And he spoke to me. He..." She collected her composure. "He threatened me before wrapping his fingers around my throat to strangle me." She pointed to the scab on her forehead, almost invisible beneath the layer of concealer she had used to hide it. "He did this to me. No one outside this house attacked me, as you seem to believe. I do not appreciate you calling me a liar, Julian."

Julian had been holding his glass of wine and he lowered it from his lips at her words, the drink suddenly forgotten. "Tessa, I understand that you are embarrassed at being attacked." He held up his hand, stalling the comment she was about to utter. "And as long as you feel that you did not need medical attention, I will not press the issue. But I am still having difficulty believing that Mr. Gray over there is a ghost," he calmly reassured. He smiled down at her softly. "Ghosts are nothing more than fairytales, love."

"He is a ghost!" Tessa persisted vehemently. She stared at him, refusing to back down from her convictions.

Julian tossed back the remainder of the liquid in his glass. "How? He is solid. I shook his hand, for goodness sakes, and a firmer grip I've never encountered." He reached out his free hand to feel Tessa's forehead, checking for a possible fever. "And I've seen the marks on you that indicate foul play. No ghost could leave bruises such as those." He twirled the empty wine glass in his fingers. "Are you sure you saw what you are claiming, love?" The expression on his face was of dire concern.

"Of course, I'm sure!" Tessa bit Julian's head off as she turned her back to the room. "And those were rather solid, icy fingers he wrapped around my throat." She stamped her foot like a rather petulant child. "And if you want proof of foul play, look at the bruises sweet Rachael is hiding!" she bit out snidely.

Julian laughed. "Tessa, Rachael is a grown woman. If she wants to have sex with that man, then that is her business." He pulled Tessa into his arms, dropping a kiss on her lips. "I really do think you are blowing this entire incident out of proportion." He brushed his fingertips along her cheek. "If it would make you feel better, I will accompany you here for all your meetings. That way you will not have to worry about some spooky ghost or strange men lurking on the docks waiting to attack you."

Tessa's eyes filled with tears. "You do not believe me. I cannot in good conscience allow her to stay here with that man. It does not feel right, Julian, so once again I will say that there is something very wrong," she cried, turning to stare at Dorian. "And that very wrong thing is the man...the ghost...that tried to kill me."

Before Julian could respond, to reassure his wife that she was wrong, he heard the tapping of metal on glass. "What is going on?" he whispered. He took Tessa's hand and pulled her back towards the sitting room, seeing a small group of guests standing around Rachael and Dorian. "Is there something you forgot to tell me?" he inquired quietly.

"No," Tessa answered.

Dorian gazed down at Rachael, an expression of total devotion plastered on his face. "Before the rest of you take your leave of us, Rachael and I have an announcement." He pulled her closer to him, raising her hand to his mouth.

Tessa paled, her hands gripping Julian's arm. "No. Oh my God, no," she murmured.

Dorian smiled at the group. "Miss Rachael Lafferty has consented to be my wife."

Chapter Eight

Julian stared at the couple with a blank expression on his face, the shock of Dorian's announcement still reeling through his mind. He felt Tessa shaking beside him, whether in rage or disbelief, he was unsure. He suspected it was with rage. What Tessa was implying was impossible. There was no way the distinguished gentleman escorting Rachael around the room could be an apparition.

He set his empty glass on a small table in the hall, watching as everyone wished the newly engaged couple well. He was trying to determine by the expression on Rachael's face if the man's announcement had been a shock to her as well. The man his wife claimed as a ghost was as polite as could be, with almost an Old-World charm, something that was uncommon even among the gentry of the modern day. Dorian laughed kindly at some stray remark as he shook the hand of a prominent publisher, before leaning down to place a gentle kiss upon Rachael's cheek.

One by one, the guests left, bidding their hostess a good night as they took their leave of her. Finally, Kitty, Julian, and Tessa were the only ones left. Kitty was in the oval sitting room of the townhouse.

Julian shook his head, choosing his words carefully as he kept his voice low. "It doesn't make any sense, Tessa, these accusations of yours. Ghosts cannot, as a norm from what I understand, have form. And if you did not see him when you turned away from the mirror that day, then how can we possibly see him now?" He raised a single eyebrow in question, clasping Tessa's hands in his, drawing them around his waist and entwining their fingers as he stood protectively in front of her.

Tessa frowned at Julian's words, her lower lip suddenly pushing out in a pout. Her own husband doubted her, and she did not like it. She leaned her forehead against Julian's. She had to somehow convince him that Dorian was more than he appeared, and that Rachael was indeed in the gravest of dangers. There was no way she could allow her friend to marry the man at her side. She knew deep down in her heart that Dorian Gray was not as he seemed.

A thought flickered through her mind and she raised her head, peering over her husband's shoulder to glare at Dorian. "Julian," she started softly as a realization dawned upon her, "is it me, or has Mr. Gray made it a point to remain in constant physical contact with Rachael?" she posed. "I wonder…"

"Tessa," Julian warned as she released him, sliding between him and the wall to step into the sitting room, stopping just at the edge of the Persian rug. He laid his hand on her shoulder, squeezing gently. "Don't you think you've done enough damage already?" he asked softly as Dorian took Rachael's hand in his and led her through the room in the steps of a lively waltz, dancing to the *Waltz of the Flowers* from the Nutcracker.

They swept past them, a cool breeze brushed Tessa's cheek as they moved along in time to the music. Tessa's stomach churned at the sight of the two dancers. The look of love that passed between Dorian and Rachael was more than she could take, and she walked over to the sideboard. She drank the glass of champagne that she poured for herself in two gulps, then poured herself another to strengthen her resolve before turning back to the couple. "Disgusting," she whispered to herself, wondering if Rachael could possibly be under some strange spell.

Kitty watched from her perch on the settee, smiling in delight as she tucked her legs beneath her. She tilted her head backward to watch the couple as they danced behind her. "Excellent form, Mr. Gray," she called, clasping her hands together in a small round of applause. "You're the first of Rachael's few beaux that at least has class."

Dorian smiled at the young witch as he spun Rachael around before pulling her closer. "A dying art, Miss Kendall, I assure you." He slowed his steps as the music ended, bowing slightly at the waist towards Rachael, her hand still clasped tightly in his. His eyes sparkled hungrily at the author as he drew her back to him, possessively tucking her beneath his shoulder.

Tessa eased her way towards them, wanting nothing more than to smack the predatory and conceited look off of Dorian's handsome face. She was shocked that Kitty of all people could not sense the danger that Dorian posed towards Rachael. She turned her attention to her friend, smoothing her hands over her skirt. She cleared her throat softly, regaining her composure and pushing down her arrogance and rage. Julian's words still rang through her mind, as she calmly spoke. "Rachael, I really must apologize for my harsh words a little while ago. It was not my intention to embarrass you."

Rachael's smile faded as she let her eyes linger on Dorian, before turning them to Tessa. There was something about the other woman's tone that set her on edge, every nerve in her body screaming for caution. She could see the hard glint in Tessa's eyes, the determined set of her jaw. It was that expression she had seen many times before as Tessa badgered publishers for more money on Rachael's behalf. When the Duchess latched onto an idea, she was a savage pit bull, until she achieved what she was going after, usually leaving the other party proverbially beaten and bloody.

"Don't worry about it, Tessa," she calmly responded, keeping her own tone clipped and short. She slipped Dorian's arms tightly around her, using them like a cloak of fleshy armor. "It's been a long day. We're all tired."

Dorian knew Rachael was simply trying to placate Tessa, noticing the sharp tone she used, matching the other woman's. Yet, he could not resist the temptation of goading the duchess. As far as he was concerned, he would never accept Tessa's apology as easily as Rachael and he knew it would be in the best interest of all parties involved to bring the situation to a head. He kissed the top of Rachael's head, breathing in her unique scent. His words were soft and casual, and, in a slightly bored tone that marred his cultivated voice, he spoke to Rachael with every intention of Tessa hearing him. "And you have worked yourself into a frenzy for these ungrateful wretches you consider friends."

Kitty coughed at Dorian's words, spitting the mouthful of champagne down her front. She attempted to stifle her laughter, enjoying the verbal battle that was sure to ensue. "And the gauntlet has been thrown," she stated in a gleeful tone, her eyes twinkling as they passed from Tessa to Dorian and back. "Imagine that. I can almost hear the skitter-skitter of metal gloves as they slide across the floor."

"Ungrateful?" Tessa sputtered, ignoring Kitty's snide comment. She pulled herself up to her full height, drawing on every ounce of aristocratic arrogance she possessed, drawing on years of cultured breeding. "Mr. Gray, I would suggest that you allow Rachael to decide who is her friend and who is not. I do appreciate having her as a friend and extend my heartfelt gratitude for her invitation to this most superb Christmas party. If anyone is an ungrateful wretch, sir, it is you." Her tone was sharp and cold eyes glared at the apparition that held Rachael closely. She softened her tone before smiling warmly at Rachael. She took Rachael's hands in her own. "You are a wonderful hostess, Rachael."

Rachael nodded silently, her mouth suddenly dry. She was torn between her growing affection for Dorian and her long-standing friendship with Tessa. They were both right in their own ways. Her eyes locked with Tessa's as her mind moved through the last few days.

Tessa had never offered to help her get ready for the party. As a matter of fact, all she had done was complain about the townhouse and the amount of work and money Rachael had put into restoring it. She had especially enjoyed whining about the fact that Rachael should've hired painters and decorators to finish the minor work instead of doing it herself and allowing her writing to be put on the back burner.

Tessa, however, had an arsenal of servants to do the mundane daily chores of running a huge estate, maids and butlers that would take care of decorating for the holidays, giving the literary agent all the time in the world for her work and social pursuits. It was a luxury Rachael could ill afford, even if she wanted to. She made enough money on the sales and royalties of her novels to live comfortably, but she was far from being rich.

The ghost that now resided with her had been more help in preparing for the celebration than Tessa ever had, even in the past. Yet, Dorian did not have the right to tell her what to do, or who she could associate with. She sighed, rubbing her temple as she found herself in a very tricky "Catch-22". Dorian held her closely, his body hard and solid against hers. Yet, she could feel the coldness spilling from him, not the warmth she had grown accustomed to over the last few days. It served to remind her that was still, indeed, a ghost. She lowered her eyes to the ground, unable to say anything.

Dorian didn't fall for Tessa's conceit and false courtesy. He entwined his fingers tightly with Rachael's as he stared at the duchess. "At least Rachael has the decency to keep her disparaging remarks about others to herself," he hissed, his breath stirring the hair at Rachael's neck.

"Oh yes, I know. After all, she is quite civilized, considering her upbringing," Tessa shot back, not caring that she was insulting the other woman. She ignored the hurt look that crossed Rachael's features and held her hands out wide, any sort of civil politeness gone. "Not that she is to blame, of course," she snapped in an indignant manner, her eyes hardening in contempt. "There are others here, though, who should know their manners from birth, let alone their place."

She clasped her hands at her waist, a sadistic smile slowly appearing on her face. "Julian, don't you find it amazing that a cultured gentleman such as Mr. Gray can conveniently forget all his manners and display all the unruly characteristics of a wolf?" she asked, glancing back at her husband before again glaring at Dorian. She ignored the pleading look of her husband as he shook his head in defeat, not saying a word. "You are very vulgar for a man of your breeding, Mr. Gray."

Dorian's expression hardened into lines of pure malice. "And you, Lady Falcon, are very uncouth for a woman of yours," he snapped sharply. His arms tightened around Rachael, holding her possessively against his body, daring Tessa or anyone else in the room to try and extricate her from his grasp. He felt her hands wrap around his wrists as he slid them higher, allowing them to rest just beneath her collarbone. He could feel her trembling and it struck his heart like a knife, sharp, quick, and painful, and it angered him even more. "But if a wolf is what

I am," he sneered with haughty arrogance, "then I have at least found my mate." He playfully nipped at the curve of Rachael's ear in defiance, letting out the softest of purrs. "Growl," he rumbled as his cold dark eyes lifted in angered defiance at Tessa.

Kitty's giggles filled the silence that had descended over the room. None of them had noticed the stereo had fallen silent, where only the crackling of the fire in the hearth and her laughter could be heard. She shifted on the settee, pulling her knees up and wrapping her skirts around her ankles as she watched Rachael's face go from a very warm pink to a brilliant scarlet.

"Why Rachael! That is a splendid color for you!" she remarked with glee and wiped at the tears of mirth in her eyes. "Really, it is," she assured, trying to relieve the tension that snapped in the air like lightning.

Tessa cast a withering glance at Kitty, one that was entirely lost on the witch. Turning her attention back to Rachael and Dorian, she lashed out at him once again, throwing caution to the wind. "The game has changed since you were a young man, Mr. Gray. Or, at least since you had a real body. One really should keep up with the times, which you clearly have not." She shifted her weight, leaning her hip on the arm of one of the wing-backed chairs, waiting to see if he took the bait.

"The game has not changed in the least," Dorian laughed as he freed his right hand from Rachael's grip, sliding it familiarly along the line of her collarbone before resting it on her shoulder. She still retained her death grip on his other arm as it leaned across her, her fingers digging deep into him as she remained silent. He waved his hand towards Tessa. "You are playing with a master, Duchess Falcon," he remarked snidely, purposefully using her formal title. He gave her a look of mock shock. "Oh, but of course. A hag such as you would not recognize that. Far be it for me, a man, who has been playing this game since the 1700's, say that the game is still the same," he remarked sarcastically, resting his hand on his chest in a parody of contriteness.

Rachael's hands tightened even more on Dorian's arm, her fingernails digging through the thickness of the sweater he wore. It was the only thing keeping her from bolting from the room. "Please! Both of you stop this!" she pleaded. "This is my home and I will not have you insulting each other within its walls!"

Tessa snorted in derision. "I believe that it is a bit too late for that, Rachael dearest." She dismissed Dorian with a haughty flick of her hand, returning it daintily to her lap. Julian had taken a seat on the opposite end of the couch from Kitty, his head cradled in his hand, embarrassed by his wife's lack of social decorum. He knew it was better to remain silent than choose a side other than his wife's. Tessa sniffed rudely, clearly elevating her own imagined superiority. "You have quite the rude and boorish buffoon for a poltergeist, Rachael." The lingering thought that had caused her entrance back into the room once again rose to the forefront of her mind as she turned her head slowly towards them. The cruel curl of her upper lip was reminiscent of a snake that was about to strike and kill its prey. She tilted her head slightly as she stared at Dorian and inquired in heartless jest, "I do wonder how corporeal he would if he weren't in physical contact with you." She saw a flicker of fear flash in Rachael's eyes and pursued maliciously in her manic verbal attacks. "As he has been all evening. That has not gone unnoticed."

Dorian's jaw clenched tightly, his eyes narrowing to thin, dark slits. Tessa's words were cutting into her supposed best friend, yet here she stood insulting the very person that was her bread and butter. Had he his cane, he would have thought nothing of giving this shrewish woman a good caning. Never in his living years would he had thought of such an act against a woman, but Tessa was testing him in a way no other had before.

"You have yet to see rude, Lady Falcon. I have been polite to you this evening on Rachael's behalf. And my form, corporeal or otherwise, has no bearing on this discussion." He kept his voice low and even, doing everything he could to keep from upsetting Rachael even more than she currently was. He let his hand slide closer to her neck, his fingers gently caressing the soft skin he found there in a soothing circular motion.

"You have attempted to sway my darling Rachael in every manner of her life since arriving in London. You have tried to convince her not to buy this townhouse and restore it. You have, by her own admission to me, tried to exert your influence on her writing. You have imposed impossible deadlines upon her." He chuckled evilly, shaking his head. His hair had come loose from its ponytail, the ribbon falling silently to the floor as his dark locks framed his face. It only added to the haughtiness that was reflected in his eyes. "That is not the sign of a friend, Madame. That is the sign of a dictator." His expression changed to one of pure hatred as he stared at Tessa. Indeed, times had changed even for him to contemplate the visage of her body falling to his feet in a heap and bloody mass. Anything to pay retribution for what Tessa was doing to his beloved Rachael.

Tessa gained her feet at his accusation, pointing to herself with both hands as she closed the distance between them, causing Rachael to cringe and press herself more firmly against Dorian. She unleashed everything she had on Dorian. "A dictator, Mr. Gray? And what would you call yourself? Benevolent? A friend?" She took a few steps away from them in the attempt to regain her composure, before spinning on one foot only to face them yet again. Tessa pointed at the couple. "After your atrocious display of unwarranted and violent jealousy I would not say you are much better than a dictator yourself!" Her chest heaved in fury, her voice getting louder and higher in pitch as she spoke. "At least

I have the benefit of not being half so possessive, and of understanding the modern world!"

Julian's mouth dropped at his wife's words and was about to stand up and reprimand all of them when Kitty reached over to lay her hand on his arm. She shook her head silently, her warm eyes flashing in warning, telling him that now was not the time to get involved, that it would only cause more heartache. He understood her unspoken warning, concerned by the paleness of Rachael's cheeks and tenseness of Tessa's posture. He was afraid that things would come to blows. If Dorian Gray was a ghost, as his wife seemed to think, and as Dorian had yet to truly deny, then Julian truly hoped the truth would manifest itself quickly and bring the arguing to a quick resolution.

Dorian's eyes widened as he laughed, a cruel and twisted sound that echoed from the high ceiling above them. "You call yourself understanding?" He tapped his lip for a second before returning his hand to Rachael's shoulder. "Tell me, Lady Falcon, when was the last time you stopped long enough to truly listen to Rachael's desires? To truly hear her?" he challenged. He waited for her answer and smirked when all he received was Tessa's silence, her chest heaving in fury.

"It is amazing what a person can discover over the course of a few days," he continued and cradled Rachael in his arms, her tears wetting the back of his hands. "When was the last time you considered her needs and not how much her next book would fill your duchy?" His temper flared and he used it to sharpen his words like the edge of a surgical knife, a talent he knew how to wield with accurate precision to gain his advantage. He canted his head imperiously. "I may be nothing more than a ghost, a nuisance in your opinion, but I do not need to be corporeal or even versed in this strange modern world you live in to love and care for someone." He dropped his lips to Rachael's neck briefly, gazing at Tessa. "Rachael is nothing more than a meal ticket to you. And if I am damned to haunt these rooms until the end of eternity, then all the better. For I will be at least making the one woman, who sees me for who I truly am happy until the end of her days," he finished with vehement conviction.

Julian saw the smug look Tessa shot him at Dorian's admission. He was a ghost. One that had attacked his wife, just as she had said. But through the entire argument, he saw a side of Tessa he did not care for. He peered over to Rachael and Dorian, and even though the author had barely said a word throughout the entire argument, he could tell that she was becoming rapidly incensed. "Tessa," he cautioned, his eyes never leaving Rachael.

Tessa stared at Dorian dumbfounded, having never heard Julian call her name. "A meal ticket?" she repeated his insult. "Don't be so crass, Mr. Gray." She folded her hands over her chest. "I didn't marry money, like some carpet bagging Yankee. If I had chosen not to assist her, then I would never have taken a step into the unwashed masses that populate society." She paused in her superiority, blinking serenely, the astounded gasp that emanated from Rachael falling upon her deaf ears. "Of which you give the distinct impression of being descended from. You belie your birth Mr. Gray."

Kitty dropped her feet to the floor and raised her hand in warning in Tessa's direction. "Be careful, Tessa. You are treading on very dangerous ground, especially for one not familiar with Dorian's history." She looked at Dorian with warmth and understanding then explained with sincere admiration, "He was born and raised in polite Victorian society but has walked and lived among those not fortunate enough to marry money. As a matter of fact, if memory serves me correctly, he has soiled those perfectly manicured hands among them." She turned her dark eyes to Tessa, eyes that were filled with sadness and pity. She adored both women, but she knew Tessa's earlier words had cut Rachael to the bone. The fact that Rachael had kept her cool this long was a testament to the woman's strength, knowing just how hurt she was. Kitty knew Rachael adored Dorian, loved him even, and she would do everything she could to keep that fire burning. She had the read the cards, she had a good idea which way the pendulum would swing, and she knew that Dorian was already totally devoted to the woman, who had brought him, and his portrait, home. She lifted her chin, disgusted at Tessa's appalling behavior. "Which is more than I can say about you," she finished softly.

Rachael stammered in Dorian's arms, her mouth moving silently as she tried to articulate her horror at Tessa's words. Her tears flowed freely down her full cheeks. Infuriated wasn't even close to what she was feeling, and when she found her voice, it was flat and emotionless. "Carpet bagging Yankee? My father was a distinguished Ambassador, Tessa, and you know that. American he may have been, but he loved my mother, an English woman might I remind you. Landed gentry." She trembled violently but held her head high in defense of her heritage. "My dual citizenship makes me considerably more than an American immigrant." She sniffed, rubbing her fingers under her nose in a childlike gesture. "Excuse me, Duchess Falcon, for being of mixed heritage. I'm sorry if the fact that my father was a carpet bagging Yankee, as you so delicately put it, makes me a pathetic human being in your eyes." Her lower lip quivered in slow boiling rage.

Julian looked up at Rachael. "She didn't mean it that way, Rachael," he said softly, trying to defend his wife, yet abhorred by her words.

"Yes, she did, Julian! Yes, she did," Rachael spat and explained to everyone present in the room, "Unlike Tessa, I've had to fight to get where I am! No, it wasn't given to me on a silver platter, since my parents had enough sense not to squander what they had! They always encouraged my brother and me to work for what we wanted! My heart and soul, my..." She sharply jabbed her own chest as she stepped away from Dorian, brushing his embrace away, causing him to disappear from Tessa and Julian's view. "My blood, sweat and tears have gone into every last piece of fiction I have produced!"

"Dear Heaven of God," Julian gasped, gaining his feet as he stared at the spot in which Dorian once appeared.

Tessa drew closer to Rachael, until only inches separated them. "Your ghost is a selfish, self-centered, violent, jealous, vain and arrogant bastard!" she spewed, poking Rachael in the chest. She whirled around at looked at Julian. "Now you believe me!"

Rachael's whole body shook in righteous fury, and she let out a short bark of a laugh that verged on hysteria. "I'd rather have a ghost, who has experienced life on the other side of the tracks and knows he's vain and arrogant in my home, than someone who pretends to be what she is not! At least he does not insult me!" She raised her hand and pointed to the door. "Get out! Get out of my house!"

Julian gathered his wits and took Tessa by the arm, knowing that his wife had definitely worn out her welcome. The sad part about the whole incident was the knowledge that Rachael was right, and he would never look at his wife in the same light again. Dorian Gray might have been a ghost, and he may very have well attacked his wife, but he wasn't upset with the man for it, a surprising fact on its own. He knew that Tessa could be hard and cold, but he never expected her to be such a shrew. His heart ached for Rachael. "Come Tessa. Before matters get worse," he stated softly.

Dorian took a step towards Rachael but stopped as Kitty gently grasped his upper arm. He looked at her in question, wondering why she had stopped him, but she simply shook her head in answer, her finger rising to her lips to indicate his silence on the matter.

Tessa didn't notice the exchange behind Rachael, Kitty's hand seemingly gripping thin air. Her tone was frosty when she finally managed to find her voice. "As you wish, then, Miss Lafferty," she stated in the most professional tone she could muster. "Do expect a notice from my assistant terminating our business partnership." She knew her next words would draw blood, but as far as she was concerned, Rachael had made her choice. "And don't bother submitting another manuscript for me to review and work on. I believe the caliber of your writing is unsuitable for the publishers my firm deals with. You may want to consider submitting them to a firm that caters to the supermarket tabloid crowd."

"You bitch!" Rachael lashed out unexpectedly and slapped Tessa across the face, watching the other woman's head snap sharply to the side.

Julian lunged forward, grabbing Tessa as she turned back to Rachael. Tessa delicately wiped the trickle of blood from her lip. "Honey," he pleaded, wanting her to stop.

"It takes one to know one," Tessa hissed as she ignored Julian and the tight hold he had on her arms. She tried to break free, but it was to no avail.

As soon as Kitty raised her hand, Dorian stepped forward, gathering Rachael into his embrace, reappearing to the others, the marked shock very evident upon Julian's face. "She does not need you to publish her work, Lady Falcon. Remember, my dear Rachael is already an accomplished author, bestselling from what I have been told. I'm sure another agent would be more than willing to step in your place and reap the spoils of this new lucrative partnership." He lowered his voice, his tone incensed as he comforted Rachael with a soft stroke of his hand over her hair. His eyes glittered, cold and dark and they left no doubt in anyone that saw them that to cross Dorian Gray could have very lethal consequences. "Don't come crawling back with an insincere apology on your lips, for I will not tolerate you here."

Julian pulled Tessa away from them, his eyes pleading with his wife. "Tessa don't do this. Emotions are high and you really don't mean it," he stammered in an attempt to atone for his wife's atrocities.

Tessa's eyes were locked with Dorian's in a stalemate as she pushed her husband aside, smacking at his hands as he tried to keep his body between the combatants. "Don't I, Julian?" she sneered. She lifted her chin, her face paling. She refused to back down, especially to a ghost. "I don't crawl to anyone, Mr. Gray. And I make no apologies for what I have said." She turned on one foot, marching into the foyer, her heels clicking loudly on the hardwood floor as she gathered her belongings and left, never saying another word as she slammed the door behind her. The glass in the foyer door shattered, raining shards that skittered across the floor in tiny rainbows as they glittered in the lights from the festive Christmas tree.

Julian stared at Rachael, who sobbed in Dorian's arms. Her face was hidden against the ghost's chest, and he approached them cautiously. He laid a comforting hand on her shoulder, gently squeezing it, avoiding the predatory look from the apparition. "I'm so sorry, Rachael." He nodded once to Dorian in respect before he, too, left the townhouse.

As soon as the door closed, Rachael pushed away from Dorian and without a word fled up the circular staircase, slamming the bedroom door with an anguished cry, the sound reverberating throughout the now silent house.

Kitty sighed and she headed into the kitchen, gathering the dustpan and broom. When she made her way back into the foyer, she found Dorian still standing there in deep thought staring at the door. She began to sweep up the shards of glass that littered the floor when Dorian knelt, holding the dustpan for her.

"Well, I must say, Mr. Gray, you put on quite a performance," Kitty complimented as she swept the glass into the pan. "A very interesting display. It's not often someone puts Tessa in her place." She shivered in delight as they made their way back into the kitchen, discarding the glass and slowly cleaning up the remains of the food that was spread out through the kitchen. "Very refreshing."

Dorian gazed towards the stairs as they made their way back into the sitting room. "I fear I may have caused more harm than good," he softly admitted as he sank into the chair.

Kitty considered him for a moment. "No. It's been coming. The more independence Rachael displays, the looser Tessa's grip on her has become." She shook her head. "One thing I have learned is Tessa is very insecure and she sees Rachael as a means to an end. Your observation was right on the mark." She gathered up her cloak from the back of the settee and allowed Dorian, who rose from his chair in a gentlemanly fashion, to escort her to the door. "You might want to get a board to cover this with until Rachael can have the glass replaced."

Dorian nodded. "I may have born into the upper class, but I assure you I can place a piece of wood over this until a glass cutter can be found."

With a quick flick of her wrist, Kitty snapped the warm, black woolen cloak out, swinging it around her shoulders and securing it with a silver Celtic knot pin. She smiled up at Dorian. "You're good for Rachael. Don't let anyone tell you otherwise." She held out her hand to him. "We'll meet again. But until then, take care of her." She allowed him to raise her hand to his lips, the soft brushing of them over her flesh making her smile. She laid her hand on the doorknob and pulled the door open, pausing long enough to wink cheekily at the ghost. "If you don't, I'll know."

Dorian suddenly found himself alone as the door clicked shut, and with a renewed determination, he set about cleaning up the party remains. He would leave Rachael alone for a while before going to her. It would give them both time to put the night's events in perspective. He glanced one last time at the door, whispering to himself. "Don't worry, Miss Kendall. I have made her happiness my life's new ambition."

TESSA HAD STORMED FROM Rachael's townhouse, leaving the remaining occupants aware of her rage. The crisp cold air only fueled her anger as she and Julian stood arguing. She had taken off up the street towards their vehicle, her chest heaving in righteous fury, ignoring her husband's calls to wait for him. She felt Julian's hand circle her upper arm and whirled on him, slapping him soundly across the face. "How dare you not stand up for me in there!" she hissed. "You allowed that...that...*revenant* to insult me without so much as blinking. I have never been so humiliated in my life!"

Julian stared at Tessa in shock. He had never witnessed such an arrogant display from her in all the time they had been married. He was humiliated. "You did it yourself, Tessa," he snapped back, and when he saw her balk, he raised his chin, his finger rising to scold his wife for her actions. "You acted like a fool in there. There was no reason to attack Rachael the way you did. She's your friend. Your star client." He walked away from her, opening the car door, slamming is shut after he started up the vehicle. He stared out the windshield, refusing to look at his wife.

Tessa slid into the passenger seat and slammed the door. "My behavior? My behavior?" she repeated indignantly. "What about her behavior?" she questioned as Julian pulled away from the curb, her voice loud and brash. "She had the audacity to introduce that thing as her escort, let alone announcing their engagement!" She laughed coldly. "Somehow, I do not think a proper wedding ceremony would be appropriate." She stared out the window, her jaw clenched tightly.

Julian's hands gripped the steering wheel tightly. "I'm sure it was simply a show, Tessa," he remarked in a strained voice.

Tessa seethed in her seat. She was infuriated with the entire situation. It galled her that Rachael would allow a ghost to influence her as much as Dorian obviously had, and in such a short time. The fool would do everything in his power to keep her from Rachael. "He will probably discourage her from writing as well," she mumbled angrily.

Julian glanced at her. "Rachael will never quit writing, Tessa." He sighed. "Is that what all this is about?"

Tessa gazed at him, her eyes narrowing into thin slits. "No," she snarled. "This is about a woman's life being in danger." She shifted in the seat so that she was facing Julian. "He is nothing more than a cold-blooded murderer."

Julian remained silent for a few moments. "And how did you come to that conclusion? If he wanted to kill you, I'm sure he would have." His voice was flat and emotionless. He knew Dorian Gray's story better than most, having studied it, analyzed it, memorized the book word for word.

Tessa snickered haughtily as she folded her arms. "Anyone who has read the book of his life knows that he murdered Basil Hallward in cold blood."

Julian slammed on the brakes, bringing the car to a halt and looking at his wife. "I didn't think you were familiar with *The Picture of Dorian Gray*," he challenged.

Tessa smiled malevolently. "I do more than just pitch books to publishers, Julian, dear." She reached up and touched the scrape on her forehead, a reminder of Dorian's attack. "I've been doing a little research on Mr. Gray. It seems that in a fit of rage and hate, he took a knife and stabbed Basil Hallward over and over, holding him still until he was dead." She held up a finger, quieting Julian. "And he enjoyed it."

Julian sighed and set the car back into motion. "Tessa, did you ever stop to ask Dorian if that was what truly happened?" He attempted to make his wife see reason. Whatever Dorian Gray had done in his past life—for his wife's accusations of him being a ghost were quite on the mark—there was obviously a reason for his spirit to be haunting the townhouse.

"Heavens, no! How could you even suggest such a thing? I have no desire to speak to that man, especially after he brutally attacked me!" Tessa moved in her seat, facing forward once again. She breathed heavily in her ire, her jaw locked, her hands clenched tightly together in her lap. There was more to her hate of Dorian Gray than what she was letting on. She was not about to tell Julian that she was jealous of the apparition; she didn't want to be looked upon as if she was a small child, who did not know how to share her toys.

But, then, she was still infuriated over the attack. Every time she gazed at herself in the mirror, she was met with her own reflection carrying the vicious bruises from Dorian's fingers. "It's only a matter of time before his true nature emerges."

"Why do you care, Tessa? You ended your professional relationship with Rachael tonight," Julian pointed out.

Tessa smiled cruelly in the dim light of the car. "I said that in the heat of the moment. Do you really think I would do that?"

Julian's eyebrows rose in surprise. "You were certainly sincere."

"Nonsense. I will call Rachael and patch things up with her." She paused. "But only on one condition."

Julian inwardly moaned. "And that would be?"

Tessa's smile grew. "She gets rid of her ghostly companion. Or I will."

Chapter Nine

BOXING DAY, 4 AM

Dorian walked into the master bedroom, pausing to gaze through the darkness. He carried a tray of Earl Gray tea and shortbread cookies, Rachael's favorites, into the room, the steam of the tea slipping through the spout of the teapot. He couldn't help being pensive. He had replayed the entire night in his head, wondering if he could have prevented the disintegration of Tessa and Rachael's friendship. He was left to consider the possibility that if he had not engaged Tessa, maybe Rachael and Tessa's friendship would not have fallen apart. He suspected the argument between the two women had been inevitable. His appearance only hastened the eventual split.

He was beginning to think that no matter how hard he attempted to atone for all the evil he had done in life, he would never find peace.

Balancing the tray against his him, he closed the door, turning to scan the room and finding Rachael. She was sitting on the bed, clutching one of her lilac-colored feather pillows. Chewing on her thumbnail, she stared blankly out the window watching the snow that was falling from the gray blue sky.

He sat the tray on the small table beside the bed before settling his tall frame in the chair next to it. He had removed the sweater he wore for the party leaving him in only the forest green shirt he had beneath it. Untucked and unbuttoned, it hung haphazardly over his blue jeans. His eyes slowly drifted over Rachael's face as he steepled his fingers in thought before speaking, choosing his words carefully, "You think she's right, don't you?" he queried in the softest of voices. "You think I'm a selfish, self-centered, vain and arrogant bastard."

Rachael had heard him enter the room, but she was too numb to acknowledge him immediately. She had been trying to make Tessa see that she needed some space, that she needed to be able to expand her horizons and not be locked into writing romance novels the rest of her life. But the agent had turned a deaf ear to her requests. Even though she was embarrassed over the verbal war that erupted, she was thankful that it was finally over. Tessa finally knew how she felt, and that Rachael now knew exactly what Tessa thought about her.

Somewhere in the back of her mind, where she wasn't in shock, a part of her giggled in glee. She was pleased that Dorian felt so strongly about her. She looked at him, dropping her hand onto the pillow she clung to. "No, Dorian. I don't think that at all," she replied, her voice hoarse from crying. She wiped the tears that had fallen from her eyes with the back of her hand as she graced him with a tender smile. "I think you really do care."

She sighed and rested her chin on the pillow, her eyes filled with longing as she gazed at him. "Never in my life have I had someone stick up for me the way you did tonight. I've always had to defend myself and fight for every last thing I ever wanted, especially when it came to matters that concerned Tessa." Her shoulders slumped tiredly as she closed her eyes. She heard the ghost shift in his seat, the sound followed by tea being poured into a china cup. "I'm tired of fighting," she murmured. "I'm just..."

Dorian paused as he set the teapot down and walked over to Rachael. "What?" he asked, taking her hand and closing it around the teacup. "You're what, Rachael?" he prompted.

"I'm just tired, Dorian," she answered, sipping her tea and staring at the liquid inside the cup.

Dorian picked up his cup of tea and moved to the bed, sitting on the edge of it facing Rachael. He took a drink, waiting, weighing his words so that she would more fully understand the life he had lived. "I understand your tiredness, Rachael," he began. "It is a bone-weary tiredness that seeps into your soul and drags you under," he finished while running his forefinger around the rim of the teacup. They remained silent for a few moments before he spoke once again. "Oscar changed the story, you know," he stated, glancing up at her through the dark fall of his hair across his forehead, the admission coming easily to his lips. He had wanted to tell her, knowing that she already suspected there were differences in the story and the true tale of his life.

Rachael remained still on the bed, her tea ignored. Her eyes met his eyes, seeing the sadness in their brown depths, her heart reaching out to him. "How?" she asked quietly as she waited. She did not want to interrupt him, afraid that he would change his mind and keep his secrets to himself. She was well aware there were discrepancies in the story, but the last few days had been such a whirlwind of activity that she never actually had a chance to discuss it with him. What she had read in his journal portrayed a man unlike the one within the pages of Oscar Wilde's masterpiece. Yet she had seen herself that he was also very much the cruel and vain man of the story.

Dorian's eyes took on a faraway look as he slipped into memory of a time long past, his voice melodic as he shared his darkest and deepest secrets. "By the time I met Oscar Wilde, I had already been an immortal for over a hundred years." He paused, gazing at Rachael for a response before he continued again. "He did not believe me, and I relayed to him the words that I have regretted forevermore." He set his teacup back upon the tray, then lay back on the bed, his eyes closed. "I still recall with vivid clarity looking at Basil Hallward when he completed my portrait. And I cried, *'How sad it is! I shall grow old and horrible and dreadful. But this picture will remain always young. I should wish it be the other way around. If it was I, who was to always be young...'* "—he turned his head and saw Rachael softly reciting the words with him.

"*...And the picture that was to grow old! For that–for that–I would give everything! Yes, there is nothing in the whole world I would not give! I would give my soul for that.*" She bit her lower lip as she finished echoing his words before looking to him to reply, "Which you did."

Dorian nodded. "The naïveté of youth." He smiled, the slightest tilting of his lips as he gazed back up at the ceiling to continue his sordid little tale. "When I met Oscar, I was arrogant and set in my ways, having already corrupted many of England's young aristocrat's. I was an enigma to them, never aging, never veering from my hedonistic and evil ways. I reveled in their blind adoration," he spat as he suddenly sat up, gaining his feet and walking to the window. He leaned his hands on the frame bowing his head. "And the murder of Basil Hallward, a murder I committed—his death by my hand, right here in this townhouse—has haunted my every waking moment," he snarled through clenched teeth, his fingers gripping the window sash so tightly in frustration that the color faded from his knuckles.

He took a deep breath, calming himself. Rachael was not blame for what he had done, and he would not take the hatred of himself that he held so close to his heart out on her. He continued with dry relief. "Oscar fascinated me. He was not like the others.

He was inquisitive and genuinely curious of the life I had led. We would talk for hours on end, sometimes spending days and weeks cooped up behind the walls of my home while the outside world moved around us." He pushed away from the window, swiping his hand over his head, pushing his hair from his face. "One night he called on me, in the sitting room downstairs. We talked about the mundane things that were required before he broached the subject of my portrait." He looked in the mirror, surprised to see his reflection was that of calm and determined young man. Gone was the anger, which had corrupted his beautiful features for so long. "And my hatred of it. He asked me: *'What does it profit a man if he gains the whole world and loses his soul?'* "

Rachael knew the quote. She had studied it and wrote many an essay on the significance of the question during her days in college. "You never did answer him," she commented. She set her teacup next to Dorian's on the tray, then, standing up, she tossed the pillow back against the headboard. She touched the lamp, drowning the room into darkness before stepping up behind him, slipping her arms around his waist and resting her cheek against his back. He was warm and solid, a comfort to her in the cold night.

Dorian had tucked his hands in the pockets of his jeans, resisting the temptation of pulling Rachael into his arms. "No. I didn't answer him," he affirmed. "It was at that moment he handed me a manuscript. He asked me to read it for he wanted my blessing to publish the words he had penned." He trembled slightly at the memory. "So, I read it. That night after he left." His voice drifted off, leaving him in a deep sigh. "The next morning, Oscar found me still sitting in the wing back chair before the fireplace where he had left me the night before. He knelt before me and asked my opinion."

Rachael walked around Dorian. She wanted to see his face, needed to see if his expression was as haunted as his voice. He was pale, the light from the streetlamp outside her window filtering through the lace curtains making his skin look like alabaster that had been covered with spider webs. His lips stood out stark against his skin, their natural ruddy color a thin slash.

"What did you tell him?" she asked, encouraging him to continue.

Dorian's jaw clenched. "I told him to do with it as he pleased." He stared over her head, his voice flat and cold. "It was a condensed version of my life, the bitterness, the fear, the depravity, the monster I had become. Anyone who knew me would've recognized his blonde curled youth for the man I had once been." He snorted ruefully. "Regardless of his change in my appearance."

"It's called literary license," Rachael whispered. She was momentarily taken aback by the harshness of his tone, but having read his journal, she understood. Oscar Wilde had put his life in stark detail, revealing to Dorian what kind of man he had become. Whereas many would have felt pity for Dorian Gray, she only felt affection and the need to make him know that there was someone who saw beneath the veneer of cruelty and conceit to the man hidden beneath.

Dorian's lips tilted slightly as he stared at his reflection in the large mirror. "Yes, but it works better when you change the name of your leading protagonist." He freed his hands from his pockets to turn and cup Rachael's face, his eyes warming as he gazed at her. "His book wasn't finished. He asked me for an ending, a suggestion he called it." Dorian shook his head recalling that moment. "I couldn't give him one."

"But you did, Dorian. You gave him his ending."

Dorian placed a soft kiss on her temple. "Oh, yes," he whispered, his lips brushing along her soft skin. The soft tone of his voice still held the flatness of undesirable memories, but it was now laced with hatred and spite aimed at himself. "I most certainly did. Between the pages of Oscar Wilde's take on my life, I was forced to face the reality of what I had done. Of what I'd become. To see what the simple wish of eternal youth had cost me."

He turned away from Rachael to pace the room like a caged animal before returning to her. "It cost me my soul, my mortality," he hissed. "I was so numb, so…cold that I knew no matter how much I prayed, how much I begged for forgiveness, I would never rest. Not until that damned painting was gone from my life. To never again look upon the image of my soul was an idea I wholeheartedly embraced." He swallowed. "So, I destroyed the painting. I took the knife that I had used to murder Basil Hallward and slashed his portrait of me into bits." His hand was moving, replaying that eventful night, slashing and stabbing the invisible portrait before him. His eyes captured hers again as he moved towards her. "It was a futile effort to regain what I had lost and to atone for my sins." He grasped Rachael's shoulders fervently, his eyes blazing. "But that wasn't enough. It was not enough of a payment."

"The painting took your soul for good." Rachael bit her lower lip to keep it from trembling. After a moment, she tilted her head up to gaze at him, composing herself before voicing the thought that rolled in her head. "Maybe, fate has something more planned for you," she offered.

"Fate?" Dorian questioned with a grim smile, the word falling from his lips laced with resentment. "Fate is a cruel task master, Rachael. It keeps us going when we no longer have the physical or the mental ability to function."

He drew a breath, his eyes sparkling as he slid his hands from her shoulders to her neck, caressing her skin, gauging her pulse as her heart fluttered beneath the pad of his thumbs. His tone softened as he spoke, going from acrimonious to impassioned as he expressed his innermost feelings, feelings which had guided many of actions while still alive. He found it easy to talk to her. "We watch our youth slip away with the sunset, never having a chance to experience it fully, too afraid to explore our more hedonistic side."

He let his hands slowly drift along her arms, then, taking her hands in his, he drew her back to the mirror that stood above her dresser. He felt her pulse quicken, heard her breath catch. He turned her to face it, taking his place behind her as they gazed at their reflections in the dim light. The shadows hid the left side of their faces where they only visibly saw half of themselves.

"And when we do explore it," his voice dropped to a velvety purr, "that side that is taboo for even us to see, we are looked down upon as being debased and immoral. We are caught between behavior that society demands and expects, and the desires of our hearts. Desires only a few of us ever dare to tread."

Rachael's eyes were locked with Dorian's in the mirror. His words struck a nerve that shook the very fiber of her being, and she knew he spoke the truth. It didn't matter what century it was. Social norms had changed very little since the days of Victoria's reign. There only were a few in the world, in the history of man, who followed what they wanted. "Like you?" she asked quietly.

Dorian shook his head, leaning forward so that his breath ruffled the hair at the nape of her neck to warm her skin. "Like us," he whispered and smiled slightly. "You are not so different from me, Rachael Lafferty. We have both been jaded by the cruel and decadent world, branded outcasts since before we were born, you because of your natural talent, me because of my questionable parentage." He nuzzled her cheek with his own, her scent wafting to his nostrils and causing his body to respond to her feminine beauty. His lips grazed her as he spoke in a low hungry voice. "They don't understand people like us. They are jealous of our talents, our beauty, of whom and what we become. They cannot see past the stature of our bloodlines."

He let his fingers pluck at the thin blouse she was wearing, having changed out of her party dress shortly after fleeing the sitting room. "The quality of our clothing." He held up her hand, stroking his thumb along her fingers. "The amount of dirt beneath our nails to what's deep within. The artist, the novelist, the lonely young man"—his voice was passionate with convictions he had never voiced before, her ears being the first to hear his feelings, to experience the strength of his emotions—"They bend us to their wills and then have the audacity to cry when we up rise and bite back," he said, as he turned her to face him.

He bit her fingers slightly, his teeth grazing at her skin. His eyes never left hers while he watched her breath quicken, her body and will yielding to him. He licked the tips of her fingers and continued, "Wondering how we became so cold and cruel." He gripped her shoulders tenderly, stroking his fingers down her cheek, along the long line of her throat, across the swell of her breast. "We surround ourselves with haughtiness and conceit, armor to protect ourselves from the sharp words and lashing tongues of those who do not want to understand us or our ways." His brown eyes bore into hers and he fell silent, feeling her heartbeat beneath his palm, its steady cadence like a beacon in the night. "Tell me I'm wrong," he whispered.

"You're not, Dorian. And for a man, who has spent his life corrupting those around him, you have certainly hit the nail on the head," she finally stated, her voice catching slightly. She didn't see the pompous aristocrat behind her. She saw a passionate man, who only wanted to be understood, who wanted to be accepted. "I don't believe someone who is inherently evil could feel as you do."

Her words startled Dorian, and he leaned back for a brief moment, before curling his fingers around her neck, drawing her closer. "You touched my soul, Rachael," he whispered, his husky voice filled with possession. "You woke me from my dark torment that day at the auction. I do not know how or even why, nor do I care, but somehow you did." He licked his lips, a slow, sensual swipe of his tongue. "I've been a slave to that portrait since the day it was finished. I do not want to be a slave to it any longer, Rachael, but if that is what I must face to remain here with you, then I will gladly accept that fate. You've shown me that I may still have something deep within worth saving."

"What?" she asked. His hand at the back of her neck was strong and sure and she slid her hands beneath his open shirt. His skin was warm against hers, the muscles of his chest rippling beneath her palms.

"My heart. It is not the cold, unfeeling thing that beats within my chest as I have believed all this time. There is still a spark of decency, of humanity, there, a flicker so faint that no one has seen it since I was a mere youth. Even I have been blind to it, for it has been hidden from me and in that I stopped believing in my own innocence." His expression softened, but the hard lines of his nature remained around his eyes and his lips. "I am a cruel and depraved man, Rachael, arrogant and calculating in my dealings with others. But not with you. I cannot bend you to my will, nor do I desire to." He paused, choosing his next words with the utmost care. "The only promise I can offer you is that of my protection and affection. I cannot offer you love, for I fear I am incapable of ever feeling that emotion." He threaded his fingers through her hair, holding her to him, reveling in the feel of her softness, of her curves, and the way she fit perfectly against him.

Rachael leaned her head on his bare chest, sliding her hands around his waist to rest at the small of his back. "Then I will take what you offer, Dorian Gray. Maybe, in time, my love for you will find its mate deep inside and you'll once again know what it means to love and be loved." She placed a gentle kiss over his heart, nestling closer to him.

Dorian rested his chin upon her head, holding her tightly against him. She had no idea what her words meant to him. Smiling softly, he kissed her, watching her in the mirror across from the bed. He noticed for the first time since his ill-fated wish that the smile upon his face was now also reflected in the depths of his brown eyes.

RACHAEL SAT IN THE chair next the bed, facing the window as the sun was rising. As she stared at Dorian's sleeping figure, she realized that she had fallen head-over-heels for the man. She knew she fell in love with Dorian Gray the day she set eyes upon his portrait at the auction house, wanting nothing more than to claim the unknown portrait of the mysterious young man dressed in fashionable Victorian garb. And that was before she even knew her secret knight in shining armor.

But her dilemma was even more complicated. She was in love with a ghost, an apparition, a being that should not exist except in bedtime stories and fairy tales.

She shifted in the chair, studying his face as she rested her cheek on her fist. Even in sleep, he retained the untainted look of youth, a man still in his early twenties, more beautiful than handsome. The hard lines of experience that appeared upon his forehead and around his mouth were gone, no longer marring his stunning features as he rested. He looked exactly like the image Basil Hallward had captured on canvas with oil paint, brush, and a precise hand. Staring at him reminded her of her own mortality when she suddenly understood his undying wish to remain forever young. It was a dark desire many humans carried deep within their hearts, to be young, vibrant, beautiful, immortal. Yet few ever have the courage or fortitude to utter those words within earshot of another human being, for fear of being looked upon as petty and childish.

Rachael tucked her feet beneath her as she shifted in the chair again, her eyes drifting from his face and dark, luscious locks to consider the rest of his body. His right hand was flung carelessly upon the pillow above his head, his left lying on his stomach. His chest was bare, rising and falling in the slow relaxed breaths of sleep. Her face warmed as her eyes drifted lower to the thin dark line of hair that started just below his belly button and disappeared beneath the sheet. She knew what was concealed beneath the thin fabric of the sheet, and it was a delectable sin. Her heart sped up at the decadent thoughts that ran through her mind as she admired him in his sleep, her eyes continuing down his length to the end of the bed. Dorian was a tall man, lanky in stature and that hid a deceptive strength. Tessa had been right in that regard. He was a very dangerous man, especially when his calculating mind was combined with the physical power he held.

Rachael didn't fear him, however. As a matter of fact, she trusted Dorian Gray implicitly. He had made passionate, yet tender love to her after his confession, then held her tightly to him, his body wrapped possessively around hers while they slept. It was almost as if it was she, who would disappear from him if he let her go. They had remained entwined in each other's embrace for the rest of the night, until she could sleep no more, her mind still in turmoil over the argument at the party.

Her argument with Tessa had hurt her more than she cared to admit, and she could not help being concerned over her career without the other woman's influence. Rachael knew plenty of agents that would jump at the chance to represent her, but she was scared that Tessa would do or say something to keep them from being interested. Considering she had pretty much declared that Dorian would remain a part of life, she didn't put it past Tessa to do something nasty.

Rachael sat in the chair and watched him in the silence of dawn. Glancing at the bedside stand, she saw it was almost seven. Standing, silently drawing on her robe, she tied it around her waist and slipped quietly from the room.

In the kitchen, Rachael set the kettle on the stove to boil. She moved to the cupboard above the end of the counter, retrieving a mug from a shelf to prepare herself a cup of soothing green tea. From the corner of her eye, she spied Dorian's journal. It was on the table, and she sat down. Opening it with one hand, she looked for the pages where she had stopped, hoping for more insight to the ghost that now slept in her bed. She carefully turned the worn and brittle pages, her eyes scanning Dorian's neat handwriting until she located the passage where she had left off. She could hear the sophisticated timbre of his voice in her head almost as if he were reading aloud to her.

> *Basil came to see me today, demanding to see that damnable portrait he had painted. I graciously showed it to him, after some deep reflection and contemplation. What he saw startled and horrified him, and for a brief moment, I found myself secretly pleased with his reaction. Is that what I have become? A man bent on the unhappiness of others, unhappiness caused by my hand or their own simple misfortune? A man, who actually*

found solace in other's misery? Or, I am so jaded to the feelings of others that I simply do not care? I do not know. I have asked myself this question numerous of times and yet, I have not found an answer.

"What does this mean?" *he screamed at me.*

I remember the high pitch of his voice at the time, a shrill call such as that of a bird as it falls from the sky, injured and dying. It grated on my nerves, sending chills along my spine. I had only one answer for him at the time. And I made no excuses for reminding him of it, regardless of whether he wanted to hear it or not.

"Years ago, when I was a boy, a mere youth, you met me, flattered me, taught me to be vain of my good looks. You and others of our rich aristocracy explained to me the wonderment of youth, convincing me to sit for you so that you could capture my innocence upon the canvas before you." *I held a rose in my hand while I spoke with him and my finger is still now throbbing from the thorn I managed to sink deep into my flesh.* "I saw the beauty of myself within your work, Basil, and in a brief moment, I made a wish. Or was it a prayer?"

"Yes! I remember it well! But it is impossible!" *He tried to explain the hideous visage before him as a result of corrosion, easily talking himself into believing that mildew had to have set into it, that his oils were tainted and caused the portrait to become as it were. But I knew better. How could I not? I had lived with the painting for far too long not to. Basil is very impressionable, even in his advanced age. I gazed at his hands, once graceful, now gnarled with the ailments of the infirm. Such a shame.*

"It is not impossible, for what you see before you is truly your portrait," I snarled. "Can you not see your ideal in it?" I asked bitterly. My mouth was dry at the time, and I knew no matter how much water or wine I consumed I would not be relieved of the parchedness that lingered upon my tongue.

"But that is the face of evil!" Basil cried, pointing to my portrait.

No truer words had ever been uttered by a man. Yes, it was the face of evil. The face of a jaded man, who had fallen into the hell of his own desires and lusts. "That is the face of my soul," I calmly corrected him. Or, at least, what was left of my soul. I could not help the tears that filled my eyes, the tears fill them, now. I am well and truly damned and no matter what anyone claims to the contrary, I will serve my time in the pits of the deepest circles of Hell for my sins.

Basil begged me to fall to my knees and pray, to repent, even going so far as to recite scripture to me. But his words fell on my deaf ears. There was no amount of praying to a God I had long ago abandoned for the pleasures of the flesh that would redeem me. I tried to tell him that, but he was most distraught. I could not console him, could not console myself. I don't know when it happened, or how, but in that very moment, I found myself hating Basil Hallward. I hated the old man that knelt at my feet, who grasped my finely tailored brown trousers with his twisted and dappled hands. He gazed up at me, his eyes begging me to recant the sins that manifested themselves upon the painting that stood on the easel behind him.

Basil then did the most curious thing in that moment. With the grace of a man many years his junior, he slowly gained his feet, his face taking on a passive expression that tore through me like a slow, tasteless poison lingering on my tongue and had been consuming me for what seemed like eternity. He turned from me and slowly walked to the portrait, covering it once again with the yard of cloth I kept it hidden under. "Show this to no one, Dorian," he whispered to me. I could barely hear him as a hansom paced beneath my window. "As a matter of fact, you should destroy it. Yes. Yes, destroy it. Atone for what you have become." He turned to me, tilted his head and studied me.

I did not see the knife in his hand, until it was too late. I had heard rumors that Basil was suffering from an illness of the mind; dementia is what I believe they call it now. I barely threw my arm up in time to deflect the knife. I asked him what he thought he was doing. "I am ridding the world of evil," he simply replied. "For the devil has taken your soul and claimed it for his own."

He rambled on about the virtues of the Bible, the atonements of sin in the Holy Sacrament, and other things I now cannot recall. In my shock, I recoiled from Basil, turning away from him and striding out of the room to call my butler. But no one came. No one except Basil. I gathered my cane, sliding free the sword that was hid-

den within its length. It was barely in enough time to deflect the artist's frantic and hurried stroke, his knife slicing deep into the flesh of my arm. We both watched in horrid fascination as the gash slowly healed itself.

"Lucifer! Devil! Spawn of Satan himself!" Basil cried.

I could only watch, the events playing out before my eyes like some sad Shakespearean rendition. Not even the Bard himself could've brought to life the drama that unfolded before me. His knife gripped tightly, Basil lurched forward and plunged it into my chest, before I could reflect his well-placed strike. He looked up at me, his eyes widening as I felt my own warm blood pool around the blade to stain the ruff of my white lawn shirt. "Be gone!" I heard him hiss as he withdrew the knife. I staggered backwards, hitting the wall.

I watched the blood on my chest cover me, haphazardly wiping it with my hand. I looked at Basil and sadly shook my head. "Do you not see?" I asked. "I am immortal. I cannot die."

He came at me again and when I raised my sword, he impaled himself upon it. I could not believe it. I did not mean to hurt the man. I pulled my sword from his flesh as he fell to his knees before me, like some petitioner before the altar of God.

I gathered him in my arms, my hand over the wound. "Basil," I whispered, seeing his life fading from him through the haze of my grief and tears that overwhelmed me. "Hold on," I begged, knowing that my words were *fruitless. No doctor could be summoned in time, no police officer. No one. I reached out and closed his eyes as he took his final breath, the blood on my hands a mixture of my own and his.*

What happened after, I still cannot clearly recall. I remember my man coming to me on the landing where I cried over Basil's lifeless body. I remember him guiding me to my room and he removed my shirt, telling me very calmly and softly not to worry, he would dispose of the garment and call the constable. It was not my fault, the death of the man, who had immortalized me in paint. My chest still hurts as I write these words, and I cannot stem the tide of tears that flow from my eyes for what I have done. For Basil's death is my fault. Another nail in the coffin of death that I will never see...

Rachael stared at the words on the pages in shock. There would be no discounting them, for they were written in Dorian's own hand. She could not understand why Oscar Wilde had not written of the death of Basil Hallward the way it happened, unless he preferred the literary flair of the book's protagonist being the murderer. Basil's death had not been in what was now her office. He had not been stabbed behind the ear multiple times, with Dorian's hand holding his head down until there was no life left in the artist's body.

He was not killed by a man, who hated him so deeply that murder was the only sane thing left for him in an insane world.

She closed the cover slowly, her heart in her throat, the loud shrill whistle of the kettle boiling piercing the silence of the kitchen. She stood up and made her cup of tea, then gazed out the window above her sink to look upon the Thames as it flowed past, its dark waters icy from the winter storm that had blanketed

London. Her mind rolled over Dorian's words written within his journal, analyzing each thought and word as she went.

It was a simple fact that Dorian had not murdered Basil Hallward. Instead, it was a matter of self-defense, even accident, that the painter met his demise at Dorian's hand, not the brutal murder Oscar Wilde had described. She was beginning to understand Dorian Gray more and more, and his search for atonement suddenly took a more pronounced place in her heart.

"It was self-defense," she whispered to herself. "Not even in this day and age are we damned for that, once it's proven."

Rachael heard the clock on the mantle chime, never realizing she had been standing at the window for almost a half hour. It was almost nine. Kitty would be awake by now, and she desperately needed to speak with the witch. She emptied her teacup, rinsed it, and set it in the drain to dry before returning to the bedroom to hastily dress. Glancing at Dorian, she placed a gentle kiss on his lips. He exhaled softly and shifted in sleep, before settling back down. It was time for answers, and she was going to get them.

Chapter Ten

BOXING DAY, 10:30 AM

Humming to herself, Rachael walked through the crisp morning air, leaving the busy docksides of the Thames behind her as she made her way to Kitty's home. It was cold and her breaths clung to the air in small puffs as she exhaled. She giggled girlishly and she purposefully breathed, just to watch the steam that curled in the air in front of her. She loved London more than any other place in the world, having decided as a small child that she would make this city her home. She could still remember walking to the local candy shop with her father, after his workday at the American Embassy, stopping afterwards to watch the *Pearlies* perform at the subway station.

She loved the old city even more now that Dorian was in her life.

By the time she reached Kitty's brownstone, she had already stopped at the bakers for some scones and heavy cream and had visited the local bookstore to buy her friend a newly released book on Ancient Egyptian spells. She only hoped the young witch had not bought it yet; she wanted to savor Kitty's excitement when she handed it to her.

Raising her hand to knock on the wooden door, it swung open on her before she could even rap her knuckles against it. "Good morning," Rachael laughed, stepping inside, breathing in the fragrance of *Nag Champa* incense that seemed to persistently hang in the air. "I come bearing scones and a gift."

Kitty raised a brown eyebrow as she took the packages, shutting the door as Rachael swept into the entry hall. "A gift? Really? I wonder what it could be?"

Rachael hung her coat on the rack near the stairs and grinned. "I wonder." Her grin broadened into a full-blown smile as she leaned down to pet Bella and Poe, the two cats demanding her attention as they weaved in and out of her legs. "I remember you mentioning it once."

Kitty squealed in delight as she stripped the bag away, the book held reverently in her hands. "Midnight reading material!" she exclaimed, hugging Rachael tightly. "Thanks. Now, come with me."

She took Rachael's hand and pulled her along the short corridor into the kitchen, skipping all pleasantries as she had more pressing matters to discuss that pertained to the author. "I knew you would be here this morning after that debacle last night." She shooed Raphael from the kitchen chair, set her book on the table, and walked over to her radio to turn down the music she had been listening to. She glanced at Rachael as she placed a cup and saucer before her friend. "And no jokes about my witchy intuition. Or I'll turn you into a toad." She poured steaming blackberry tea into the cup and set the kettle beneath its cozy on the table. "Sip it."

Rachael had barely sat down when the younger woman ordered her to drink. "Kitty, I..." she stammered.

Kitty held up a hand. "Just sip it." She proceeded to slice open the strings on the baker's box, setting the scones on two plates, then pouring the heavy cream over them and slathering them with orange marmalade. She returned to the table and stared at the two cats that had taken up residence in her seat. "Raphael! Michelangelo! Scat!" she snapped, waiting impatiently as they stretched, meowing their displeasure that their slumber had been disturbed. With flicks of their tails, they finally jumped from their perches, allowing Kitty to sit down across from Rachael. She watched eagerly as Rachael sipped the tea, before pulling her cup and saucer across the table and discarding the rest of the tea in the small pot beside her.

"I wasn't finished with that," Rachael protested, just as Raphael jumped into her lap. Making himself comfortable, he curled up into a ball. Lazily scratching his head, he purred at the gentle attention. "What was that for anyway? And do I get another cup to drink with my breakfast?"

Kitty slid her own cup towards Rachael, then she studied the tea leaves in the bottom of the cup she had retrieved. "Satisfying my own curiosity," she mumbled, never looking up at Rachael. With a soft grunt of satisfaction, she set the cup aside. "Come with me," she demanded pushing away from the table and walking past Rachael, all of the cats except Raphael following her.

Rachael swallowed the mouthful of scone she had just taken. "Can we eat first? I'm starving!" she complained, beginning to wonder why they just couldn't sit down to a nice morning cup of tea.

"Bring it with you," Kitty called from down the hall.

"Bring it with me," Rachael grumbled. Raphael looked up at her through slitted cat eyes. "Bossy, isn't she?" Patting him on the head one last time, she gently set him on the floor and gathered up her plate and the cup of tea. She had only wanted to talk to Kitty about Dorian, girl-talk as it were, not to get any supernatural advice. But Rachael knew that supernatural advice was exactly what she was about to get, whether she liked it or not.

She sighed as she stepped into Kitty's sitting room and glanced around the room. Laid out on the coffee table were five Tarot cards from a *Celtic Dragon* set Kitty seemed to prefer. The smell of lavender filled the air, soothing and aromatic, and she loved the ambiance of the room, with its small devotional altar before the fireplace and colorful gypsy scarves draped across the paintings of mythical creatures, which were hung on the walls. More scarves were draped over the table lamps, casting the room in a warm glow that enhanced that numerous candles glowing all around.

"Kitty, I..." she started, taking another bite of her scone.

Kitty gently pushed Rachael into one of the Queen Anne chairs across from the couch, the table between them. She curled her own legs beneath her as she settled on the overstuffed couch and faced Rachael, smoothing her skirts over them as the four cats settled around her. "I know, I know. You don't believe in this stuff. But considering you have fallen, hard I might add, for a ghost, you might want to listen." She looked at Rachael and smiled mischievously, pointing at her. "And don't deny it. You are in love with Dorian Gray."

Rachael snorted, licking marmalade off her fingers. "I wasn't going to deny it. As a matter of fact, I wanted to ask you about—" She was cut off again by Kitty's waving hand and stopped the young witch with a passing thought. "Why do I have a feeling I'm missing something here?" She set her empty plate on the floor, the four cats jumping from their spot next to Kitty and converging on the cream that remained, as if it were their last meal.

Kitty stared at her cats for a moment. "Why can't you take care of the mice in the basement with that much gusto?" she chided softly, before she sighed, shaking her head. "Yes, you wanted to talk to me about Dorian. I already knew that." She waited for a moment, expecting some sarcastic comment from her friend. "Insert comments about the pagan here," she finally quipped, teasingly.

"No. I would prefer not to be turned into a toad," Rachael teased back, leaning an elbow on the arm of the chair, her chin on her fist.

Kitty blinked at her innocently for a moment, before chuckling. She pointed to the cards between them. "You were the last person to touch this deck, last week as a matter of fact. The day Dorian appeared."

"So?"

Kitty stroked Bella's head, as he jumped back up into her lap and licked the cream from his whiskers. "On a whim, I picked them up this morning and those cards fell out," she replied seriously, her free hand waving over the cards that were laid out between them.

Rachael shook her head, jumping slightly as Poe and Raphael both hopped into her lap. "And that means what exactly?" As she rubbed her cheek against Poe's head, he ruffled against her in affection, his fur soft and warm. She made a mental note to find out if her unusual houseguest would mind a cat. It would be nice for a change to have a pet of her own.

Kitty stared at Rachael. "And to think you've wrote about Tarot readings in your works. Let me reconnect the dots for you." She leaned forward and pointed to the first card. A dragon was perched on a castle balcony, watching two lovers. "The *four-of-wands*. It means you're happy and rested from a long period of tiring past endeavors. You are successful and have found new love." Her eyes twinkled in delight as she watched Rachael's face redden. "See? There's that lovely shade of red you wore last night."

Rachael glared at her. "That's not nice, Kitty."

Kitty laughed. "It's the truth and you know it." She pointed to the next card, tapping her finger on it. It was the *two-of-cups*, a water dragon pouring liquid from a chalice he held in one clawed foot into another chalice that was being held by two lovers. "Once again, a great love is possible, with the chance of some future announcement that has resulted from a commitment you have made."

The hand that petted Raphael stilled. "You can't be suggesting that these cards are talking about Dorian and me?" She knew very well that the card was referring to the announcement Dorian had made during the party, and she shook her head vehemently.

Kitty folded her hands in her lap, a smug, thin-lipped smile on her face.

"He's a ghost!" Rachael objected.

"And?" Kitty asked leaning forward on the couch. "Okay, I'll admit, he's a bit less corporeal to most, but he's madly in love with you and you, him." She closed her eyes for a moment, her hands up. "Hear me out, Rachael. I haven't been wrong yet." She opened her eyes and held up the third card for Rachael to see. It was the *nine-of-cups*. The Tarot deck's wish card. "I don't need to explain this card to you, or its significance." She paused for a moment, setting the card down and picking up the two remaining cards. "Now, when these fell out of the deck, I knew they were indicating you."

Rachael stared at the two cards her friend held up, a cold chill running down her spine. "Kitty, this is...very disturbing."

Kitty shook her head. "No. Actually it's very reassuring. The *king-of-cups* represents a strong, loving masculine presence in your life."

"It could be referring to my brother," Rachael stated nervously, suddenly trying to point the conversation away from her. She only wanted to talk about Dorian as idle chit-chat, not in relation to the future with her. Or had she? The question popped into her head without any warning. Why did she want to discuss Dorian with the witch? A cold chill slid down her back.

"It's not and you know it." Kitty traced her finger along the dragon that circled the throne before she dropped the card with the others. She held up the last card, the *five-of-pentacles*. It showed the lovers apart. She carefully chose her next words. "I know you love Dorian, and he loves you, although expressing it openly will not be his strong suit when he is corporeal to others." Her last words died on her lips, the momentary silence heavy between them.

Rachael could tell something was bothering Kitty and the ominous feeling that had settled in the pit of her stomach was foreboding. "Then, what's the problem?" she asked softly, hoping Kitty could disperse the feeling.

"Both of these cards indicate emotional turmoil, Rachael."

"That's not a surprise. Last night was a perfect example of that," Rachael laughed nervously, waving her hand dismissively. Yet the feeling of disaster would not leave her, and she couldn't help but to wonder if everything was all right at the townhouse. She had left a note for Dorian, so that he wouldn't worry when he discovered her gone, and she knew that he would be interested in her day and would greet her with fervor when she returned. So, why did she feel like there was a dark cloud looming over her?

Kitty reached up and pulled her long hair through the ponytail holder she'd plucked from her wrist. "Honey," she couldn't meet Rachael's eyes as she spoke, "I'm afraid something bad is going to happen before this..." she tapped her finger against the *nine-of-cups*, the wish card "...happens."

Rachael paled at her words. "You mean to Dorian?"

"Yes."

Rachael stared at the cards, her heart beating erratically in her chest. "I don't want to lose him, Kitty. There must be something we can do so that he can remain on this plane of existence." Her eyes locked with the witch's, who simply shrugged.

Neither woman heard the front door open and close. Tessa stood standing frozen in the hall, for she had heard everything about the last two cards as Kitty explained to Rachael. She listened intently, her calculating mind filtering the information for her own use. She had hoped to talk to Kitty to discover a way to rid Rachael of the ghost that inhabited her home. When she heard that Rachael loved Dorian, and he her, it made her even more determined to make Dorian simply disappear.

Tessa continued to listen to the conversation as it drifted towards her from the sitting room.

"He said he wanted to be free of the portrait, to no longer be a slave to it, but not if it means he can't be with me," Rachael informed, her voice filled with sadness. "He's still plagued with guilt over Basil Hallward's death as well."

"I thought he killed Basil Hallward in cold blood?" Kitty asked.

Rachael shook her head as she looked at the two cats, now sleeping her lap. "No. I believe it was an accident. I read the whole encounter as he described it in his journal."

Kitty twirled her hair in thought, her dark locks wrapping and unwrapping around her forefinger. She had spoken with Dorian at length before the party started the night before, and he was every bit the gentleman Oscar Wilde portrayed him to be. But she, like Rachael, was able to see through the veneer of charm and wit to the lonely young man beneath. It was the way his eyes followed Rachael as she finished the last-minute preparations that had made Kitty's heart ache.

"I might have an idea, and I can't promise it will work, but I might be able to help the both of you." She stood up and walked around the table to stand before Rachael, taking her hands. "But only if Dorian agrees. Go home, tell him what I showed you, and then bring me back something that personally belongs to him."

"How?" Rachael asked as she stared up at Kitty. Her body tingled at the thought of helping Dorian. It was a glimmer of hope and if anyone could accomplish the impossible, it would be Kitty.

Kitty shrugged. "First, we'll free him from the influence of the portrait. After that, we'll see what happens."

In her hidden listening place, Tessa's eyes narrowed as she ran her leather gloves through her fingers, then she slipped back outside, silently closing the door behind her so that she would not be heard. She turned right as the brutal wind whipped at her hair and headed towards the museum to meet Julian for an early lunch. Maybe, she could get rid of that ghost first. She didn't believe what Rachael had said about reading the *real* incident in Dorian's journal. What would a ghost be doing with a journal in the first place? And where did it come from? For all anyone knew, he could be filling her head with lies, simply to get what he wanted—whatever that could possibly be.

Tessa walked slowly along the street, ignoring the bustling people about her as she headed for the street corner. She told Julian that she had read Dorian's story, but didn't reveal to him that she had also researched ghosts and poltergeists. It was very interesting reading. The fact that he was able to physically cause someone harm put Dorian into the poltergeist category. Knowing his history, Tessa considered him very dangerous. There was no telling what he was capable of, especially if angered.

There was absolutely no way she was going to allow him to remain on this earth. Between his brutal attack, and the way he showed her up at the Christmas party, Tessa felt that he needed to be crushed like a bug under her shoe. She saw him as no more than a conniving spirit, vicious, evil, dangerous. She smiled slightly as she waved her hand, hailing for a taxi. To her, Dorian Gray was no more than another competitor, vying for a piece of

Rachael Lafferty. There was nothing in this world that Tessa Falcon enjoyed more than squashing and ruining her competitors.

RACHAEL KICKED THE repaired foyer door closed with her foot, gazing back briefly at the piece of wood that now was secured to the frame. She smiled as she juggled her packages, tossing her keys onto the sideboard. The Christmas tree was still lit, the small lights twinkling slowly, illuminating the antique ornaments that belonged to Dorian. Turning on one foot, she walked into the sitting room, glancing at the stereo. Soft strains of Bach flowed through the speakers that were strategically hidden throughout the rooms, utilizing its unique shape and the high ceilings.

Dorian sat in one of the chairs before the fire, a book propped open on his knee, totally engrossed in the words on the pages. He looked up slowly, a warm smile spreading across his face. "Well, nice to see you're happy I'm home," she commented. She jerked her head towards the tea setting between the chairs. "Expecting company?" she teased lightly.

Dorian leaned his wrist casually on his knee above the book, his eyes half-lidded as he gazed longingly upon Rachael. "Only you. You're the only company I need these days." He slipped the thin ribbon that laid across the arm of the chair into the book and closed it before standing; looking like a graceful cat, he unfolded himself from the chair with poise. "And how can I not be happy to see you?" he inquired, closing the distance between them, his lips finding hers in a searing kiss until he finally released her with loving compassion. "Did you have a good day?"

Rachael took a deep breath. "Yes. As a matter of fact, I had a wonderful day."

Dorian nodded. "How was Kitty?"

"She was well. Come on. I have to get these groceries put away." Rachael strode through the room into the kitchen, Dorian not far behind her. She placed the bags on the center island and removed her leather jacket as Dorian laid his book on the table. "We had a very insightful conversation, and I'm thinking about getting a cat," she remarked casually, smiling up at Dorian to gauge his response.

"A cat?" Dorian asked as he peered curiously into the bags. He reached into one of the sacks, removing the items and setting them aside for Rachael to put away. "I think a cat would be a very good companion for you. I never had one myself." His brow drew down as he discovered a box in the bottom of the second bag. He lifted it, turning it in his fingers.

"Hey, hey! Wait your turn, little boy!" Rachael scolded, smacking his hand as she snatched the box from his fingers, ignoring the shocked look that appeared on his beautiful face. She tucked it into the pocket of her shirt before opening the freezer door to load the food she had bought into it.

Dorian stared at her in disbelief, before he answered her in his haughty voice, "Little boy? I'll have you know, madam, that it's been quite a few centuries since that particular moniker has been applicable." Slipping around the center island, he caught Rachael and backed her into the counter, pinning her between it and his body as he wrapped his arms around her, resting his hands on the granite top. He leaned into her, his voice smooth and seductive with a clear, radiant point. "And I don't like being made to wait. For anything."

Rachael laughed as she pushed his searching hands away, wiggling away from him. "Well, you are going to have to wait until I'm damn good and ready to give it to you." When he slid along the counter with her, she shifted her weight and stomped on his foot, ducking under his arm. She scooted around the back of the table, keeping it between them, the look of amusement on his face making her laugh even harder. "I think I'm in trouble."

"You minx," Dorian growled seductively, his eyes twinkling with mischief intent. "You want to play? Well, let's play." He took a step to the left causing Rachael to dodge to the right. As soon as she did, he reversed course, catching her around the waist before she could escape through the doorway, and swung her around. "Finished so soon?" he taunted as he nipped gently at her ear.

"I'm only getting warmed up," Rachael answered as he set her back on her feet. She was about to break his hold when she caught sight of the book he had been reading. She quickly perused the spine and flushed in embarrassment when she realized it was one of her own creations. She lunged for it, and Dorian pulled her back against him, right as she snatched it from its resting place.

"Where did you get this?" she asked in chagrin, holding the book up for him to see.

Dorian easily pilfered the book from her hand, holding it above their heads as she jumped for it. "I found it buried in the back of your bookshelf." He smiled smugly down at her, his eyes narrowing slightly in merriment. "It's a very intriguing story." He took a step away from Rachael.

"It's trash, Dorian, give it here," Rachael snapped, wiggling her fingers towards him in a gesture that brooked no argument.

He took another step back, forcing her to follow, the book still firmly in his grasp. He was very interested in the story within and had been so mesmerized by it that he had almost finished it in a single sitting, something he had not accomplished in a very long time. "Why, Rachel, I do believe you're embarrassed by this fascinating piece of fiction." He glanced at the book, running his fingers lovingly over the dust jacket. "And this is hardly trash, my sweet."

Rachael was getting upset. "Dorian, give me the book," she demanded crossing her arms over her chest.

Dorian gazed at her, his dark eyes twinkling in the light of the kitchen. "No," he casually answered. He moved to the center island, leaning against it as if he were preparing to give an important speech, and then opened the book. A box of chocolate truffles sat on the counter, and he peered into the box, taking his time to select and enjoy one of the confections, before returning to the page he had been reading when Rachael had come home. "Ah yes. Here we are:

> *With silken garters, the Baroness tied her Lord's hands to the posts of their spacious bed, securing them above his head with a seductive smile that invoked images of forbidden pleasures.*
>
> *She dragged her well-appointed bosom down his length, his moans of torment making her smile even more as she forced herself between his legs, her hands drifting along to caress his muscles as she gently bound his feet to the opposite posts. She leaned over him, tempting him with her body as she retrieved a candle from the candelabra.*
>
> *"You've been naughty, my Lord," she commented as she dribbled a small amount of wax along the planes of his stomach. He hissed before letting out a hearty groan of pleasure.*

"Oh my," Dorian's eyes lifted from the pages to look at Rachael as he laughed with mild amusement, studying her. Her head was hung, her hair hiding her face as she gripped the back of the chair before her tightly. Frankly, he was shocked at the scene, the decadence, the descriptiveness. It was the most erotic thing he had ever read, and the fact that his own dear Rachael had written it made all the better. "Can we try that?" he asked huskily.

"*No!*" Rachael protested as her head jerked up to stare at him, her voice cracking. Her face was a brilliant shade of red. "Give me the book, Dorian, please?"

Dorian shook his head. "This is so erotic, Rachael. Passionate and debased." He let out a short chortle as he held the volume up. "And a best-seller, according to the cover." He approached her with slow, even steps, catching her chin in his hand and forcing her to gaze at him. "You should be proud of this, not embarrassed." The tone of his voice had changed to a more serious note, but Rachael still wouldn't meet his eyes.

"It's a tawdry, Gothic novel, not even my best work." She swallowed hard, lightening her grip on the chair. "It wouldn't even have been worthy of your perusal in the 1890's."

Her comment sent Dorian into a torrent of laughter. "Oh, yes, it would have been worthy. As a matter of fact, I've nearly read the entire book in one sitting, something only a writer of exceptional expertise can inspire." He took her hand and led her back into the sitting room, guiding her to her favorite chair before tossing the book into his. He stoked up the fire, adding another log to the blaze before settling across from her in the other chair, picking up the book and resting it on his lap. "Yes indeed, my sweet Rachael, you would have been the talk of London with this book." He shrugged nonchalantly as he fingered the pages of the novel. "Granted, you might have been blacklisted, but you would have been famous."

"Blacklisted?" Rachael gazed at him in skepticism. "Somehow you are not reassuring me, Dorian."

He raised a graceful hand in a dismissive wave, his expression one of infinite patience, as if he were explaining the ways of the world to an obstinate child. "Being blacklisted back then only raised your worth. The aristocrats, especially the ones that seemed to favor my company, men and women alike, would've devoured your tale of decadence." He leaned his chin on the backs of his fingers as he gauged her reaction to his words. "You would've been invited to all of the best parties of the elite. Possibly even been invited to Buckingham Palace for a private audience with the Queen."

His eyes shone as he continued speaking, impressing upon Rachael that things were not as innocent as they seemed during Victoria's reign. His smirk only grew, his words borne out of his own personal experiences. "They would've engaged you in friendly conversation and then gladly tell morbid little tales behind your back, heightening everyone's curiosity about you and your book. The elite would have read your book in their clubs and during their afternoon tea socials, at sewing circles, and in the spas, anywhere." His eyes bore into her, seeing the potential before him and wishing she had been alive during the height of his own corruption. "Oh, yes, my beloved Rachael. You would have been famous," he finished and gave a lusty growl.

A comfortable silence fell between them as she absorbed his words. He had sparked her imagination with his description of the times, seeing in her mind's eye a posh men's club with snifters of brandy and expensive cigars, a haze of smoke settling in the air, and one man reading of her words from the pages of a leather bound volume. The tall tales that would've circulated behind her back wouldn't have bothered her then, much as they didn't bother her now. She kept to herself anyway, having reminded Tessa on numerous occasions that the nasty rumors and tabloid articles about her social life meant nothing to her.

She finally looked over at Dorian, who was watching her, his expression carefully guarded as he observed her like a hawk. "You would've made one hell of a literary agent, Dorian," she complimented quietly, a sad smile tipping her lips as she stood up. She walked over to him, pressing a soft kiss on his cheek. "Thank you."

"For what?" he asked, catching her hand in his and raising it to his lips.

"For the truth," she simply answered, cupping his cheek in her hand before pulling away with a sigh. "I need to get dinner ready. You may not need to eat, but I do. And I'm hungry."

Dorian stood, catching her hand once again as he escorted her into the kitchen. "At the moment, you are the only thing I am hungry for."

Rachael chuckled as she let go of his hand, moving over to the far counter and the head of lettuce that she had set out to chop into a salad. "You can't live on sex alone, Dorian."

Dorian sniffed arrogantly. "Speak for yourself. In case you have forgotten, I'm a ghost." A door slammed somewhere in the townhouse, causing him to turn abruptly, his eyes catching Rachael's. He raised a finger to his lips, telling Rachael to remain quiet. "Stay here," he whispered as he slipped out of the kitchen. He moved through the townhouse as quietly as a cat, the advantages of being no more than an apparition. The stereo had long since finished playing Bach, and the house was filled with an uneasy silence as he checked every room, every nook and cranny he was able to move through.

Rachael waited in the kitchen, her heart pounding in fear, Kitty's admonition of danger fresh in her mind. Her fingers wrapped around the butcher knife in its rack on the counter as she peered through the window above the sink to see if anyone was racing away from her home.

"I hope you are not planning on using that on me," Dorian whispered in her ear, his breath warm on her neck.

She yelped as Dorian spoke, turning and baring the knife she held, raising it above her head to strike as he caught her around the waist. The knife clattered to the floor. "Damn it, Dorian, whistle or something next time, please?" she hissed breathlessly, pushing her racing heart back into her chest and gulping air in an attempt to calm herself. She rested her forehead against his chest. "Well? Did you see anyone?"

Dorian stroked his hands along her back soothingly. "No. Whoever it was is gone. I would suggest making sure the house is locked up tight tonight." He gazed over her head, checking the street outside for his own satisfaction. Something gnawed at him in the back of his mind. "By the way, my penknife is no longer in your office. Did you by chance move it?"

Rachael had forgotten about the knife he had used to tack his dinner invitation to her office door. It had seemed like a lifetime ago, that night when they first made love. She shook her head. "As far as I can remember, it was on my desk. I might have knocked it to the floor." She looked at him curiously. "What made you think of that?"

Dorian released her for a moment, bending down to pick up the butcher knife. "This." He held the knife up before rinsing it in the sink. He picked up the head of lettuce and the cutting board, moving them to the center counter and began to prepare their salad.

"Oh," Rachael mouthed silently with a sly grin. "I'm sure it's up there," she reassured and opened the refrigerator to retrieve the chicken she had left in there for dinner. She set it on the counter, watching as he sliced the salad into fine pieces. "You didn't bring any friends with you, did you?" she teased softly, still uneasy over the mysterious slamming of the door.

Dorian's lips twitched as he swiped the lettuce into the two bowls before him. "I'll never tell." He wiped his hands on the dishtowel and leaned on the counter. "I'm tired of waiting. What is in the box?" he asked, changing the subject and attempting to set them both at ease.

Rachael reached into her pocket and withdrew the box. "A late Christmas present." She ran her fingers over the lid before sliding it over to Dorian with a shy smile. "Open it."

Dorian did as she instructed and gazed at the gold men's bracelet that was nestled in its velvet lining. "This is...exquisite, Rachael," he said softly. The simple gesture was more than he ever expected, and it melted the last of the ice that had gripped his heart. He cleared his throat, his emotions very evident. The bracelet meant the world to him and he gazed up at her, his brown eyes filled with warmth and tenderness. "Thank you," he whispered huskily.

Rachael picked up the bracelet and clasped it around his wrist, tickled that it fit him perfectly. "You're welcome. I saw it and just couldn't stop thinking about how it would look on you. So, I bought it." She watched as the gold glimmered in the light, accentuating his long fingers and perfectly manicured hands. Her eyes met his and they leaned towards each other in a soft kiss.

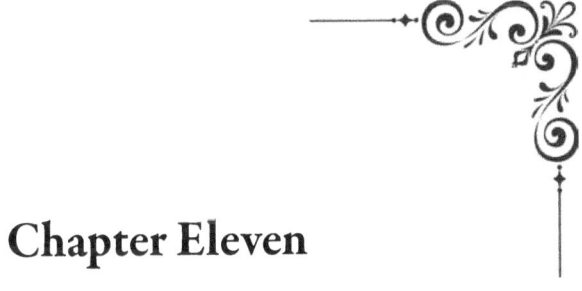

Chapter Eleven

D ECEMBER 29, 11:30 PM

Kitty stood at the top of the stairs, staring at the door. Something had awoken her, but she was not sure exactly what it was. When the bell rang, she knew that someone was there, waiting to gain admittance into her home. She made her way down the stairs, stepping over Poe, who was sleeping on the bottom riser, as she rubbed the sand from her eyes. She gazed at the clock and groaned. She had no idea what time she dozed off, but visitors this late at night were never good, especially in her profession. She swung the door open and froze, her mind trying to register the urgency of her night visitors. "Tessa, Julian. What are you doing here?"

Tessa rudely pushed her way past Kitty, reaching out to flip on the light. She shrugged off her coat as the witch blinked at the sudden brightness. Grabbing Julian and tugging him into the house, Tessa closed the door, locking it. "We don't have much time," she stated hurriedly as she made her way into Kitty's sitting room, turning on lights as she went.

"Sure, come on in," Kitty mumbled sarcastically as she trudged along behind the duchess and her husband. She reached up to stroke a hand over her head in the attempt to smooth down her bed head. "Time? Time for what?" she asked, lighting the candles while moving through the sitting room. She turned to

Tessa, who was chasing two of the cats from the couch, upsetting the felines from their nighttime nap. Kitty sighed, a combination of her tiredness and disgust at the Duchess's behavior. "What is going on? And it better be good." She leaned against the wall, blinking to clear the sleep from her eyes.

Tessa crossed her legs, smoothing her black slacks. "We just came from Rachael's. She is an absolute mess."

Kitty's brow furrowed as she gazed at Tessa. "She let you back into the house?"

"Let me?" Tessa snorted as she waved her hand with a haughty air. "Please, she called us begging to come over."

Kitty sat down in the chair Rachael had sat in only two days before, watching Julian pace the room, his steps silent on the thick carpet. She turned her head towards Tessa, her eyes still upon Julian, who seemed very uneasy, yet he remained silent.

"She was fine this afternoon when I spoke to her. What happened?"

Tessa's eyes narrowed. "Dorian Gray," she snarled, the venom in her voice indicative of her hatred of the ghost. She leaned forward, her expression earnest. "We stopped there tonight after she called. Since I don't normally hold a grudge…" She ignored Julian's grunt of disbelief. "…I felt it best that we see what had her in such a right state. She came to the door in tears." Tessa laid her left hand over her heart, looking up to the ceiling. "Kitty, her face…" She paused dramatically. "Her left eye was bruised and swollen shut and her lip swollen." She closed her eyes, shaking her head, crocodile tears filling her eyes. "That damned ghost! He is a coldblooded murderer and a vicious poltergeist, and I just know he is going to kill her!" She sniffed pathetically. "She simply cannot see it. He is a snake and has charmed his way into her heart, and she cannot see it."

Kitty turned in her chair, retrieving a box of tissues, and handing them to Tessa. "Is she all right?"

Tessa dabbed at her eyes to hide her anger and to feign her worry. "*No!* Of course, she's not all right." She sniffed, folding the tissue in her hands. "She had her coat on and was on her way to see you. Dorian has turned on her. She never expected him to be so evil." She snuffled, wiping her nose. "You know, I never meant what I said to her the other night. I was just so scared, so concerned for her well-being. I would never truly dissolve our partnership, and you know she means the world to me. She's just so…innocent, and I'm sure he's taking advantage of that."

Julian rolled his eyes at his wife performance, mouthing, "She's full of shit," over Tessa's head. He saw the imperceptible nod and slight tilting of Kitty's lips, knowing that the witch agreed.

Tessa continued, "She knew you could help her get rid of him." She pulled her purse into her lap, digging into the bottom of it. "She asked us to come over right away on her behalf and talk to you." She reached out and dropped two items into Kitty's hand.

Kitty stared at Tessa's gift. It was Dorian's penknife and the dinner invitation he had penned. Something was not right; she could feel it deep down to her bones. There were no evil vibes coming from the items she held, no strange misgivings that permeated the cold, hard steel of the knife. She could only sense warmth from them. She glanced sideways at Julian, who was perusing her bookshelf in fake interest. He wouldn't meet her eyes. As a matter of fact, the man would not look at either one of them.

"Where is Rachael now?" Kitty asked, picking up the receiver of her phone, her fingers poised above the buttons.

"She's at ho—" Julian started.

"Our house," his wife intervened, glaring at her husband. "She was too afraid to remain in that horrid townhouse." Tessa shredded the tissue in her hands. She closed her purse, setting it aside, the strap draped across her knee. With one hand, she clutched the tissue, playing with the leather strap of her purse with the other. She continued her tale without meeting Kitty's gaze directly. "Julian and I managed to get her settled with a cup of tea in the guest room. I gave her a sleeping pill to help her relax, and we made sure she was asleep before we came here." She stared at Julian before meeting Kitty's eyes once again. "She asked us to come here."

Kitty set the phone back on the cradle. "Yes, you said that already. Don't you think it could've waited until morning?" She had a sudden distrust of Tessa and knew that the woman was lying to her.

Tessa shook her head, her red braid slapping the back of the couch. "No. He's so vicious. There was no way Rachael could've been with him one more night. Who knows what else he would've done? I mean really, you know his story." She sniffed and lifted her chin. "He killed a defenseless old man in Oscar Wilde's story. For all we know, he could force himself upon Rachael or do other terrible things to her." She leaned forward in the chair earnestly. "You've said it yourself that these types of...things are best settled at midnight."

"What types of things?" Kitty asked suspiciously.

Tessa waved the tissue. "Spells and such."

Kitty nodded. "Spells." She looked pointedly at Julian. She could see that the lie his wife was telling was not sitting well with him, yet he never refuted Tessa's words. She kept that little fact to herself as she stood up. Kitty had an idea and Rachael would be furious with her for acquiescing to Tessa's request, but she knew that this was the only way to solve the problem between the two women. "I'll be right back. I need to gather up the items I'll need, and we'll cast the spell," she reassured Tessa with a soothing tone.

"Don't you need Rachael here?" Julian asked hopefully, dropping the suggestion when Kitty shook her head.

Kitty slipped from the room and sighed, mumbling curses to herself as she walked into the kitchen. Her distrust of Tessa only grew, and she realized that it had actually started after witnessing the fight at the Christmas party. Tessa showed her true colors that night, and, no matter what Tessa said in the contrary, Rachael deserved to be happy. She knew Dorian's story as well as Rachael, and even though he seemed to attempt to strangle Tessa, Kitty knew that Dorian was too much of a gentleman to strike a woman, most especially Rachael.

Kitty marched back into the room, her face set into lines of determination. She rearranged the candles around the room, setting them in the four corners, each one representing the directions of the compass. "Julian," she called out, watching him startle at his name, "please hand me the pot on the shelf." She set three more candles on the coffee table before Tessa. She added the tarot cards from Rachael's reading days earlier, before setting the small censer on its stand, lighting the small candle beneath it, fragrant water already contained within its black depths.

"What do you need us to do?" Tessa asked in fascination. She had never seen Kitty cast a spell before.

"Sit there," Kitty snapped. "And be quiet." She turned off the overhead light and approached the first candle, lighting it. *"Air, Fire, Water, Earth, Elements of Astral birth, I call you now, attend to me!"* She moved to the next candle, lighting it as well. *"In the circle, rightly cast, safe from psychic curse of blast, I call you now; attend to me!"* She moved to the third candle, remaining silent before approaching the last one, her mind fully in tune with the powers she called. *"From cave and desert, sea and hill, by wand, blade, cup and pentacle, I call you now; attend to me! This is my will, so mote it be!*" She reached out and snuffed out the match with her fingers, moving to kneel at the coffee table.

"What was that for?" Julian whispered, noticing that the air within in the room seemed suddenly charged with energy. It made the hair on the back of his neck stand up. He gazed at Tessa to see if she noticed the atmospheric charge, but she was oblivious to it.

Kitty laid out the herbs she had gathered. "I have cast a protective circle. Stay there until I tell you that you can move." She waited as the four cats settled around her. "They can travel across the line without bothering it." Her eyes flashed. "You can't."

Julian nodded, laying his hand on Tessa's knee as he sat beside her. "We want this to succeed. We'll stay here until you tell us otherwise."

Kitty nodded. She ignited another match and lit the three candles around the censer, one black for a lack of falsehood, one white for purification, and one purple for divine power. She took a pinch of herbs between her fingers and closed her eyes, dropping them into the water. *"Eight eyes gaze through the night, the moonlight upon the land so bright, following one as fair as sight, his soul encompassed by evil blight."* She opened her eyes and picked up Dorian's knife. Opening the blade, she dipped it into the pot, stirring the herbs. *"Mihi proderas."*

Tessa looked at Julian. "What did that mean?"

Julian let the Latin roll around his head for a moment, the translation becoming quite clear: *Mihi proderas* simply meant *come to me*, and he suspected Kitty was attempting to bring Dorian more fully into the world, instead of getting rid of him.

"I don't know," he answered her, keeping the knowledge to himself. He wanted to see the witch succeed, instead of his wife.

Kitty ignored their soft exchange, continuing with the spell. *"Upon atonement a face so fair, in death his corpse left lying bare, his soul within the image's care, to rest inside the devil's lair."* She added another pinch of herbs to the pot, stirring them once again. *"Mihi proderas."*

"What is she doing?" Tessa hissed only to have Julian hold up his hand, quieting her.

"The Fates have judged the man by fire, to walk again a ghosts aspire, warmed by a kindred desire, and freed from the funeral pyre." The herbs sizzled as they hit the water, sending up a small wisp of smoke. Kitty never wavered as she repeated, *"Mihi proderas."*

Julian's eyes widened as the candles flickered within the room, the power growing around them. He felt a coldness fill the air, and he watched Kitty intently.

"A forbidden love to save his soul, to be with her their one strong goal, against the odds they stand alone, tempted by fate to finally atone. Mihi proderas." Kitty lifted the hand-written note and held it over the white candle, setting it aflame, before dropping it into the caldron. *"From the dark a man will come, to finish what now has begun, to live a mortal's life he won, to age and wizen beneath the sun."* She looked up at Tessa and Julian, a small smile creasing her features. She added another pinch of herbs, stirring them, before taking the pocketknife from the pot. *"To replace the lost the Fates do call, another one not innocent shall fall, to supplant he that has atoned, and in his place forever roam."* She snarled the words one last time, *"Mihi proderas."*

"Is it done?" Tessa asked, her eyes wide with glee as she leaned forward. Her mind was so intent on removing Dorian forever that the witch's words never registered. Her nose wrinkled at the odor wafting from the pot between them.

Julian looked at the two women, one intent on destroying someone's life, the other determined to save it. He could feel the strength of Kitty's power as he sat there silently. He gazed upwards over Kitty's head at one of the gypsy scarves, which danced over the pictures that hung there. His heart skipped a beat nervously.

Kitty didn't answer Tessa. She took Dorian's knife and sliced open her palm, allowing four drops of blood to drip into the mixture. *"Atonement fulfilled by love."* She added herbs from a second pile to her right. They sparked, causing a small fire in the pot. *"Atonement accomplished by guilt."* The herbs popped as she added more, the smoke pouring from the caldron. Her eyes locked with Tessa's. *"Atonement sought through fear."* She allowed four more drops of blood to drip from her hand. *"Atonement exchanged by maliciousness."* She closed her eyes, her head dropping back as she added the last pinch of herbs, her voice loud, her arms outstretched. *"Atonement's love was won!"*

She was aware of her old grandfather clock in the entry hall chiming, striking midnight. As the last chime sounded, she released the last pinch of herbs, watching as everything seemed to slow down. The herbs fell and the pot exploded, the mixture splattering the table, Tessa's perfectly pressed pants, Kitty's t-shirt. *"This is my will, so mote it be, Blessed Goddess hear my plea."*

The candles extinguished as a gust of cold air flowed through the room from an unknown source.

Tessa and Julian both shivered, a tingling sensation coursing down their spines. They stood as one, both trembling as they watched Kitty open the circle.

"It is done then?" Tessa inquired softly.

Kitty couldn't even look at the duchess. She was disgusted with her. She wrapped her hand with the towel she had carried into the room. "Yes. Now get the fuck out of my house," she hissed in a low and menacing voice.

Tessa and Julian did not need to be asked twice. They hurried from the room, both of them shaken by the spell and the power the young woman had raised in the circle.

Kitty followed the couple and leaned on the door. She watched as Julian helped his wife into their car, before casting her a knowing glance. He knew that she had changed the spell, but he didn't know how. That was exactly the way she wanted it, because then Tessa couldn't say that he was in cahoots with her.

She closed and locked the door, before slowly walking back into the sitting room. She sat down on the couch, the cushions still warm from her visitors, and picked up the tarot cards, rubbing her fingers over them as tears filled her eyes. Raphael, Michelangelo, Poe, and Bella joined her, rubbing against her in an attempt to comfort her. "Forgive me, Rachael," she whispered before allowing the tears to overcome her.

"IT'S YOUR MOVE."

Dorian looked up upon hearing Rachael's soft words, and he and smiled. "So it is. I'm sorry," he remarked as he lifted his knight and captured her bishop. The firelight cast soft shadows across her delicate features, and he studied her, memorizing every detail. His eyes traced the curve of her cheek, following the line of her jaw down her slender neck before continuing lower, stopping at the provocative swell of her breast that was just visible between the edges of her tailored white shirt. He stroked his goatee, sighing in contentment as they enjoyed the solitude of the townhouse.

Rachael contemplated her next move. If she wasn't careful, Dorian would have her in checkmate. Again. She had managed to lose three straight games against him, and her determination to beat him at the game of strategy only grew. She tapped her finger on the table contemplating her next move when she looked up to find him gazing at her from beneath heavy-lidded eyes.

"What's on your mind, Dorian?" she inquired. "You've been too quiet tonight."

Dorian leaned back in the chair and steepled his fingers. "I've been reexamining the events of my life. A habit of mine that I have attempted to break my entire life." He snorted softly, a wry sound. "And, apparently, in death."

Rachael moved her queen, setting up a gambit that usually worked. "What exactly have you been trying to reexamine?" She glanced up at him from her position on the floor. They had slid the coffee table over so that they could play, and she leaned back, rocking on the pillows she was sitting on. "Come on, tell me. There are still things about you I don't know."

Dorian raised an eyebrow as he leaned his arms on his knees. The gold bracelet she had given him sparkled in the firelight on his wrist. "Are you sure you want to know?" he teased casually, blocking her gambit by capturing her unprotected queen. "Check."

Rachael sat up, not a bit surprised by his move. "Dang it. You figured out what I was going to do."

"Rachael, you've been playing that same move since our first game," Dorian offered by way of explanation.

Rachael grunted. "Brat," she teased and moved her king. "And, you are avoiding my question."

Dorian shrugged. "I was just thinking about a conversation I had with Oscar. It was after Basil's untimely demise." He slid a pawn forward. "He commented that I had not changed and that I would always be a friend to him. He did not feel that I needed to change my ways to atone for what I had done." His expression grew sad, wistful even. "I remember how I longed for my unstained youth."

"Isn't that what got you in trouble in the first place, Dorian?"

Dorian nodded. He poured them each a fresh cup of tea from the pot that had been sitting on the table between the chairs, then sipped from the teacup in his hand. "Very much so, my sweet Rachael." He sighed, leaning his chin in his hand. "Do you believe that someone could enjoy murder?" he pondered the question out loud to her.

Rachael's eyes widened. "Who are you planning on murdering?"

Dorian laughed. "No one. Simply a hypothetical question." He waited for her answer, watching her over the rim of his teacup.

Rachael's eyes locked with his. "I suppose so. But you didn't murder anyone, Dorian."

"I murdered Basil Hallward," Dorian stated plainly, taking on the responsibility of his own actions so long ago.

"No, you didn't. By your own admission, in your own hand, you said that Basil's death was an accident." She bit into a shortbread cookie, thinking. "That is not murder, Dorian. That was self-defense."

"Then what about the murdering of oneself?" he whispered.

"Suicide?"

Dorian simply nodded towards her, the slightest inclining of his head. His hair brushing his shoulders softly, his brown eyes softened as he gazed at the woman he found himself in love with.

Rachael watched him, shaking her head in confusion. "What are you getting at, Dorian?"

Dorian reached out and moved his last chess piece. "Checkmate," he stated softly and stood up, walking over to the fire, gazing into the flames as they danced in the grate, dispelling the cold air that drifted from the flue. "Do you think that one could...murder themselves by their deeds?" He glanced at her. "By the actions of their life?"

Rachael stared at him. "I guess it would be based on how you define suicide, Dorian." She packed up the chessboard, tired of playing the game and losing. She could think of more pleasurable things they could be doing, and her lips tilted at the thought. "It's a matter of semantics. Now, in your case, no. How you lived your life would not be a good definition." She stood up, setting the table back where it belonged. "You enjoyed life. You didn't live it with the intent of killing yourself."

Dorian tilted his head thoughtfully. "To cure the soul by means of the senses and the senses by means of the soul," he commented. "Is that what I did? Attempt to cure myself of a horrid mistake made in the vanity of youth?"

Rachael approached him. "Dorian, there are people in this century who live their lives in far worse and debased ways. You questioned your actions, but we all do that."

"And we all do not have a portrait that decays with every sin you commit either," he answered, reaching out to tuck a lock of her soft hair behind her ear. "Perhaps, I did live my life in such a way that I looked for a reason to end the torment."

Rachael chuckled and stepped into his embrace. "Why? To what purpose? You were a rich young man, favored by members of the aristocracy. You had everything to live for. I cannot see even you contemplating the end of your life in such a way."

Dorian stroked her hair and laid a gentle kiss on her forehead. "You have a way of making things seem so clear," he whispered. "To have had you at my side during those days when I was alive, I would've been the envy of every young man. My fate may not have been what it was."

Rachael rubbed her cheek against the soft fabric of his shirt. "Oh, really?" she laughed softly. Gazing up at him, her eyes danced in amusement. "Who's to say you wouldn't have pushed me away, tossed me aside to the curb because of something I did that you did not care for?"

Dorian looked at her, his brow furrowing. "I don't think I would have. You would've been the talk of London, and, under your influence, I might not have allowed Basil the opportunity to paint my portrait." He stroked his finger along the line of her jaw. "And, I beg to differ with you, Rachael."

"About what?"

He lifted his chin slightly, gazing down his nose at her. "My untimely death."

Rachael sighed. "You're giving me a headache, Dorian. Get to the point."

"I did commit suicide."

She threw her hands in the air as she stepped away from him frustrated. "Dorian, you didn't know that you would be killing yourself by slashing your portrait." She laughed ruefully. "If every wish was granted, this planet would've ceased to exist a long time ago." She turned and looked at him, her hands planted on her hips. "You did not commit suicide, Dorian."

Dorian stared at her. "You believe it to be that simple."

"It is that simple. You had no idea that slashing your portrait would cause you to die," Rachael said again and held up a finger. "You did not..." She paused, noticing the color had faded from Dorian's cheeks. "Dorian?"

Dorian grabbed the mantel piece, trying to catch his breath as the clock upon the mantle chimed. Breath caught in his throat and he gagged before gasping, gulping down air.

"Are you all right?" Rachael immediately returned to his side, cupping his face with her hand.

"No!" Still gasping, Dorian took a staggering step away from the fireplace as the clock chimed again. "Something...something is very wrong." He managed to make his way to the wing-backed chair, sinking down into it hard. His eyes were filled with panic, his pupils dilated in fear as he looked at her. He glanced at the clock, which chimed for the third time, noticing its hands rested on midnight. He peered at Rachael, remembering her trip to Kitty's house earlier in the week. The clock chimed once more. "Dear God, Rachael, what have you done?" he asked, clutching the collar of his shirt, feeling as if his throat was constricting.

"What are you talking about?" Rachael reached out to take his hand, her fingers suddenly meeting air as they passed right through his flesh. "You're fading," she cried horrified, her eyes growing fearful. The clock chimed again.

"I can see that!" Dorian snapped as he attempted to touch her. His eyes flickered around the room, resting on the clock that chimed for the sixth time. "The room...it is growing dark. Tell me you are not the cause of this," he pleaded, his ghostly eyes catching hers. He knew about Kitty's proposal, but they had never agreed on a course of action, afraid of attempting anything for this exact reason. The clock chimed for the seventh time.

"Dorian, I never left the house today. Kitty couldn't have performed any spell without something of..." Their eyes met, Rachael's hand flying to her mouth. "Your pocketknife," she whispered. The eighth chime rang through the room.

"That *bitch*," Dorian hissed.

"Who?" Rachael shook her head. "*Who*, Dorian?"

"Tessa," he gasped. "The day we heard the door close, the day you spoke with Kitty. She has a key to your home!" he insisted as loud as his voice could carry over the loudness of the ninth chime. They both looked at the clock. "She must have...convinced...Kitty that you were...in danger." He turned his brown eyes back to her, tears filling them. "I cannot stop this."

Rachael reached for him, grasping cold air as her own tears fell from her eyes. She shook her head vehemently. "Kitty wouldn't do this to me!" she cried. On the tenth chime, she fell backwards, her hands shaking as she covered her mouth in grief. "Don't you dare leave me!"

Dorian reached out to her, dropping to his knees. He leaned towards her, his tears falling from his eyes as he placed a soft kiss on her lips. "I have no choice," he whispered against her skin, closing his eyes so that she could not see the pain and sadness within them at the eleventh chime.

Rachael felt the slightest brushing of his mouth upon her skin, a caress of cold air as he faded, growing dimmer before her. "No," she whispered, rocking back and forth.

Dorian's voice floated to her ears as clear as bell, his words searing into her heart and mind forever. "I do love you, Rachael Lafferty. I will for all time."

Rachael watched as her world slowly fell apart around her. She saw his hand reach one last time to stroke her cheek. She caught the glint of gold from his bracelet and her eyes followed it as it fell in slow motion to the Oriental carpet on the last stroke of midnight. The only sounds in the room were her sobs and the muffled thud of the gold as it hit the carpet right as the clock on the mantle ceased to tick. She sat frozen for a moment, before a heart-wrenching scream tore from her throat, *"Dorian!"*

Anger filled her, and she called out to him again, willing with all her might to return him to her. *"Dorian!"*

The world tilted and fell in, on, and around Rachael when in her rage and fury, she found her feet. She ran into the foyer, her eyes falling on the beloved portrait at the stair landing to find nothing there. The canvas stood blank, only the muted background and Basil Hallward's scarlet autograph remaining in the gilt frame. *"No!"* she screamed in terrified realization. Dorian Gray was gone.

She whirled around, her hands finding the boughs of the Christmas tree. She screamed as she pulled, the tree crashing down to the floor, sending the ornaments and lights scattering everywhere. The angel on top smashed into a thousand pieces at her feet. She spied Dorian's sword cane in the corner. In an instant, his cane was in her hand, the sword sliding free from the hilt, her eyes drifting to the canvas that was now empty. She threw the scabbard away as she marched up the stairs to the landing.

The sword was still gripped tightly in her hand when Kitty found her the next morning, sitting in the corner of the landing, despondent, her eyes red and her tears dried on her cheeks. The tattered remains that were once the picture of Dorian Gray, the portrait Rachael so loved, lay scattered around her, shredded.

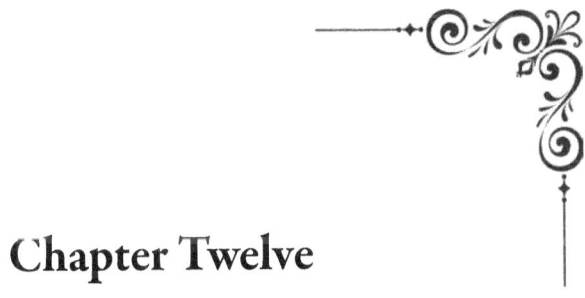

Chapter Twelve

DECEMBER 31, 1:00 PM

Rachael sat with her legs curled beneath her in one of the wing-backed chairs before the fire, a cup of soothing Chamomile tea cooling in her hands. The gold bracelet she had given Dorian was wrapped around her wrist, its luster already faded even though he had been gone for less than two days. The metal was cold against her skin, echoing the feeling of the old townhouse without its former owner. Boxes were strewn from one end of the sitting room to the other, white sheets waiting upon the risers of the spiral staircase to cover the furniture. She had stopped long enough to take a break from her packing, the love of the Victorian townhouse gone. It had vanished with Dorian.

The door to the foyer opened as Tessa and Julian walked in without any announcement. The duchess gazed through the room, noticing the now bare Christmas tree still in the corner. It was completely without ornament, stripped of the antique decorations Dorian had given Rachael. The boughs looked forlorn without the glass trinkets and white lights.

Tessa noticed the portrait was missing from the landing and suppressed the smile that threatened to grace her lips. She hung her jacket on the coat rack, brushing her hands against each other, before turning towards the sitting room. "Rachael? Rachael, dear, we need to talk," she called as she walked into the room.

Rachael didn't bother to look up. Instead, she sipped her cup of cold tea. She ignored the woman, who was standing before her, and reached out to lovingly run her fingers along the silver top of Dorian's sword cane. It leaned against her chair, that and the bracelet she'd given him, the only items she had left of her ghostly lover. She kept the cane close to her, always. She didn't bother wiping away the tears that slid down her cheeks.

Julian glared accusingly at Tessa, before slipping past her to stoke up the dying fire. The room was cold, and he wondered if Rachael even noticed the goose bumps that were rising on her arms. Picking up the teapot on the table next to the author, he checked it and saw steam rise from the hot liquid inside as he lifted the lid. He replaced the delicate china top, before leaning over Rachael to refresh the tea in her cup.

Kneeling next to her chair, he placed the teapot back onto the table. "Kitty said you were upset, which is understandable. Do you want to talk about it? Do you want to tell us what the matter is?" he asked as tenderly as he could. He still carried guilt in his heart, not for what Tessa had apparently done, but for not standing up for what he believed would have been right.

Rachael shook her head. "There's nothing the matter." She sighed deeply as she set the teacup back on the service. Uncoiling herself from the chair, she stood up holding her chin high, picking up Dorian's cane and carrying it with her. "Excuse me. I need to finish in here."

Tessa had taken a seat in the chair across from Rachael, and she watched as the young woman made her way to the pile of sheets on the stairs. "Are you going somewhere?" she inquired innocently.

Rachael stopped in her tracks, settling the end of the cane on the floor, leaning tiredly on it, before turning to look at Tessa for the first time since she had entered the townhouse, uninvited.

She kept her expression a blank mask, not revealing the torment that was coursing through her or how deep Tessa's betrayal had stung. "Yes. As a matter of fact, I am," she replied evenly. "I'm leaving London and returning to the States."

Tessa was shocked. She knew Rachael was upset, devastated at Dorian's disappearance, but she never expected her to simply pack up and leave. "Whatever for?" she gasped in dismay, rising from the chair. "You love it here. The townhouse is your pride," she protested.

Rachael stared at her. "Do I?" she retorted emotionlessly. "Is it?" She canted her head in thought, her eyes narrowed into thin slits of violet colored ice. "Oh, yes, I forgot. I do love it here and this place..." she sarcastically responded as she motioned to the walls surrounding them with her free hand "...is my pride, because you say it is so. Forgive me for...questioning you." She snorted in disgust before continuing past the staircase to the bookcase behind it. She set Dorian's cane on the shelf and retrieved another of her pewter dragons, wrapping its delicate and perfectly shaped wings in cotton, before covering the whole piece in bubble wrap. She knelt down to place it in the box at her feet and moved on to the next one.

"Rachael, I'm sorry for the disagreement we had Christmas. I didn't mean what I said," Tessa started, taking a few steps towards her. She stopped when Rachael spun around to face her, pointing an accusing finger at her.

"Yes, you did, Tessa," Rachael snapped and shook her head. She chuckled ruefully, propping her hands on her hips, gazing towards the high ceiling of the sitting room. "You are ruthless, and you are not happy unless you get your way." She dropped her head to look at the duchess. "I've compromised more of my writing for you, and you've taken more than your fair share of the cut, not counting the numerous pounds of proverbial flesh that went with it under your venomous tongue."

Tessa gazed at her, blinking. "I only asked you to change things, so the books would sell." She ignored the disgruntled sigh that came from Julian behind her. "Sometimes the story needed..."

"No!" Rachael objected sharply, cutting off Tessa's diatribe. She closed the distance between them until mere inches stood between them. *"No!"* She pointed at Tessa, poking her finger hard in the fleshy part of Tessa's shoulder. "After I changed *Rake Notorious* to suit you, I submitted an unedited version of the manuscript to another agent."

"You did what?" Tessa gasped in shock, her face reddening at Rachael's proclamation.

Rachael smiled the first real smile that had graced her face in days. It had been her little secret until now, a gem she had hoped to never use. But if Tessa Falcon wanted to be the haughty gold digger that she truly was, so be it. "Very easily. I stuck it in an envelope, slapped a stamp on it, and stuck it in the post box across from Trafalgar Square." She folded her arms over her chest, knowing she would have the last laugh. "And you know what? They wanted it. Oh, how they did want it." She lifted her chin. "They praised my imagery and the back-story details that you insisted I remove." Rachael allowed her temper to flare, her voice taking on a dangerous edge. "But I let you pitch it to the publishers, like a naïve idiot, instead of taking their extremely generous offer." She returned to the bookshelf to continue packing her treasures.

"Yes, and you made the best-seller list," Tessa pointed out, still recovering from Rachael's sudden revelation.

Snorting, Rachael set another dragon into the box. "The infamous list." She gripped the shelf tightly. "Tessa, have you ever once read any of my books, after I made your suggested changes?" she inquired. She already knew the answer. She wanted, no, needed to hear Tessa's admission.

The question took the duchess by surprise. Rachael had never questioned her business practices before, and she had a very uneasy feeling that the conversation was going to turn uglier than it already was. "Well, I...that is to say..." she stammered, her face flushing slightly. She looked to Julian for support, but he remained silent, perched on the edge of the chaise lounge near the staircase.

"You haven't," Rachael simply answered for Tessa, never looking at the woman.

Julian was genuinely intrigued by the entire conversation. He had never had a need to look into his wife's interaction with any of the author's she represented. Now, he was wishing he had. "How can you be so sure, Rachael?" he asked as he sipped the wine he had helped himself to a few moments earlier.

Rachael slammed her hands against the shelf she had been gripping. "Because if she had, then she'd know that I never changed a word of any of my last four novels just to suit her warped sense of what my fans want and don't want to read!" she bit out as she looked at Julian.

Tessa gasped, her hand flying to her chest. "Rachael!"

Rachael savored the shock that was evident in Tessa's voice. She traced a finger along the spine of one of her many books waiting to be packed. "I've been a blind fool and to tell you the truth, Tessa, ending our business partnership was the best Christmas present you could have ever given me," she stated, her voice shaking and cracking with emotion.

Tessa regained her composure, pouring herself a glass of wine and sipping it as she gathered her thoughts. "I was only looking out for you," she finally admitted, pouting slightly. "Just like with

Mr. Gray." She peered at Rachael and asked curiously, "Where is he anyway?"

Rachael dropped the dragon she had been holding as soon as the words left Tessa's mouth. The creature of fantasy shattered when it hit the floor, porcelain skittering everywhere. Her chin quivered. "Why don't you tell me?" she whispered, her voice unable to hide the hurt and pain.

"Well, how would I know?" Tessa caustically answered. "It's not like I can see him."

"Tessa," Julian warned, reaching out a hand to grip his wife's wrist. He shook his head slightly, freezing as Rachael's eyes bored into both of them.

Rachael took a shuddering breath as she turned to face them fully. Her face was dark with fury, pent-up emotions flooding to the surface, painting her face with lines of righteous outrage. "Oh, you *know*. You were in my house the day after Christmas. You took the note Dorian wrote me and his penknife from my office."

Julian stood up, setting his glass of wine aside and stepping between the two women, in case the argument escalated to blows. "Rachael, how can you accuse Tessa of such a thing?" he asked as he glanced back and forth between them, torn between loyalty to his wife and the wrong done to Rachael.

"I'm insulted you would even utter such an untruth," Tessa gasped.

"Don't play shocked, Tessa Falcon!" Rachael reached into her pocket, withdrawing a tan kidskin glove. She rubbed the soft leather in her hand with her fingers as the color drained from Tessa's face, giving her all the proof she needed. "It almost worked, except you left this on my desk." She strode forward and slapped Tessa across the face with the glove, before throwing it at her. "You had Kitty exorcise Dorian from my home!" she screeched at the woman she'd once trusted. "How you talked her into it, I don't know. And I don't want to know. You betrayed me, Tessa!"

Tessa rubbed her stinging cheek, her eyes gazing downward to see the glove at her feet. "It was for your own safety," she whispered in explanation.

"My safety?" Rachael huffed. "*My safety!* Dorian would never have hurt me, you stupid fool!" Her laughter echoed through the sitting room with a maniacal edge to it. Her eyes glimmered with the sorrow of losing her one true love.

"Then explain the bruises on your wrists, Rachael," Tessa cried out as she grabbed her friend's hands, pushing the sleeves of her sweater up to reveal her wrists.

Rachael jerked her hands back, laughing. "Good Lord, Tessa! We got a little wild between the sheets one night." She shook her head. "You cannot tell me that you and Julian have never explored some of the more interesting sexual fantasies?" She watched as Julian's face reddened in embarrassment, the museum curator actually turning away and coughing. A cruel smile crossed her lips, but she pounded her chest with her fist as her glare returned to Tessa. "We were in love. And you took that away!"

Tessa never wavered in her convictions. "He didn't know love, Rachael! He was a domineering man...ghost...apparition, revenant...whatever you wish to call him. He would've ruined your life!" she disagreed, her voice rising to high squeal.

"Like you? Like you do by forcing me to do things your way? I don't think so." Rachael marched across the room, bounding over boxes to the bookcase next to the fireplace. She reached up and pulled her hard-covered volume of *The Picture of Dorian Gray* free from its place. "You didn't understand him. You didn't try!" She pointed with the book at Tessa. "All you saw was someone, who stood between you and your puppet." Tears filled her eyes as she retrieved Dorian's journal from the mantle. "I saw him for who he was, a lonely young man scared of his own mortality. A man, who wished to remain young and in the prime of his life." She returned to Tessa, shaking both books at her. "A man, who regretted every evil deed he had done that ruined his life!" She slapped the books together, a dull thud in the room as she shook her head.

Tessa stared at her. "Everyone wants to remain young, Rachael. And no wish could ever make someone as evil and debased as Dorian." She snorted in derision, then added in a conceited tone, "I wish to remain like this forever." She paused, running her fingers through her thick hair as her words hung on the tension that filled the room. "But we age and grow old." She swallowed as the words left her lips, a sense of foreboding filled her as the fire in the hearth suddenly flared widely, the lights flickering around them, threatening to plunge them into darkness. Somewhere upstairs a window crashed open, shattering the glass, and allowing the cold winter air to enter the house.

Rachael looked away with a short bark of laughter, oblivious to everything other than her distress and rage. "You don't understand. I saw myself in him, Tessa."

Julian looked at Rachael briefly, before turning his gaze away, the pain in Rachael's voice breaking his heart. "Rachael..."

"No, Julian, don't. Don't try to soften her delusions," Tessa interrupted, holding her hand up. "She is clearly on the verge of a nervous breakdown to be speaking such rubbish." She raised her hand to her temple as a headache settled there, before gracing Rachael with a look of utter pity. "I can arrange a quiet retreat in Portsmouth, dear. The sea air will do you some good and you can rest..."

"I don't want to rest, damn it, *you selfish bitch!*" Rachael yelled. Her tone made Tessa step back in fear. "I want to refocus my life. I want to write what I want to write and not conform!" She pointed to herself. "I have that luxury, and I refuse to be anyone's puppet any longer." She raised her head in pride and proclaimed, "I, like Dorian, regret the mistakes I have made in my life." She pushed the two books into Tessa's hands. "Read them. Memorize them. Analyze them. Know them word for word," she hissed from clenched teeth in a low, dangerous tone. "And when you do, you'll understand just what you have taken away from me."

"I don't see..." Tessa began.

"No. You don't. Until you see the regret Dorian carried with him from the day he cursed himself, you'll never see. I'm on that same path, Tessa, right now. Albeit, my path is considerably less violent, but the same nonetheless." She took a step back. "Having had him in my life has at least made me see that I can step off that path and onto another one, before it's too late." She was seething with anger. "Remember this, Duchess Tessa Falcon," she spat, "as far as I am concerned, you killed Dorian Gray, murdered him in cold blood, holding him down until he was no more!"

She turned away, tossing her long hair over her shoulder as she moved over to the bookcase. Silently, she bent down to pick up the shattered pieces of her dragon. She never uttered another word to Tessa or Julian, nor did she bid them goodbye when they left.

NEW YEAR'S EVE WAS usually a time for festive celebration, a time of rebirth and renewal. But not for Rachael. She had continued packing her possessions after Tessa and Julian had said their good-byes earlier in the day and now, she sat once again in the chair by the fireplace. The townhouse was dark and cold, just like its owner who had restored it to its timely grandeur.

The only light that shined within came from the hearth, the fire shading the sitting room in dark flickering shadows. A blanket was draped around her shoulders, and she wanted to sleep. But sleep had become elusive to Rachael ever since the night Dorian disappeared, and, when she could sleep, her dreams were laced with passion and pain, always ending the same. Like a ghost, she relived that night Dorian disappeared from her life over and over.

Kitty and Julian had joined her, respecting her wish that no light be shed in the house. Tessa had remained home, having come down suddenly ill. Kitty suspected the duchess was too embarrassed by her actions and words to face Rachael directly. The young witch gazed at her friend, the changes in the once vibrant woman staggering. She felt terrible for her part in the despondency Rachael had sunk into, and she knew no amount of apologizing could make up for it. She still didn't understand everything about Dorian Gray, having never had the opportunity to read his journal as she had promised, but she knew that he had left a lasting impression on the author.

And her cards never lied.

Rachael and Dorian were meant to be together, except this was not quite the way in which Kitty had envisioned it. She pushed the plate of cookies Grace had sent over towards Rachael. "Why don't you have a cookie? The sugar ones are great, and you really need to eat," she prodded.

Rachael leaned her head in the corner of the chair, her eyes closed, deeply absorbed and lost in her depression. "I'm not hungry," she whispered. Her words to Tessa had struck a chord deep within her own soul. She knew it would be a matter of time before she snapped out of the depression she had fallen into. She only needed to allow her heart to heal and that would take time. But could time heal her heart? Perhaps not, for her heart had been shattered and broken, much like the angel that had once graced the top of her Christmas tree and the little red dragon she had dropped.

Julian gazed into the glass in his hands as Kitty slipped past him. "Tessa sends her regards," he uttered softly, hoping to at least spark some emotion from Rachael. "I believe she has come down with that nasty flu that is going around. She was very pale when I left her."

Rachael opened an eye and considered Julian. "It takes a while to get over it," she remarked unsympathetically and closed her eyes again with a sigh.

Kitty emerged from the kitchen and glanced at the watch upon her wrist. It was almost midnight and she took Rachael's hands, wrapping them around the mug of herbal tea she had brewed. She was very concerned with the dark circles that had formed beneath Rachael's eyes, the sallow hue of her cheeks that seemed to have appeared overnight, and her lackluster hair. "Drink up while it's still hot," she coaxed. "It will help you sleep."

Rachael looked into the teacup. "What? No leaves for you to read?" she commented caustically, turning away from the woman. Even Kitty's betrayal stung deep.

Kitty let the gibe go. "Not tonight," she whispered as she stroked her hand over Rachael's head in a sisterly fashion.

Julian's watch beeped from its place upon his wrist, signaling the first stroke of midnight and he stood up, clearing his throat before speaking nervously, "Happy New Year, ladies. May it bring us joy and love and many successes." Outside, the streets were filled with revelers. Fireworks exploded over the Thames, their booms muffled by the thick walls of the townhouse.

"Here, here," Kitty agreed, trying to keep her voice light. Her smile faded as Rachael's expression crumbled, her face hidden by her free hand, midnight having the worst and most ominous effect on Rachael. It reminded Kitty why she hated clocks, now.

This time Kitty's watch sounded as it hit the last stroke of midnight and was immediately followed by a loud knock on the door that led onto the dockside street. It echoed through the empty, cold townhouse, and the occupants froze for a brief moment. Julian chuckled nervously. "Probably some partygoers going about knocking on the doors. I'll get rid of them." He set his glass aside, hastening from the room, happy to be doing something other than wishing he could remove Rachael's pain.

Kitty sat down next to Rachael's feet, fussing with the blanket and making sure her friend was warm. "I'm going to Brighton in the morning to pick up some supplies. Why don't you come with me? A change of scenery might perk up your spirits."

"No," Rachael whispered, dropping her hand from her face. She sipped at the tea Kitty had prepared, tasting cinnamon and allspice in the liquid. It was a comforting combination that tried to ease a dying soul, and she closed her eyes, missing the shocked expression on Julian's face as he reentered the sitting room.

"Rachael," he began, his voice cracking. "There is someone here to see you." His hands were shaking, and his face was white as a ghost. He tossed back the rest of his wine in one gulp, and then poured another, trying to calm his suddenly rattled nerves.

"Get rid of whomever it is," Rachael stated flatly.

Kitty's eyebrows drew down as she looked at him. "What's the matter?" she asked as she stood up.

Julian waved to her in answer. "Rachael, you really need to go to the door." He looked at Kitty in question, the confusion on his face evident.

Kitty's lips tilted slightly, and she sent silent thanks on the wind. "You can't keep your fans away, can you?" she joked good-naturedly with Rachael as she took the blanket.

Rachael sighed and stood up, taking the blanket back from the witch and wrapping it around her shoulders, defiantly wanting to remain in her own cocoon of depression. "Don't blame me for my rudeness, then," she commented dryly as she shuffled her way through the sitting room and into the foyer.

The shock of the cold air in the stairwell made her mood grow even darker and by the time she made it to the front door, she already knew what she would say to whomever it was that was waiting for her. She had no intention of being polite or nice. She jerked the door open so hard that it banged against the wall, leaving a mark. "Can I help you?" she snapped in irritation, in no mood for festive cheers and good will.

The cruel words she was about to utter died on her lips as she took in the man's clothing. He was standing with his back to her, dressed against the weather in a finely made tan camel wool coat. A stylish man's hat was protecting his head from the snow that was once again swirling from the sky. It stuck to his shoulder-length brown hair. His trousers were expensive, and, even without seeing it, she could almost guarantee that the crease in the front was in the exact center of the legs. Even his boots were shined to perfection, a surprise in the weather of winter London. He turned slowly, revealing a pair of long fingered hands encased in shiny black leather, hands gripping an elegant walking stick. His deep brown eyes sparkled at her in longing, and he smiled at her tenderly with full, red lips.

"I hope so, Miss Lafferty." He took a step forward, forcing a shocked Rachael to step back as he entered the house. He removed his hat with a flourish. "I do hope you are still considering my proposal for becoming my wife."

Rachael's mouth moved but no words came out as she stared at him. The blanket slipped from her fingers as she reached out to touch his face. He captured her hand in his, kissing her palm, his flesh warm and solid beneath hers. "Dorian?" she whispered, afraid that she was hallucinating.

Dorian nodded and pulled her into his arms, his mouth finding hers without hesitation as he kissed her with every fiber of his being. Her lips were soft against his, softer than he remembered, and she tasted of cinnamon and allspice, an intoxicating combination. He could not recall her being so lush and delectable when he kissed her as a ghost, and his heart skipped a beat at the joy of holding her in his arms, tasting her flesh, breathing in her scent. Being a mortal was much better than being a ghost. Everything around him was so much clearer, sharper, warmer. He felt her soften against him, her body responding to his own and he leaned back, taking in her flushed cheeks and swollen lips. "You did not answer my question."

"But...how?" She licked her lips, tasting him there, an essence that lingered and was sweeter than any wine.

"My doing," Kitty answered from halfway down the stairs. "I would've spared you the grief, Rachael, but I had to make sure he wouldn't fade away again." She nodded to Dorian as she descended the steps the rest of the way. "I told you that the cards never lie. He is here to stay and has been given a second chance."

"With you," Dorian added.

Rachael looked at him, still in shock as she threw her arms around his neck. "Yes, I'll marry you, Dorian Gray," she cried, the tears that streamed down her face this time ones of joy. "Welcome home, my love."

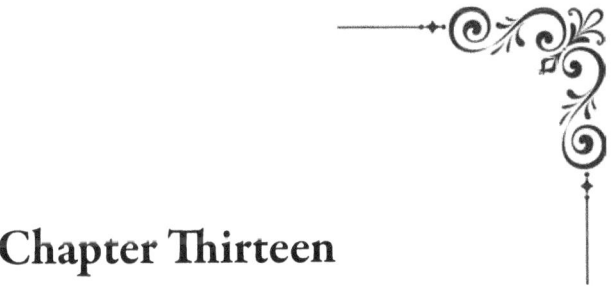

Chapter Thirteen

JANUARY 2, 8:00 PM

Dorian walked into the sitting room with a cup of hot tea in one hand, the daily newspaper in the other. He had spent the day shopping with Rachael, returning to the townhouse with numerous boxes and bags of clothing that he would need now since he was no longer just an apparition. As much as it appealed to his warped sense of humor, he simply could not see himself going around London in nothing more than the skin he had been born with. He looked at Rachael as he tucked the paper beneath his arm, and then loosened the collar of his red silk shirt. "What is this television I have been reading about?" he asked softly. "It sounds intriguing."

Rachael sat on the floor with her brand-new laptop computer perched on the coffee table. She nodded as she continued to type. "Some would probably say that about TV, yes. Personally, I think they are the worst invention on the face of this planet. Dampens the mind leaving hardly anything to the imagination." She looked up at her fiancé as he passed, smiling. It was still hard for her to believe that he had been returned to her, in the flesh, and mortal. Yet here he was, standing before her. He had insisted that she buy the laptop, understanding that, if the moment presented itself on their honeymoon, she would have the urge to write. He had already aided her in unpacking her belongings, knowing she would never leave the townhouse now that he was there. It even seemed as if the townhouse, itself, had returned to life upon his return. It was a comforting thought. "Although," she amended in afterthought, "it is handy for watching movies."

"Movies," Dorian repeated as he sat down. "I'm beginning to think things were much simpler in my day."

Rachael laughed and replied, "They were." They both turned to gaze through the room at the knock that resounded from the foyer door. "I wonder who that could be." She started to get up when Dorian motioned for her to remain seated. She settled back on the floor, her eyes following him as he started forward.

"I shall find out," he replied as he strode past. His heels clicked on the hardwood floor in a measured and even tone. He opened the door, stepping back. "Julian. This is an unexpected surprise."

Julian stepped into the foyer, disheveled and looking worried. "I need to speak to Rachael," he said quickly, turning the hat he held in his hands. He gazed at her as she approached. "Oh good, you're here. Tessa...Tessa is in the hospital. She's very...sick," he finished. He gazed earnestly at Rachael. "The doctors are saying that she's dying." His face crumbled, tears sliding down his wind-reddened cheeks.

Rachael stared at him in stunned silence. "What? You said she had the flu, Julian. How could she be dying?"

Julian shook his head, wiping his face with his handkerchief. "I...I don't know, Rachael. She asked me to get you right away. She wants to talk to you, to...smooth the hard feelings between you, in case the worst happens."

Dorian had retrieved Rachael's coat and held it ready for her. "You cannot think that way, Julian. For Tessa's sake," he reasoned in a calm and soothing tone. He slid her coat over her shoulders before gathering his own outerwear from the coat rack. "I know there is no love lost between Tessa and me, but not even I am so cold hearted to wish her ill." He buttoned up his coat and laid his hand on the small of Rachael's back. "I will call for a cab."

Julian shook his head. "There is one already waiting." He put his hand on Dorian's arm, stopping the man before he exited the foyer. Rachael had already slipped past them and was waiting outside. "I didn't have the opportunity to tell you that I am very glad you decided to come back to Rachael, no matter how it happened."

Dorian considered his words for a moment, before nodding. "Let us go see your wife, and we can discuss this later." He motioned for Julian to precede him out the door, making sure the townhouse was locked up before following.

The cab ride to the hospital was made in total silence, Julian gazing forlornly out the window in the passenger seat. Dorian could see the worry on the other man's face, and he truly understood what Julian was going through. He could not imagine losing Rachael, and the thought made him grip her hand tightly in his, stroking his thumb soothingly across the back. He looked at her, seeing the worry in her eyes, before leaning towards her. "I'm sure she will recover," he whispered, his breath warm on her ear. "You must not allow yourself to believe otherwise."

Rachael nodded, watching the heavy traffic that clogged the winter streets of London. "But what if she's not?" She peered at him, her brow furrowed in worry. "I may be upset with her, but I don't want to see anything happen to her, Dorian."

Dorian settled her hand in his free one, stretching his arm behind her and gathering her into his arms. He rubbed her arm as she settled her head on his shoulder, watching through the windshield of the taxi as the snow began to fall once again. There was nothing he could do or say to alleviate her concern, so he remained silent until the cab pulled up to the front door of the hospital. They followed Julian through the pristine corridors, the smell of antiseptic permeating the ward they entered. He coaxed Rachael to follow Julian into the private room at the end of the hall, hanging back in the corridor.

Rachael stopped just within the doorway, her eyes wide at the sight of Tessa lying in the bed. She looked so small and frail, the freckles that covered her face very apparent in the harsh light above the bed. Intravenous lines ran into her hand, an oxygen line crossing her face to provide her with enough air to survive. Her hair was spread across the pillow, creating the illusion of dying embers of a fire. She could not believe that the woman lying there was her friend, that she was no longer vibrant and headstrong, her fiery spirit all but extinguished.

Rachael moved towards her, taking her free hand in hers. It was cold, her fingers feeling like alabaster in her palm. "Tess?" she called softly. She watched Tessa's chest rise and fall in shallow breaths. "Tessa, it's Rachael."

Tessa's eyes fluttered open slowly. Her pupils were big, covering nearly all of the deep green that was her irises. "Rachael," she whispered hoarsely. She attempted to smile, only to stop halfway before grimacing in pain. "Rachael, I'm sorry," she continued when the pain passed.

Rachael sniffed. "For what? You have nothing to be sorry for."

Tessa turned her head slowly, looking at Rachael. "Yes, I do. I took him away from you. And, I tried to control you. That was wrong of me." She took a shuddering breath. "You were so right. You were right about everything."

Rachael stroked her hand over Tessa's forehead, brushing a lock of hair from her face. "*Shh*," she whispered. "You conserve your strength, Tessa. We can talk about this when you're better, okay?"

Tessa weakly squeezed Rachael's hand as she breathed in pain. "Monica...Monica has the last...manuscript," she wheezed. "I have...left instructions to...send it on to the publishers."

Rachael laughed sadly. "Always the businesswoman, you are." She looked at Julian in question, but he simply shook his head. He sat across from her, his hand gently cradling his wife's. "I'm sure they'll follow your instructions to the tee, and if they don't, well, you'll just have to give them what for when you're better." She smiled and nodded at Tessa, ignoring the foreboding that caused her stomach to clench. She had to remain optimistic, if not for Tessa's sake, then for Julian's.

Tessa swallowed. "No. You...will have to...do that for me." She winced and shifted in the bed. "I'm dying, Rachael. The...doctors cannot...find out what is causing this..." She closed her eyes with a deep sigh, her hand falling limp.

"Tessa?" Rachael called in a panicked voice. "Tess?"

Tessa's eyes opened again. "I'm still..." She began to cough, blood flecking her lips.

Julian turned away, muffling his sobs in the crook of his arm. Once composed, he gazed at Rachael. "It's some form of cancer. The doctors do not know what caused it, or why it has spread so quickly," he whispered in explanation. "They have had her on a morphine drip since New Year's Day."

Rachael's mouth opened in shock. "Why didn't you tell me sooner?" she questioned in dismay.

"She asked me not to," Julian answered.

"I...didn't think you...would care," Tessa whispered. "I said some very cruel...things to you in the last few weeks." She held Rachael's hand as tight as she could. "Promise me something," she gasped. She reached for Rachael with her other hand, motioning for her to bend lower. "Promise me."

Rachael leaned forward. "What, Tessa? Just tell me what you need."

Her hand shook as she cupped Rachael's cheek. "Do...not...leave London. Stay...here and...keep writing. Find inspiration...in...the townhouse."

Nodding, Rachael laid her hand over Tessa's. "All right, Tessa. I'll stay."

"He...he would've...wanted it." Tessa looked at Julian and motioned to him weakly. "Give her...give her the books...back."

Julian stood and bent over Tessa, caressing her head lovingly. "Not now, dear. There's time for that later." He placed a soft kiss on her temple. "You rest now, and you can give her the books back later."

Tessa nodded, letting her hand fall to her side limply. "I'm...tired. Thank...you for coming, Rachael," she whispered sincerely.

Rachael's hand covered her mouth as the tears slipped down her cheeks. She closed her eyes, swallowing past the lump in her throat and the heaviness in her chest. She looked at Julian, her heart breaking as he stared forlornly at his wife lying in the bed, helpless, too weak to fight the disease that had spread so mysteriously through her small frame.

Rachael turned, seeing Dorian standing outside, watching the entire scene through the glass window. She shook her head, her resolve to be strong crumbling. She wanted to do something for Tessa. She was powerless to change what was going on. She simply stood there, hoping her presence was at least a comfort to the dying duchess.

Dorian stepped just inside the doorway, his coat draped over his clasped hands, watching as Tessa opened her eyes one last time.

She gasped as her throat constricted, her eyes staring at the open doorway in terror. Her hand reached out towards Dorian as she began to convulse, her face frozen in a mask of horror as her eyes locked on him as the monitor behind her began to beep out an unsteady rhythm. Nurses and doctors pushed past him into the room as the heart monitor flat-lined.

Dorian held out his hand to Rachael, and he wrapped his arm around her as they were chased from the room. He held her as they watched through the window, watched as the doctors and nurses attempted to restart Tessa's heart.

He kissed the top of her head as she buried her face in his chest. "Come, Rachael," he whispered. "There is nothing we can do for her now." He led her away from the room just as the doctors pronounced Duchess Tessa Falcon dead, a remorseful expression creasing his handsome features with the realization that his was the last face she saw before she died.

TESSA'S FUNERAL WAS a solemn affair. Members of the literary world flocked to Stratford-Upon-Avon to pay their last respects. She had insisted upon being buried in the small family plot close to Shakespeare's birthplace, where the narrow streets of the city were lined with vehicles near the graveyard. The weather was unusually warm, yet rainy, typical British weather that only added to the sadness of the day. By the time Julian, Rachael, and Dorian returned to London, the rain had turned yet again into snow.

Dorian stood at the foyer door with Julian. "Are you sure you don't want to spend the night? I'm sure your home will be full of memories that you most assuredly do not wish to face at this time."

Julian nodded politely. "I'm sure. I do appreciate the offer, Dorian, but I'd rather go home. There are some things I must attend to and I would prefer to grieve alone."

Dorian offered, "Well, then, if you need anything, don't hesitate to call."

Julian shook his hand. "Thank you. Take care of Rachael for me," he requested before turning to leave, quietly slipping back into the dark night.

After Dorian closed the door, he tucked his hands in the pockets of his trousers. Strolling through the quiet townhouse, he found Rachael in the kitchen, standing at the center island with a lost look on her face. "How are you holding up?" he asked, standing opposite her. He waited, knowing she was still in shock.

Rachael shrugged with an exhausted sigh and gazed up at him. "I'm numb, Dorian," she admitted, before taking the tea towel in her hands and wiping it across the counter. She turned away from him, reaching for the dishes in the drain and putting them away, trying to remain busy so that she didn't have to face the pain in her heart. "Not counting that scene in the hospital, our last words to each other were said in anger and in spite." She closed the cabinet door harder than she intended causing the dishes inside to rattle.

Dorian moved to her, taking her in his arms. "It is not your fault, Rachael. You did nothing wrong."

She looked up at him, her arms wrapped tightly around his waist. "How can you say that? How can you say I did nothing wrong when I...?"

He laid his fingers on her lips, silencing her. "You stood up for yourself, something you should have done from the start. You expressed your dissatisfaction with the events surrounding your life. Tessa, I'm sure, respected that. Otherwise, I do not believe she would have asked to see you to apologize."

Rachael laid her head on his chest, knowing he was right. She then realized that it was the first time she actually heard his heart beating, making the moment even more surreal than it already was. She sighed. "I don't know if I can keep the promise I made to her."

"Of course, you can." Dorian tucked his forefinger beneath her chin and tilted her face up to look at him. He cupped it gently between his hands, wiping away the tears on her cheeks with his thumbs. "You have no reason to leave this house, no matter how many memories, good or bad, it may hold." He smiled gently at her. "And the memories we make together here will far outweigh the bad ones. We've already had a very good start on that."

She chuckled slightly, her face flushing as she looked away, feeling a bit guilty for the warmth that spread through her body at his hungry gaze. "You're right. You're right. I'm sure she knew that."

He turned her in his arms, tucking her beneath his shoulder as he led her from the room. "Of course, I am." They walked through the house together making sure the place was secure for the night. "We will take it one day at a time and together." He paused on the landing, looking down at her. "And I would be willing to postpone our wedding, if you feel it is too soon, considering the circumstances. Although we did announce our engagement at your delightful Christmas party."

Rachael thought about it for a moment. "No. Deep down, Tessa probably was happy that I had found someone I could call my own. I'm sure she'd want us to keep our plans."

"Then it is settled," Dorian answered with a smile and took her hand, leading her into the bedroom. He let her go and turned down the comforter. "Why don't you take a long bath and soak for a while? It might make you feel better."

She shook her head as she moved over to where he sat on the edge of the bed. "I'd rather let you make love to me," she whispered as she threaded her fingers through his thick hair. "Make me forget for a while, Dorian. Make the pain disappear for a time."

He settled his hands on her hips and gazed up at her. "How can I say no to such a request?"

He did exactly as she asked, taking his time and making sure she thought of nothing else except the euphoria only he could bring upon her. Afterwards, he lay on his side watching her as she slipped into an exhausted sleep, sated, content. He placed a loving kiss on her forehead before slipping out of the bed.

Pulling on his robe, Dorian slipped from the bedroom, leaving the scent of sex still lingering in the air of their room. Like a cat on padded feet, he made his way downstairs, finding the pack of cigarettes he had bought earlier in the day. Lighting one, he inhaled deeply and enjoyed one of his less debased vices. He walked back into the foyer, running his fingers across the leather binding of his journal that lay atop Rachael's copy of Oscar Wilde's book that outlined his life. He held his smoke between his lips as he carried both books back into the sitting room, replacing them on the shelf where they belonged. He sat down in the chair before the fire, his mind replaying the events of the past few weeks.

He never told Rachael what had happened to him after he faded away. He wasn't even sure himself. He remembered the dark cold that he escaped from when he stepped from the portrait, and remembered regaining consciousness, with a start, in Kitty's house, as the young witch was bending over him, gazing at him in satisfaction. But anything between the time he had returned to the dark and awakening, nothing. He stood up, flicking the remains of the cigarette into the dying fire before climbing the spiral staircase.

Dorian knew there was more to his sudden corporealism than met the eye, and when Rachael explained to him what had happened to cause his disappearance, he became even more intrigued. He could only wonder what Kitty had done in order to allow him to return to the land of the living as a mortal man. He had asked Kitty numerous times to tell him, but she remained evasive, assuring him that it worked and saying to move on with his life. She had left for a trip to Russia the next day, forcing both him and Rachael to wait for her return in order to gain any answers.

He continued down the dark corridor until he came to the door that led to the attic. He reached up and found the key on the top of the doorframe where he had always kept it, his fingers closing around the cold metal. He unlocked the door and returned the key to its home before cautiously opening it and stepping through. He climbed the stairs, his steps silent on the risers until he reached the top. Extending his arm, he pulled the chain above him, illuminating the room with the single, bare bulb that hung from the dormer. He gazed around, finding the gilt frame right where Kitty had placed it, after finding Rachael desolate and broken beneath the ruined canvas.

Dorian stretched his hand out and paused, unsure if he wanted to see what was beneath the purple fabric that was draped over the frame. There should've been canvas shreds spilling from it at his feet, but the hardwood floor was bare, with only the tracks in the dust from Kitty's feet. He gathered the fabric in his fingers and jerked it away. He stared at it sadly, shaking his head slowly, at the mysteriously restored portrait.

The colors were once again vibrant as he let his fingers drift over the rough edges the paint caused. The background was still the same and he lifted the portrait from the easel it was resting on, carrying it back to the light to study it in more depth. He began to laugh, a haunting sound in the silent and close air of the attic. There was no humor in the sound, only remorse. "I do believe I won this round of the game," he stated to the figure in the portrait. He returned the canvas to its resting place, studying it a few moments more. "But, at what cost?"

He turned away, extinguishing the light before he exited the attic to return to Rachael's side.

The canvas still retained the scarlet signature of Basil Hallward. Only this time the canvas did not hold the image of a young Victorian aristocrat caught in the prime of his youth, before evil could touch the features of a man considered more beautiful than handsome.

This time, the canvas held the image, and the soul, of Duchess Tessa Falcon.

Epilogue

LONDON, DECEMBER 22, 2120

The British Museum of Art was always busy, even with Christmas being only a few days away. The renovations on the historic building had added a wing and four more floors, the glass tower behind the museum proper a marvel of engineering genius. Climate controlled conditions, paintings behind hermetically sealed glass facades, comfortable benches for the patrons of the arts, all of it had been added over the course of the last century, a gift from the late Duke and Duchess Falcon. It was sad that neither of them had seen what their generous duchy had brought to fruition.

A small tour group of teenagers made their way along the moving walkway with the tour guide, stopping at a small alcove on the third floor of the Falcon Wing. Their tour guide, a young woman with a flair for dramatics, turned to the group and indicated to a darkened portrait behind her. "I will warn you all now that it is unwise to make any wish that will bring you youth or prosperity, for you may not always receive your wish in the way you expect." She pressed a button on the small remote in her hand, bringing the lights up slowly on the portrait in the alcove. "The portrait behind me has been dated by experts to be over four-hundred years old," she began.

The students gasped as they gazed at the woman in the painting. She was leaning against a wing-backed chair, her hands clasping the back of it, a conceited look on her face. Her red hair was perfectly fixed, a black clip holding its long locks in place as they flowed down to drape over her right shoulder. She wore a sky-blue blouse with a gold chain, and her rings seemed to sparkle on her hands. A pair of black slacks and high heels completed the elegant ensemble, the barest wisp of a gold ankle bracelet just visible on one leg.

One of the students raised his hand. "Excuse me," he started, "but I have studied the art of the 1700's. This portrait could not have been painted then. Her clothing is too modern."

"Well pointed out. And there have been many who have attempted to discredit the painting as a clever hoax. I assure you; it is not." The tour guide nodded and stepped slightly to the side so that the students could view the painting better. "No one seems to recall who this young woman was, but the painting is, indeed, from the 1700's. It is now referred to as the *Curse of Dorian Gray*, for no one seems to be able to determine why this woman is dressed in modern clothing in a painting that has been authenticated as an original work by Basil Hallward. As you can see, the artist's signature is still in the lower corner." She pointed to the scarlet slash that was indicative of Hallward.

"Dorian Gray. We read his story in class," a girl commented. "It was said that he wished to remain young forever, and that, when he did, his portrait aged when he did not."

The tour guide smiled. "And when, in a fit of desperation, he destroyed his own portrait..."

Another of the students took up the story. "He disintegrated and the painting returned to the way it was."

"Correct." The tour guide held up her hand. "But the story doesn't end there. A little over a hundred-years-ago, the portrait once again changed. How or why, no one knows. It defies logical explanation." She took a small laser pointer form her pocket and aimed it the protected painting. "There are shadows in the background, here and here, that indicate there was something else at one time on this canvas."

"Are you saying that this was the actual picture of Dorian Gray?" the first student scoffed.

"It could have been. But we have no way of knowing." She lowered the pointer. "All we know is that this is an original work by the renowned Basil Hallward, complete with all its mysteries." She started to walk along the path, the electronic walkway once again moving. "Now here, we have another portrait..."

The tour guide's voice faded as she and her small group moved away from the alcove. The room was left in silence, the eyes of Tessa Falcon staring down into the open area. A young man entered the room, his hands holding those of two young boys, ten and twelve, respectively. A hat hid his face, his hands gloved, his clothing elegant and refined. His companions were dressed similarly, marks of aristocracy and upper crust society.

"Is what she said really true, great-grandfather?" the older boy asked.

"Which part?" the man asked as he gazed down at the youngsters.

"About making a wish and the portrait aging while you did not?" the other inquired.

Dorian Gray slowly looked up at the portrait that he had found restored in the attic of the Victorian townhouse he shared with his beloved wife, Rachael. "Oh, yes, Michael. Jonathan. It's true. And there is so much more to the tale," he purred with enthusiasm, making the boys curious.

Had anyone seen them, they would've wondered why the boys referred to the man that was accompanying them as great-grandfather. Dorian Gray looked nothing like a great-grandfather. As a matter of fact, he could have been their older brother, for he did not look a day over twenty-five. "So much more," Dorian whispered.

Somewhere along the line, Kitty Kendall's spell did not go quite right, for Dorian Gray, once returned to the living, had never aged.

And he was quite content with remaining a young and beautiful immortal.

About the Author

Born and raised in upstate New York, with a brief and very influential stint living in Great Britain, Beth A. Freely calls Texas her home with her husband Daniel, daughter Caitlyn and cats, Peanut Butter and Toast.

Beth has more than 10 years of writing experience as a copywriter and published author. She enjoys shooting pool, riding horses science fiction and comic book hero movies.

She holds a Bachelor's Degree in Journalism and Mass Media Communication with a minor in Marketing as well as a Master's Degree in English and Creative Writing.

In 2005, she was the First Place Winner of the ArcheBooks Publishing Novel Writing Contest, Women's Fiction Category with her novel *Behind The Eyes Of Dorian Gray*. It was originally published under the name Beth A. Carpenter.

She is the owner of The Muses Funhouse.

Read more at https://bethafreelyrauch.com/.

About the Publisher

At The Muses Funhouse, you will find the professional copywriter you need to produce the engaging content you want. From search engine optimization to website reviews, you will receive first-class service from the start of the project to the end. From news-based articles to leadership commentaries, educational blogs to press releases, social media to whitepapers, The Muses Funhouse will produce your content quickly and competently.

CPSIA information can be obtained
at www.ICGtesting.com
Printed in the USA
FSHW021545190321
79603FS